SINS OF THE FATHER

A MAFIA THRILLER

VINCENT B. DAVIS II

Dedicated to my grandmother, Mary Hutchison, who lived through Prohibition and the Great Depression, the Moon Landing and the birth of the Internet.

You are so missed.

CONTENTS

JOIN "THE BUREAU"!

The Bureau is your connection to Vincent's growing library of crime thriller books. It's like having a direct connection to the Chief of Police with top secret clearance where you get the inside scoop in real time.

Just scan the QR code below!

PART 1

HEARINGS BEFORE THE
PERMANENT SUBCOMMITTEE ON INVESTIGATIONS
OF THE
COMMITTEE ON GOVERNMENT OPERATIONS
UNITED STATES SENATE
EIGHTY-EIGHTH CONGRESS
FIRST SESSION
PURSUANT TO SENATE RESOLUTION 17
SEPTEMBER 27, 1963

Chairman: Do you recall spending much time with Vincente Consentino in the early nineteen thirties?

Mr. Valachi: Who now?

Chairman: I said Vincente Consentino, often called "Sonny."

Mr. Valachi: Oh yeah, Sonny. Yeah, I spent some time with him.

Chairman: And was he involved in the war your organization found itself in?

Mr. Valachi: Yes, he was. He wasn't part of my family, though.

Chairman: Mr. Consentino wasn't part of your criminal organization?

Mr. Valachi: That's correct.

Chairman: Did Mr. Consentino take part in any of the murders you've recollected for us?

Mr. Valachi: What now?

Chairman: Did Sonny Consentino ever take part in any murders, that you know of?

Mr. Valachi: I need a drink of water.

Chairman: Well, take a drink, then. I ask again, was Sonny Consentino present for any of the gangland killings you've described?

Mr. Valachi: I don't remember.

Chairman: You don't? You've said otherwise, previously, under oath.
    (Mr. Valachi receives counsel from his attorney.)

Mr. Valachi: Yes, he was.
    Chairman: Vincente "Sonny" Consentino was involved in gangland murders?

Mr. Valachi: Yes.

Chairman: And how many murders do you believe him to have been a part of, to the best of your recollection?

Mr. Valachi: I never bothered to count them.

Chairman: You never what?

Mr. Valachi: I never bothered. To count them, I mean. There were several, I think.

Chairman: Was he involved in other criminal activity, like bootlegging?

Mr. Valachi: Not really. He didn't seem to care much about all that.

Chairman: He didn't care much about what?

Mr. Valachi: Bootlegging, making money and everything. Sonny wasn't like the rest of us.

Chairman: How do you mean?

Mr. Valachi: He didn't go out with us much. He didn't have a girl. He'd rather go to bed early so's he could be at the earliest service of Mass. He'd rather watch the New York Stock Exchange than the horse races. He stayed to himself most of the time.

Chairman: And what would Mr. Consentino do with his time?

Mr. Valachi: One time I visited him and he was cleaning his piece.

Chairman: He was cleaning a gun?

Mr. Valachi: Yeah. He was cleaning his pistol and helping another guy load rounds into a tommy-gun drum.

Chairman: Do you know what Mr. Consentino's purpose was in doing this?

Mr. Valachi: Not really. But back then, we were at war. And Sonny took it all very personally. He had one objective, and anybody who got in the way was gonna wind up in a Chicago overcoat.

Chairman: If they got in the way they would wind up in what? Explain for the court what that term means.

Mr. Valachi: A Chicago Overcoat is what we called a coffin. Sonny and his crew put a lot of their enemies in coffins.

Chairman: I think this is a good place to recess until 1:30.
   (Members present at time of recess: Senators McClellan, McIntyre, and Mundt. Whereupon, at 11:15 a.m., the committee recessed until 1:30 p.m. on the same day.)

ALONZO

The sun warmed his face, and a gentle breeze carried the smell of salt in from the sea. Alonzo Consentino closed his eyes and lifted his head, savoring every second. With two toddlers at home, and another child due any day, he found it nearly impossible to make his regular after-dinner trip to the shore for some fresh air. He had made a habit of it since he was a child, but moments like these were simply fading away beneath the growing list of chores presented by his wife, and the need for attention from his twin boys.

He was exhausted. He plopped down on a grassy patch over-looking the beach, and delicately placed his straw hat over his eyes.

"Papà! Papà!" the voice belonged to one of his twins. In his weary mind, it was just his imagination. "Papà!" When Alonzo heard the voice of his eldest twin, Enzo, yet again, he pounced to his feet. He sensed distress in his boy's voice, and adrenaline and fear surged through his limbs.

"What? I'm over here. What is wrong? Is it your mother?"

"*No.*" *Enzo doubled over, making it known that he was strug-gling for air.* "*There is a boy here. He asks for you.*"

"*A boy?*"

"*Yes! A boy, bigger than me. And he's hurt, Papà. He is bleeding everywhere.*"

"Madonna mia," *Alonzo whispered beneath his breath. He swept Enzo in his arms and took off through the pastures to his home.*

"*Rosa!*" *Alonzo pushed through the screen door and ran toward the kitchen.*

"*We're in here.*" *He sensed more irritation than fear in his wife's voice. The fear of finding someone dead in his home dissipated, and it was replaced by a far more terrifying fear: the aroused anger of his rotund pregnant wife.*

"*Piddu?*" *Alonzo asked as he rounded the corner, finding a young man lying on his dining room table, his wife Rosa hovering over him.*

"*Mr. Consentino, I am so sorry. I am so…sorry,*" *the boy sobbed.*

"*He bled all over my table cloth, Alonzo. And your little Vico used up half of our bedsheets trying to stop the bleeding.*" *Alonzo strategically neglected to respond to his wife. She threw up her arms in exasperation and left the room.*

"*Why have you come? What is wrong, Piddu?*" *Alonzo used the calmest voice he could muster, despite his irritation.*

But the boy's tears continued, and they grew more wretched as time passed. He blubbered. The boy must have been thirteen by now, Alonzo thought. What could possibly cause this much commotion?

"*Let me see your wound? We can patch it up.*" *He noticed that the boy's hand was wrapped in a cocoon of bedsheets and clutched tightly beneath his opposite arm. Without much opposition, he pried the boy's hand free and unveiled the wound. Blood spurted up from empty stubs where the boy's fingers once were. Only the thumb and pinkie remained.*

The blood gushed out so violently and forcefully that Alonzo had to struggle to get the wound wrapped again.

Before he could finish, Piddu ripped his arm away from Alonzo.

"That's not why I am here!" He sucked wind, and tried to tamp down his tears. "They killed my ma and pa! They killed them both."

Alonzo's knees nearly buckled. He had to prop himself up on the table. "Who did? Are you sure? Who killed your parents? Are you absolutely sure?"

"Yes, I'm sure!" The boy now wrapped up the wound himself, then sat up. He shook from the cold of blood loss. "It was some men. My pa called them the Armettas…or Arm…Are…"

"The Armettas? Why would they do something like this?"

"They said my father insulted them. They said he slighted them, so they killed them both while we ate dinner." He brandished his mangled hand once again. "And they did this to me so I couldn't kill them when I'm older."

Alonzo's eyes flickered cautiously toward the door. "Piddu, why did you come here? What do you expect me to do? The Armettas are associates of mine, just like your father was. You must have spent hours coming from Palermo. Was there no one back there who knows how to stop the bleeding?"

"No, we were visiting here. We were only here for the week, to see the festival of San Biagio down by the water. And they killed my parents, here in Castellammare del Golfo. I came to you because you are in charge here! And I beg for you to help me!"

Alonzo backed away from the boy, his eyes blinking in disbelief. The breath caught in his lungs.

"Well?" Piddu pleaded.

"I'll see what I can do, but now you need to rest. And someone has to stop that bleeding."

Piddu nodded. It took only moments for his adrenaline to subside. And when it did, he collapsed back onto the table, leaving Alonzo to patch up his wound and contemplate what he knew could cause far greater pain than the loss of a few digits.

ALONZO

After spending the first thirty years of his life on the Sicilian coast, Alonzo Consentino considered himself quite the seafarer. By the time he neared Ellis Island, this was disproven.

Night and day, he fought back the urge to vomit, and once or twice, he snuck away from his wife and three boys, pretending to take a smoke in private, and only then would he empty the contents of his stomach into the Atlantic. His nausea was alleviated temporarily when he remained in the family's lodgings with the other immigrants, but pellagra and malaria were rampant, so he kept himself and the rest of the Consentino clan on the deck of the steamboat as often as he was able.

Once they had arrived at the port, and were safely out of the Armettas' dangerous grasp, Alonzo had taken as much time as possible to discuss with others what they

should expect in America. He was surprised to find himself
nervous, but he had never left Sicily before. The Americans
could have all been ten feet tall, for all he knew.

Several travelers who had already been to America and
were now returning with enough money to establish themselves in their native country told Alonzo all he needed to
know about his entrance to America. Very little of it was
encouraging. At first, he was unsure if he should believe
the nightmarish stories they told him. All the papers said it
was the land of freedom, hope, and boundless opportunity.
But these men all shared stories of inhumane living condi-
tions, violent prejudice, and limited job opportunities.

Something wasn't adding up, but eventually, Alonzo
began to believe the travelers, although he was determined
that his story was going to be different.

The most important thing they had told him was that
he needed to claim that he had a job prepared for him
once he arrived at Ellis Island—or risk being rejected.
They also said he would have to contact a "padrone," one
of the wealthy Sicilian immigrants who could help them
find a place to live and a job…for a fee. Alonzo balked at
the idea of having to approach, hat in hand, some two-bit
immigrant for provision in the States. Then he remembered he was going to be nothing but a two-bit immigrant
the moment he stepped on the boat. Regardless, he
intended to stay as far away from important Sicilians as
possible, for obvious reasons.

For all Alonzo's preparation, there was nothing he
could have done to prepare for the seasickness. Looking
around at the diseased wretches in the living quarters
beneath the deck, he was forced to at least be relieved that
his plights weren't as bad as theirs, but comparisons didn't
hold much weight when his guts felt twisted up in knots
and he couldn't keep his stale bread down.

He couldn't let the boys see, though. He made sure to smile and talk about how majestic America would be. The twins, Enzo and Vico, couldn't have been more delighted to make the move. For them, it was all one big adventure. For little Sonny, things had been more difficult. He wasn't so sure about this nation so far away from Sicily's coast.

The travelers, packed in like sardines on the deck, began to cry out in awe as land was spotted in the distance.

"America!" Some of them shouted. Alonzo only exhaled in relief. He was beginning to think he would never see the promised land.

He bounced Sonny, who was latched on to him tightly, and pointed into the distance.

"Look, we are here!" Alonzo said with feigned excitement. "Isn't it lovely?" Sonny turned his face away and lowered his eyes. Alonzo craned to look at him. He was pouting like a child, but there was something about Sonny's demeanor that was adult-like, informed, wise.

"Mamma doesn't want to go to America," Sonny said, his voice barely audible. He was quite right. Rosa had never said it aloud, but she had made it known that this voyage to America was not her choice. She was a dutiful wife and mother, though, and when Alonzo said that they had no other options, she packed their bags as instructed, and they left as soon as they could.

But that didn't stop her from drinking.

Alonzo could hear it in her voice, and he could smell it on her breath when she infrequently came close enough to Alonzo for him to notice. The twins weren't very perceptive, and if they had picked up on their mother's discontent, they didn't care. Sonny, only two and a half, seemed to read his mother like a book.

"Yes, she does, Sonny, she will just miss Sicily. Look here." He eased Sonny to the floor and fumbled through the pockets in his tweed jacket for a flyer he'd received from an orphan boy at the docks before their departure. "I bet we will see this in just a few moments."

"It's a lady. A statue of a lady." Alonzo's heart warmed with his son's spirits. He knelt to Sonny's level so they could both scan the horizon from the same vantage point.

"That's right! The *Statua Liberta*, and she represents everything this country stands for." Alonzo smiled until Sonny followed his example, then pinched his cheek.

"Like what?"

"Like what? Like what!" Alonzo picked Sonny up again in mock anger and swung him around. "Well, fresh starts!"

"And what else?"

"And…well, liberty, of course!"

"Uh-huh."

"And opportunity! Opportunities we wouldn't have had back home." He paused and watched as Sonny's face lit up.

"I think I can see her! Way out there."

"Only one way to find out." Alonzo hoisted his boy up with ease and perched him on his shoulders.

"That's her, I can tell." At first, Alonzo was simply playing along for the boy's sake, but as others began to point out the statue as well, his own excitement grew.

"And it says in this flyer that even if you can't see it… ah, even if you can't see it, she has broken chains at her feet to represent freedom and all the things that we'll be able to do here."

"Your father is clawing at his coffin," Rosa said from beside him. He hadn't noticed her approach. She took a long drag on her cigarette, another of her new habits.

"My father would be happy that I'm giving these boys the best chance at a good life that I can," he said beneath his voice, although he knew Sonny would hear. Rosa exhaled but didn't respond. She was wrapped up in a warm coat like it was winter, and she was shivering. It wasn't Sicilian hot, sure, but Alonzo believed it was just another way for her to let him know that she disapproved. "Where are Enzo and Vico?"

Rosa nodded her head to the side. "Playing dice with the other privileged youth."

It was true that very few of the boarders came from any kind of wealth, as they had. Most of them were farmers from Mezzogiorno escaping the natural disasters that had destroyed their crops, Sicilians escaping the oppressive taxes of the northern Italians, or anyone seeking to avoid the rigorous military subscriptions. Whether Rosa liked it or not, though, they were all equals now.

"Maybe you could invite them to look?" Rosa flicked her cigarette over the edge and sauntered off to collect the twins.

"Papà?" Sonny said, craning his head to see Alonzo.

"Yes?"

"Will the people here look like us?" he asked, a tinge of hope in his voice.

"Not exactly, Sonny. But there are a lot of different kinds of people here. You'll make plenty of friends."

"Okay, good," Sonny said as he continued to watch the growing horizon. "Papà?"

"Yes?"

"And will they talk like us?"

Alonzo let the silence grow. "No, they won't." He didn't know what to say. He couldn't say much.

And he couldn't say a word of English. None of them could.

Little Italy, Manhattan—October 3, 1907

Their new apartment in Little Italy wasn't much: two bedrooms, one small stove, and a community bath down the hall. At the end of the day, Alonzo was just thankful they had found a place at all. The first landlord they'd approached, who owned a little apartment block on Mott Street, had turned them away. "No Sicilians allowed," he had said. For a time, Alonzo feared he would actually have to approach one of the infamous "padroni." But, after prayer, supplication, and a fair amount of promises to God, Alonzo found an opening in a tenement in Mulberry Bend. There were nearly one thousand other tenants lodged there, but at least they had a roof over their heads. It was better than the horror stories Alonzo had heard from some of the travelers back at the docks.

At least there was a stoop, which was where Alonzo spent most of his time installed in a wicker chair. No longer able to spend time on the Sicilian coast, he took to the porch with a copy of the *New York Times*. He could hardly read English, and he didn't know anything about baseball, but every update he could find on the New York Highlands—or "the Yanks," as some called them—was the highlight of his day.

"Lonz." His wife's voice carried from the doorway. He ashed his cigar and turned to her.

"Yes, *mio tesoro*?"

"You need to talk with your son." Sonny appeared behind her. "Go on, love." She patted her son's back, and he moved forward like a convict called before a judge.

"What's wrong, pal?"

"Mom is upset with me." His eyes were wet, and he rubbed his wrist over his nose.

"Did you do something wrong?"

"I told her I don't want to wear short sleeves to school anymore." His lip puckered, and tears began to materialize in his long eyelashes.

"Come here." Alonzo helped his youngest onto his lap. He didn't know exactly what to say. What was Rosa concerned about? "And why don't you want to wear short sleeves? It's been hot out."

"Just because…" Alonzo followed Sonny's gaze to his little arms. Sonny began to sob as Alonzo rolled up the sleeves.

"I don't want the other boys to see the bedbug bites. They'll make fun of me. They already don't like me because I'm Sicilian and not Italian, and they'll make fun of me because I'm poor. Everyone makes fun of me except Antonello, and that's because he is even more poor than me."

"Hey, hey." Alonzo pulled his Sonny closer to him and buried his son's head in his chest. "Don't you ever be ashamed of who you are. You come from good people, and you have a family that loves you very much. Don't ever forget that." He lifted Sonny's chin.

"Okay…"

"I mean it. Don't listen to those kids. They just say those things because you're new. They were probably just like you—they've just been here a little longer."

"Do you think so?"

"I know so. It was just like that in Sicily, and it's just like that anywhere. You'll be the neighborhood hero before you know it."

"I bet they'll like my playing cards." Sonny pursed his lips to hide a growing smile.

"That's my boy. Do you have your cards?" It was a simple fifty-two-card deck that Alonzo had spent a very precious nickel on to cheer his boy up. Sonny looked up and finally let his smile shine, putting his little hands on his father's face.

"I take them everywhere I go."

"Let's see them." As Sonny pulled them out, Alonzo picked up his cigar and wedged it between his teeth. "I'm going to show you a game. It's one my father taught me. Did you know I used to play cards with my father too?"

"Really?"

"Yes. It was our favorite thing to do. He was an important man, and he didn't have much time at the house. But when he would come home, he would always wake me up from my bed and ask me to play cards with him. It is the happiest memories I have with your grandfather."

"I wish he was still alive so he could teach me."

"Me too, Sonny, but I can teach you." Alonzo pulled up a nearby chair and dusted it off. As Sonny plopped down on it, Alonzo pulled over a side table and began to deal the cards. "And you know the funnest thing about cards?"

"What?" Sonny was already giggling in anticipation.

"You get to say bad words." Both father and son let out a laugh. "No, really! You can say whatever you want when you play cards. That's the rule. But you don't tell your mother, and you don't ever say them when you aren't playing cards. Got it?"

"Got it."

"Yeah, or I'll pop you." He smiled and ruffled Sonny's hair. "Look. I got some bad cards. A Two and a Four.

That's no good… Shit." Sonny's face lit up with shock. "Do you have good cards?"

"Nope." Sonny looked back and forth between his cards and his father, and a mischievous grin only a child could wield split across his face. "Damn it." He erupted into laughter, and Alonzo encouraged it by tickling his sides.

"I love you, pal." He pulled his son in with a firm hug and gave him a kiss on the head.

ALONZO

"Ever since your father died, you have led this family with honor and toughness. The Consentino family has never been more respected. Why do you now doubt yourself?" Alonzo's uncle Umberto leaned back in his old leather chair, munching down on an unlit cigar.

"Because I don't know what to do, Uncle. What if I start a war? The Armettas are powerful. They have many friends, and I consider myself one of them." Alonzo couldn't keep his feet from tapping.

"You call them friend? Well, you also considered Piddu's father a friend, and the Armettas knew this. Yet they killed him and his wife without consulting you or asking for your permission. What kind of friend does that?" a young associate, Turridru, added in from the shadows of Umberto's dusty workshop.

"Mind your place." Umberto slammed his hand on the weathered wooden bench between them. *"But still, I agree with the boy."*

Turridru threw up his hands in exasperation and paced around the room. *"I am grieved that they did this. I am insulted."*

"As you should be. Do you not believe this deserves reprisal?" Umberto may have never desired to lead the Consentino Borgata, but if he had, he would have been a fine leader. Ruthless, determined, and bearing a sense of ethics that couldn't be questioned.

"But you didn't answer me: What if this starts a war?"

"It will start a war, Don Consentino," Turridru said.

"He's right. That goes without saying. The Armetta family will want to exact reprisal. And they will seek to do so. The only real question is whether or not you are willing to accept the consequences of doing the right thing. Are you prepared to shed blood, willing to risk your own blood, to avenge the death of an ally your father held dear?" Umberto added.

"You should have seen the boy, Uncle," Alonzo said. "It was awful. They mutilated his hand. Made him watch as they emptied their guns into his parents… What kind of insult could have been so offensive that this was warranted?" Alonzo genuinely wanted to know. If there was just cause, he would leave well enough alone. He would return to his home and make sure that Piddu was well, and then he would send the boy on his way.

"Does it matter, Don Consentino? It doesn't," Turridru said. "No matter what the offense was, Piddu's parents were your allies, and the Armettas killed them without pause. Either to send a message to you or because they do not believe you have the spine to do anything about it."

"Quiet, damn you!" Umberto turned to the young man and shouted before convulsing into a fit of coughing. "Who does this young man think he is?"

"He's right, Uncle," Alonzo said.

"I know he's right, but he needs to mind his station."

"I brought him here for a reason. I wanted his counsel as well."

"More fool you, then. He's reckless." Umberto turned and scowled at Turridru, who met his glance with a furtive smile.

"I am tired of this." A beam of light entered the old workshop as Turridru's father, Ignazio, hobbled in on his cane. "Alonzo, your *father... Do you remember your father?" He fumbled his way to the table, using his cane to guide him, since his eyes were no good.*

"Of course, I do."

"Well, I'm having a hard time believe you, boy." Ignazio poked his cane at Alonzo like a weapon. "Have you heard how I became part of this Borgata?"

"We've all heard it, Father. A thousand times," Turridru spoke up, hiding his irritation with feigned cordiality.

"Your father entered my florist shop to buy some flowers for his own father's grave. A miscreant came in and was going to kill your father right in my place. So I shot him. Dead. I shot him dead, close enough to your father that he lost his hearing for a week. And he invited me, and my entire family, into yours, because of what?"

"Because you—" Alonzo began.

"Because of action. There were bad men in the world, and I put one of them down like a rabid dog. Action. What will you do now? Bad men live, and you have a choice to make. Will you do something about it, or will you sit here sniveling about right and wrong?" The blind old man plopped down on Umberto's newest wooden bench, snarling. Alonzo thought if anyone needed to mind his place, it was Ignazio. Old and blind he may be, but what right did he have to give lessons on how to run a Borgata?

"And if my own people die because of it? If the Armettas retaliate?" Alonzo asked.

"Than you live with the consequences." Ignazio had already struggled to his feet and was hobbling for the door, making it clear that he deemed this a waste of his time by shaking his head and wagging his fist. "Or you can send a message to all of Sicily that your friends can be killed with impunity, that your father's legacy means nothing, and that this Borgata is nothing but a guise. Your choice." Ignazio departed, slamming the door behind him with what little force he could muster.

"I'll do it, Don Consentino. Say the word, and I'll do it myself," Turridru said, stepping closer to him. Alonzo looked to Umberto, who

only lowered his head and said nothing more. Alonzo assumed that his diplomatic uncle agreed with Ignazio. He felt he was the only one who had misgivings. If that were the case, the decision was already made.

Castellammare del Golfo—February 27, 1905

Alonzo trailed behind his ambitious young companion Turridru. He could keep up, but this was his least favorite part of running a Sicilian Borgata, a network of family allies that looked to him for protection and guidance. Betrayal was tantamount, and couldn't be ignored. Revenge was necessary. Blood demanded blood.

"They're in there." Turridru nodded toward a local delicatessen that was owned by a cousin of the Armettas.

"You're sure it's only the three we're looking for?" Alonzo asked, trying in vain to hide his reluctance. He couldn't afford to show weakness in front of this young man, but what else could he do?

"I'm sure, Don Consentino. I've trailed them for a few days, and this is where the three young men get lunch every afternoon. Father saw them enter not thirty minutes ago."

Alonzo nodded for his friend to lead the way. With one hand, he clutched the sawed-off shotgun hidden beneath his suit coat. With the other, he rubbed his fingers over the rosary that dangled from his neck. Before they reached the door, he tucked the rosary back into his shirt, and then quickened his pace.

Turridru kicked the door with as much force as the eighteen-year-old could muster. Alonzo rushed in behind him.

Chairs scraped violently against the linoleum floor as the Armettas struggled to their feet. Alonzo pulled violently at the trigger. The shot reverberated to his elbows, to his shoulders. Smoke from the tip of his weapon obstructed his view.

Blood cascaded across the room as the body of the first man tumbled back over the table, sending wine and a bowl of grapes and cheese across the floor. Alonzo shot again at a second man who tried to duck behind his fallen brother, pellets of buckshot ripping through his chest.

The third brother drew a pistol and pointed it at Alonzo.

As the man braced to pull the trigger, a bullet shredding through his cheek. Turridru paced over to Alonzo, his pistol still smoking.

"I'll check the back. The owner is here somewhere."

"No, let's go," Alonzo said. Turridru shot him a look, and stood firm. Alonzo rushed to the man Turridru had shot and rolled him over to his stomach. He was still sucking in air, but his moments were numbered. Alonzo pulled a dagger from his belt and shoved it into the man's back, at the spine.

It was a message. The Armettas had betrayed them, and this was the result.

"Let's go." Alonzo bolted for the door, his mind returning to his pregnant wife and his two boys at home. Turridru followed behind him, and they made for the door as quickly as they had entered. Behind them, the owner shouted a curse, and two blasts of a shotgun rang out.

Alonzo sprinted with a vitality he didn't realize he possessed, and Turridru trailed him closely.

"We shouldn't have left their cousin alive!" Turridru shouted as they passed through a field to where two horses had been staged.

"We had a point to make, and we made it."

SONNY

"I don't like that boy. I never have." Sonny's mother's voice carried in through the screen door as he attempted to pay attention to his cards. "I heard some of the other parents talking. They said they've seen Antonello smoking cigarettes."

Sonny swept up the cards and moved farther from the door.

"That boy shows up every day with fresh bruises. His father is beating him, Rosa. Badly," Alonzo said.

"So we're supposed to let him influence our son because he has a bad home life?"

"We can help him," Alonzo insisted. Sonny moved farther away still.

"We should help him. I feel bad for him too. But he is eight going on nine. Why does he want to spend time with our Vincente so much? He's only five, Alonzo. And they're from Naples. You can never trust a Neapolitan."

"That's your mother talking, Rosa. We don't have Sicilians or Neapolitans anymore. We're all Americans." Sonny heard his mother's sardonic laugh carry through the screen door.

"They don't think that. And neither do you. We shouldn't even be here. My cousin in Buffalo says the entire community she's in is from Castellammare del Golfo. The Bacchiegas say that Williamsburg in Brooklyn is full of our kind. So why are we here?"

Sonny slid his cards into his pocket and tried to find a toy to play with, anything he could do to distract himself from their fussing.

"I don't want that anymore, Rosa. We left for a reason. As long as we're around other Sicilians, they'll know who I am. They'll know who we are."

"And that's such a bad thing?"

"No, Rosa. But you know exactly what I mean."

"So being around Italians is better? If we were around our own people, maybe you would be able to at least find a decent job." Sonny's mother opened the door and began to enter before pausing. Sonny pretended he hadn't heard anything until he perceived something was wrong. Headlights spilled into the dark tenement foyer and engulfed his mother. "Who is that, Lonz?" Rosa stopped in her tracks.

"Go inside, Rosa. Shut the door."

"Come on, baby boy. Let's go upstairs," Rosa said, extending her hands to carry him up to their tenement.

"I can walk," Sonny said, double-checking to make sure all of his things had been gathered up. His mother ushered him up the stairs, but he stopped. "I forgot a card."

"Hurry and get it. You need to clean yourself before bed." Rosa pointed her finger as Sonny hurried down the stairs.

Sonny hadn't forgotten any cards. He felt bad about lying, but he couldn't go upstairs if something was going on outside. Pretending to look for a Jack of Hearts in the dark, he peered out the window. A black car had pulled up out front. Several men were in the vehicle, and most of them had remained seated. The motor of the automobile continued to rumble. One of the men, however, took his time walking up the concrete stairs to greet Sonny's father. Sonny watched, heart racing, as his father straightened with tension until the man drew near. Eventually, his father's posture relaxed, and he embraced the strange man with a hug and kiss.

"Sonny, have you found it?" Rosa called from the stairwell.

"Still looking," he called back, his eyes glued on the doorway. His father talked with the man for a brief moment, until the stranger reached into his three-piece suit. He pulled out a thick envelope and handed it to Alonzo. Sonny's father waved his hands in resistance at first, but eventually took it and bowed his head. Sonny couldn't hear the words they spoke, but after a moment, the stranger held out his hand. It was marred badly, and only a thumb and perhaps another finger or two remained.

Sonny shook with terror, and bolted up the steps.

"Did you lose another card, Sonny? We can't afford another deck."

"No, I found it, Mamma." He clung to her leg as tightly as he could, allowing her to carry him up the stairs. He shut his eyes and tried to force out the image of the Hook-Handed Man.

Little Italy, Manhattan—February 17, 1910

It was a happy day.

It wasn't like most days. Even Sonny's mother was smiling and cheerful. His father was singing Sicilian folk songs at the top of his lungs, and Enzo and Vico were playing nice as well.

Sonny sang along with his dad and took advantage of his mother's geniality by dancing around with her in the kitchen.

"Go on, now. Go on. Get your things—as soon as your father is ready, we'll be leaving." Sonny's mother smiled at his playfulness but waved him from the kitchen. Sonny stopped by his favorite place in the kitchen before he left, his mother's china cabinet. It was the only part of their tenement that reminded Sonny of the wealth and prosperity of their time in Sicily that his brothers so often talked about. Vico told Sonny that the china set was the only nice thing that his mother had had time to grab when they were preparing to leave for America. Sonny didn't remember it well, and had been fairly confused about what was going on at that time, but he was glad his mother had remembered them. There were only three pieces left, and his mother often lamented that she had once had many more. One was chipped and cracked from the long sea voyage, but the family was still proud of them. The only thing his father had brought that wasn't of functional purpose was his rosary. Sonny loved to play with it when his father fell asleep shirtless on their couch after returning from some day job or another.

That was about to change, though.

Alonzo had just purchased a building down the road, and he was opening a barbershop. One just like Sonny's grandfather had once been the proprietor of back in Castellammare del Golfo. Sonny had never seen his father so youthful. Alonzo seemed to bounce on his toes, and a jolly tune was always flowing from his lips.

His brothers questioned where this good fortune had suddenly come from. His mother didn't seem to be interested in its roots, but simply in the fruit it might bear. But Sonny knew. He was just a boy, and none of the others thought he was smart. But he had seen it. Their recent fortune had something to do with the strange man who had shown up at their door. It had something to do with that envelope the man had slid into Alonzo's hands. He just knew it. He also knew better than to ask questions or to mention it. He simply hoped he never had to see the Hook Hand again.

The *Consentinos* traveled the six blocks by foot, but when they arrived, Sonny found his excitement none depleted.

"Here she is." Alonzo turned and took a deep bow before the windows of his new prize, "A.C. Barbers" freshly painted in yellow letters at the top. A white pole that looked awfully like a candy cane twirled just before the window with a bright light above it.

"Come on!" Enzo hurried through the doorway as Vico followed in close pursuit. Sonny entered last, slowly and curiously, holding tight to his mother's hand. He stopped and admired the room, mouth agape. Mirrors lined the walls, and barber chairs were stationed before them, a white towel draped over the back of each.

"What do you think?" Alonzo asked Rosa, along with a wet kiss on the cheek.

"Well, you've got your work cut out for you, Lonz."
She was joking, but Sonny could see from the pursed grin
on her face that she was almost as delighted as her
husband.

"I can't get this damned thing to work." The low,
rumbly voice came from a man in the back of the shop
perched over a phonograph. The man spoke in English,
but Sonny knew he had said a bad word. He craned his
head and, noticing the children, apologized for his
language.

"Rosa, boys, this is Oscar. He is going to work with us."
Alonzo began to speak in English, a new talent he seemed
anxious to show off. The man shook their hands one by
one, and finally knelt by Sonny.

"And you must be the oldest?" Enzo and Vico were
appalled by the comment, but Sonny simply analyzed the
man and didn't reply. He had a funny look about him, with
pale-white skin and bald spots atop his head. Bifocals twice
the size of his eyes hung on the tip of his nose.

"He doesn't talk much," Rosa said, shaking her head.

"He's just a little shy. Say hello, Sonny." Alonzo patted
his back and squeezed his shoulder.

"I'm not the oldest."

"Yeah, I am," Enzo shouted with great pride.

"No, you aren't. Vico is just as old as you." Sonny
scrunched his nose at Enzo. It was their age-old argument.
Enzo was born a few minutes before Vico, and had clung
to that narrative to justify his rightful place as the eldest
brother. Vico never protested.

"Well, you might not be the oldest, but do you want to
be the first to get a snip?" Oscar snipped his scissors, and
his eyebrows danced emphatically.

"No, me!" Enzo tugged at his sleeve.

"I want Papà to cut my hair," Sonny said.

"Alright, Sonny Boy," said Alonzo, now speaking in Sicilian, as he picked his youngest up underneath an arm with ease and swung him into a nearby chair. "Look here." He fished through his multiple layers of winter clothing to find a sharp razor with an ivory handle. "This was your grandfather's. See his initials there?" Sonny reached out and ran his fingers over it. "Be careful, it's still sharp. This little blade will run this entire building." He waved his arms as if overlooking a kingdom. "And, one day, maybe it'll be yours, if you want to cut hair like your papa." He winked and ruffled Sonny's unkempt hair. "We've got to fix that." He swung the chair around and started to work. Sonny watched him in the mirror, amazed. He didn't know if he wanted to cut hair, but he wanted to be just like his papa.

HEARINGS BEFORE THE
PERMANENT SUBCOMMITTEE ON INVESTIGATIONS
OF THE
COMMITTEE ON GOVERNMENT OPERATIONS
UNITED STATES SENATE
EIGHTY-EIGHTH CONGRESS
SECOND SESSION
PURSUANT TO SENATE RESOLUTION 17
SEPTEMBER 28, 1963

SENATOR MCCLELLAN: I have a question for Mr. Valachi.

Chairman: Go ahead.

Senator McClellan: Did Sonny Consentino ever talk much about his childhood?

Mr. Valachi: No, not really. Why does that matter? He turned out the way he turned out.

Chairman: Answer the question, Mr. Valachi.

Mr. Valachi: He never talked about it much. His brother Enzo did some, but most of what

I knew came from hearsay, what I heard from others.

Senator McClellan: Go on.

Mr. Valachi: His father was a connected guy in Sicily. Apparently, he was pretty important and had a lot of connections. They moved here when things were getting a little rough across the pond, and I think he tried to get away from that life. I heard once that they moved to Little Italy because there weren't many Sicilians there.

Senator McClellan: Sonny's father, Alonzo, wanted to break from his criminal organization ties?

Mr. Valachi: Yeah, or at least he wanted it to seem that way. I don't know. All of it caught up to him pretty quickly.

Senator McClellan: In what way?

Mr. Valachi: They were poor, and then suddenly they weren't. I wasn't around for any of this, you see. But I heard from others that he might have still been connected. It would be hard to go from being a wealthy man in your homeland to being a poor man in a foreign place. I assumed he did what he had to.

Senator McClellan: Do you believe Sonny became connected to your organization through his father?

Mr. Valachi: I don't know. He was already involved when I met him. So were his brothers.

Senator McClellan: Did they have a good relationship with Alonzo? Did they speak of him often?

Mr. Valachi: Like I said, Sonny didn't talk about personal stuff very often. When he did, though, yeah, his father came up a lot. They called him "Sonny" because of his likeness to his father. In Italy, that nickname usually goes to the firstborn. But Enzo wasn't much like their old man. I always got the impression they didn't have much of a relationship. Sonny was different, though.

. . .

Senator McClellan: That is all.

Chairman: Thank you, Senator.

ALONZO

The screams were horrifying. Perhaps even worse than when Rosa had given birth to their first two boys.

Alonzo waited anxiously in the foyer of their home, biting intensely on his knuckle. He bowed his head and tapped his feet like he was running for the hills.

"Brother! I came as soon as I heard." Alonzo's brother, Giuseppe, hurried to his side and kissed his cheeks.

"They say there are complications, Giuseppe. She's been in there all day."

Giuseppe looked down and contemplated what to say. Alonzo's youngest, and only surviving, brother had always been an eternal optimist, but there wasn't much he could say. He fingered the petals of the roses he had brought for Rosa, and sat down on the dusty old bench beside Alonzo.

"Then let us pray for the baby. That it will be strong," Giuseppe said.

"What about Rosa? What if something happens to her?" A

tremor enveloped Alonzo's body, and a sort of moan escaped from deep in his chest.

"It will not be so. She is tough, your wife."

Rosa's cries picked up in the other room, and so did the voice of the midwife.

"Brother"—Alonzo turned to him and finally found the courage to take Giuseppe's hands between his own—"what if we are being punished because of the bad things I've done? What if God punishes me and makes this child crippled, or lame?" Tears fell from his eyes. He couldn't ever remember crying in front of his little brother.

"Hail Mary, full of grace…the Lord is with thee…" Giuseppe began, cradling his older brother in his arms like their mother had before she passed. "Pray for us sinners now and at the hour of our death."

Giuseppe's words left a hollow pit in Alonzo's gut. Giuseppe seemed to consider this and fumbled through the words. He had always been a devoted Catholic, quick to point out God's sovereignty, but he had a shortage of prayers in his arsenal for moments like this.

Rosa's screams died down to low groaning. Then the cries of a baby took its place.

Alonzo jumped to his feet, and hesitated before the doorway into the bedroom.

"Rosa!" he shouted as Giuseppe came behind him and grabbed his shoulder. He received no reply.

After what felt like hours, the door crept open, and the midwife slid out and closed the door behind her.

"The baby has been born, Don Consentino." She bowed her head. A gentle smile lined her face, but it was etched with worry and perhaps sadness.

"Is it alive? Is it healthy? Is Rosa safe?"

The midwife bounced her hands vertically, indicating that he should quiet down. "The baby is alive. A baby boy, in fact."

Giuseppe let out a gasp of relief, but Alonzo was still panicked.

"*You have not said that the baby is healthy. How is Rosa? Rosa!*" *The midwife sidestepped to keep him from the door.*

"*You don't want to go in there, Don Consentino. Very bloody, all around. Your boy will most likely live, but when he was born, the umbilical cord was wrapped around his neck, and he struggled to breathe. I'll need to keep an eye on him.*"

"'*Most likely…*'" *The words were wrenched from Alonzo's chest like a dagger. He thought again about the things he had done and felt guilt sweep over him like a coastal current.*

"*What about my sister-in-law?*" *Giuseppe asked.*

"*She must rest now. She is very weak and has lost a lot of blood. This birth wasn't as easy as the last. The baby had shifted in her womb. I'll get back to her. I'll let you know if we need anything.*" *She bowed and stepped back into the room, letting the door swing shut in front of Alonzo's face.*

"*Let us keep praying, brother,*" *Giuseppe offered, but Alonzo shrugged the hand from his shoulder and strode away from him as if he were a ghost.*

Creaking began from the steps near the entryway. Both Consentinos halted and watched as Piddu slowly made his way down the stairs. He was still living in their home, a constant reminder to Alonzo of what had happened to him, and what Alonzo was forced to do because of it.

"*Is it over?*" *Piddu asked genuinely, a tinge of hope in his voice. Alonzo met his gaze until Piddu's smile completely faded. Then he turned and walked away.*

ROSA

Rosa shielded her eyes from the sun as they exited onto the steeple steps. Family and friends lined the way, clapping and cheering as if it were a wedding. Instead, she held up her precious baby boy, who she had named Vincente after her father. No one had yet called him that, though. She had taken a few days before selecting a name. She had pretended that her two favorite male names had already gone to her first two sons and she couldn't think of anything else. Alonzo had gone along with it, saying that he refused to name him. It should be for Rosa to decide.

Her true intention was to put off naming the boy as long as she could. She knew it was wrong, but she couldn't stand the thought of naming the boy if he were to pass away in his infancy, as it looked like he might. She kept this quiet because, in her heart, she knew she would suffer whether the boy was named or not. Just as she had suffered through the two miscarriages and the stillborn before.

Regardless, in the interim of the child's birth and the receiving of his name, he had been dubbed "Sonny Boy." It made sense. While

Rosa was too tired and too weak to get to her feet care for the baby, Alonzo was already curled up beside the crib. He fell asleep with one hand on the baby's belly for the first three nights. Alonzo had always been a devoted father. Rosa had never seen a man, so fearless and brave, be as nurturing and loving to his children. She loved him more than she could say, and certainly more than she actually would say. Perhaps it was just better left unsaid.

Despite the boy's resurgence and growing health, Rosa made it clear that she wanted to have the baby christened as soon as possible. Through tear-filled eyes, she implored her husband, "If something happens, I want to know that I will be with my baby in heaven." She meant if something happened to either her or the baby. Just after the delivery, either seemed plausible. Alonzo had argued that nothing would happen; he wouldn't let it. Eventually, he capitulated, and began to make arrangements.

Now, just four days after the troubled birth, she ushered the baby through the halls of their ancestral church, where her family was buried. And yet, it was not a somber moment. It was a celebration. As she stepped carefully down the stairs, gripping the steady hand of her husband for balance, the christening felt more like a festival than a Catholic Sacrament.

"He looks just like his big brother!" her aunt Margarete said, dabbing a tear from her eye with a white handkerchief.

"He's built like a bull," Uncle Umberto said, proudly slapping his nephew on the shoulder.

"Perhaps he'll grow up like his great-uncle, then!" Alonzo's contagious laugh rang out as he leaned to kiss the man.

Giuseppe stood at the end of the throng, another bouquet of flowers in hand.

"Or perhaps he'll turn out like his favorite uncle, if I have anything to do with it." Giuseppe's bright smile matched his brother's.

"Not if I have anything to do with it." Alonzo leaned in and embraced his brother.

Their celebration was halted as tires screeched in the distance. A black automobile pulled up in front of the chapel, and a man jumped out, a machine gun resting on his hip.

Bullets began to fly. Rosa, with her mother's instinct, turned and protected the baby. Alonzo pounced on top of them, shielding them both with his body. Rosa's shrill cry rang out over the bullets. The throng of gatherers cowered to the ground, and some scurried off. Only a few met the assailants.

Without delay the armed man pounced back into the vehicle, and it sped away.

"Come back here, you son of a bitch!" Giuseppe's voice carried as he took off after the vehicle, the nickel of his pistol shimmering in the early-morning sunlight.

"Giuseppe!" Alonzo cried, jumping to his feet.

"Lonz, Lonz!" Rosa cried, tucking the baby into her breast.

"Are you okay?" he asked. "I'm not hit." He looked himself over to make sure.

"Your ear." She dabbed at it with her fingers. The bullet had only grazed him. Alonzo stood to survey the scene.

Then, in the growing silence, they heard gurgling.

"Uncle!" Alonzo took over across the courtyard to where Umberto had tried to fight the hit men. He was perched awkwardly against the brick wall, Latin scriptures inscribed behind his head. He tried to speak, but only blood poured from his lips.

He began to sink farther down the wall, and in a fit of epileptic rage, he shook to the ground and moved no longer. Alonzo clung to his chest, checking for a heartbeat.

"No, no, no..." Rosa watched in horror as her husband tried to nurse him back to health. It was too late. Alonzo stood and turned to them, a pained look on his face. He whimpered and tears welled in his eyes. "Uncle..." he said, quietly. Then his body bolted upright as he apparently remembered his brother. "Giuseppe!" Alonzo ran after his brother, his voice carrying as he faded into the distance. Rosa remained behind on the steps, weeping alongside her baby boy.

SONNY

Sonny had never been more excited in his young life. Buying the barbershop was small peanuts compared to getting a baby sibling.

It seemed like no time after Alonzo started his new business that his mother delivered the news: she was expecting another baby. Enzo and Vico shrugged. They had already received a little sibling, and they weren't very interested in another. Sonny, however, was thrilled. He asked to feel his mother's belly often, and he liked to postulate what the baby's gender would be, and what it would be like. A baby in the family meant that he wouldn't be the youngest, and it meant that he would have a companion like Enzo had Vico had each other. It meant he would have a friend, bringing his grand total of friends up to four: his Italian friend Antonello, his father, his mother, and the soon-to-be-born baby.

"You know, Sonny, when you were born, we didn't have

a place like this." Alonzo pointed around the hospital waiting room with the brim of his hat.

"Really?"

"Yes. We didn't have any good hospitals nearby, so your mother had you right in our bedroom."

"Ew." Sonny scrunched his nose, to his father's amusement.

"Maybe, but that's how we did it. It was hard on your mother. But we made it through unharmed." He leaned over and patted Sonny's shoulder.

"Where did Mamma give birth to us, Papà?" Vico asked, his head tilted.

"Let's see…Sonny Boy was born in 1905, and he was born in a bed. You two rascals were born five years before, in 1900, so I will bet you were born"—he tapped his lip with his forefinger, and looked up inquisitively—"probably in a barn somewhere." Enzo and Vico shouted out with mock indignation and clamored across Sonny to pick at their father.

"Shh, shh. We have to stay quiet," Alonzo said. Enzo and Vico snickered, but obeyed.

Sonny didn't like it when the silence grew. The sounds of the hospital were scary. All of it was foreign and strange. His feet tapped against the linoleum beneath him until his father's hand rested on his knee to slow them.

"Are you nervous, Sonny Boy?" Alonzo asked. Sonny nodded. "That's okay. I am too."

"It doesn't look like it," Sonny replied, and his father chuckled.

"Maybe it doesn't. But I am. But we've been through this before, and it was very scary last time. But God got us through it then, and I bet he will now. You know what I do now instead of tapping my feet?" Alonzo materialized the rosary he had clutched in his palm. "Do you want to pray with me?" Sonny shook his head. He didn't want to pray. He didn't want to do anything except see his mother and his new sibling. "I know how you feel. I didn't want to pray when you were born either. But your uncle Giuseppe made me." Alonzo began to put the rosary back in his pocket, but then hesitated. "Have I ever told you about who this is?" His finger traced along the beads to a silver disc in the center, which bore the image of a bearded man clutching to a cross.

"No."

"This is Saint Bernard of Corleone. Boys, listen to this." He waved to get Enzo and Vico's attention. "He is a Sicilian, like us. He was a soldier once, and he was very mean and angry, and he did a lot of bad things."

"He did?" the boys asked, confused about why such a man would appear on their father's rosary.

"Yes, he did. But after a while, he realized he was doing a bad thing. He realized he was putting those he loved in danger. So he went far away, where God talked to him and told him to change his life."

"God *talked* to him?" Sonny asked.

"Yes. You could say that. God talks to many of us, if you listen."

"Doesn't he just talk to the priests?" Sonny asked, noticing a look of surprise and pride in his father's eyes.

"Most of the time, yes. But sometimes he whispers in our ear and tells us what to do. He informed this man that he was doing some bad things, and told him to change it. So he did. Now he is a saint of the Catholic Church."

"Is he still alive?" Vico asked.

"No, he died a long time ago. He's with God now."

"I wish I could have met him," Sonny said. The silence returned, and the twins lost interest. "Papà, I think I would like to pray. Thank you for making me pray, like Uncle Giuseppe made you." Alonzo pinched Sonny's cheek.

"Of course. Your uncle was a good man, and he taught me many things."

"Where is he now?" Sonny asked. Alonzo turned to his boy, his face now as stonelike as the Statue of Liberty's.

"He's with God now too, Sonny Boy."

Little Italy, Manhattan—April 9, 1911

Sonny was afraid that if his father pulled his tie any tighter, he would suffocate.

"Stop squirming, Sonny. There, ready to go." Alonzo stood up and went to help Enzo and Vico finish getting dressed.

"I thought you said today was a holiday?" Enzo pouted and tugged at the collar of his coat.

"It is a holiday. That's why you boys don't have to go to school today."

"Then why is everyone so sad?" Vico asked.

"Because a great man has died, and today we are going to tell him thank you." Sonny had heard his mother say before that to wear black was a bad omen for a Sicilian, and it could only be worn in times of mourning. It didn't seem that they knew this fellow, but apparently, they were mourning regardless.

"How can we tell him thank you if he's already dead?" Enzo asked as Alonzo finished with his tie. Rosa walked over and popped him lightly on the mouth.

"That's disrespectful. Never say anything against the dead. You'll pay for it. Now hurry up and get ready."

"Rosa," Alonzo said, gesturing to the small flask in her hand, "before a funeral?"

After Alonzo had dressed his sons to his liking, the family made its way out onto the street. People were pouring out of their tenements from all directions. They were all dressed in black as well, and wore gloomy faces.

"Where are we going to tell the dead man thank you?" Sonny asked.

"Hush now. We're going to Old St. Patrick's." Alonzo held a finger to his lips. The walk to their church was usually only a few minutes' walk, but not this morning. The throng of people continued to grow, and everyone moved slowly, as if afraid of what they would find at the cathedral.

A man approached and kissed Alonzo on either cheek.

"Damned shame, isn't it?" the man asked, beginning to walk along with them, his wife and son following close behind. After a moment, Sonny recognized him as Mr. Bacchiega, one of the few other Sicilians who lived in Little Italy, but it was hard to recognize him in that black suit.

"It is. He was a hero." Alonzo's voice was barely audible, out of respect.

"I heard that he died poor, and that they had to raise money just to give his wife, Adeline, something to live on." Mr. Bacchiega shook his head.

"Well, yeah. The bulls make their living on bribery and outright theft, and Petrosino was an honest man. Of course, he was broke," Mrs. Bacchiega said from behind them. Alonzo declined to respond. Sonny noticed that his mother had also been silent most of the morning, and he didn't know what that meant. She instead smoked cigarette after cigarette.

As the steeple of the cathedral rounded into view, they stopped. The line was backed up for half a mile to Old St. Patrick's. More people piled in behind them, and waited. Everyone was keeping their voices quiet, but a general murmur of confusion and sadness could be heard throughout.

"Good morning, friends." Another man approached and greeted Sonny's father and Mr. Bacchiega. Their party seemed unperturbed, but Sonny started shaking. He recognized the man. He recognized him by the bushy mustache that hovered over his lips and his mangled hand. The Hook Hand was young but appeared ageless, like an ancient black shadow.

"I wouldn't call it a good morning," Mr. Bacchiega said after half accepting a kiss.

"That's a matter of perspective." The Hook Hand shrugged his shoulders.

"You got a lot of balls even showing up here, Morello," Mr. Bacchiega said, his wife reaching forward and placing a concerned hand on his shoulder. The Hook Hand held out his hands, a coy grin splitting across his face.

"A few years away from Sicily, and we forget our manners, don't we? *Don* Morello will do." The Hook Hand tipped his gray fedora and walked off.

"Papà?" Sonny clutched his father's hand.

"Quiet," Alonzo whispered.

A horse-drawn carriage appeared down the road. The crowd's murmuring dissipated. The policemen marching before it passed by, and the hearse followed behind it. The carriage was transparent, and, inside, a coffin could be seen clearly, the stars and stripes of the American flag draped over it. As Verdi's *Messa da Requiem* began to play in the distance, women in the crowd dabbed their eyes with handkerchiefs. Some of the men saluted.

Alonzo only lowered his eyes. Rosa lit another cigarette.

"I heard his corpse was so filled with bullets, they couldn't even give his wife an open casket," Bacchiega said, whispering to Alonzo, who, in return, shot him a look that immediately silenced him.

After the hearse arrived at the cathedral, Alonzo led the boys away, back toward their tenement. They still wanted answers, though, and Alonzo seemed to know it.

"That man was a policeman. Do you know what a policeman is?" Alonzo asked his boys.

"Yes, Papà." Enzo rolled his eyes.

"Someone who fights bad guys?" Sonny looked up, only half sure of his answer.

"That's right. His name was Joseph Petrosino. And he was like us, from across the sea. He fought against a lot of bad men, and did a lot of good things for New York."

"But the bad men won?" Sonny asked. His father exhaled and thought for a moment, which concerned Sonny even more.

"They didn't win. There will always be bad men. And sometimes even good men can do bad things. They'll always be around. But there will always be men like Petrosino to protect us."

"I hope so, Papà."

Little Italy, Manhattan—June 15, 1911

. . .

Sonny spent all the time he could at his father's barbershop. With school out, and not much to do, he pitched in all day when his father would allow it. He occasionally took the day off to play baseball with Antonello and some of the other boys in his neighborhood, but he liked to be around his father more than anything. Watching Alonzo talk with the important men that came in for a haircut or a hot lather shave was all the compensation he needed.

He even got to stay up later. Sonny smiled to himself as he swept up the hair from the last haircut of the evening, imagining that Enzo and Vico were being scolded by their mother to get into bed and turn the lights off. But Sonny got to stay out as long as his father left the lights on, and Alonzo often left them on until late, allowing some of his busier associates to come by after a long day of work.

The lights were off now, a little after 9:30 p.m., but Alonzo always said that they couldn't leave until the job was done.

"Cut the music, Sonny Boy, it's almost time to go," Alonzo said, nodding to the record player and making for the door. As he reversed the sign from "Open" to "Closed," blinding headlights swept through the barbershop. The car came to a stop just before the place.

"Pops?" Sonny had begun calling him the New York City version of "Papà" to fit in with the other boys in the neighborhood.

"Don't worry about it. I'll tell him we're closed. Go grab the trash from the bathroom." Sonny propped the broom against the wall and hurried to do as he was told, but kept the doorway in his line of sight. He grabbed the bag of trash, tied it, and threw it over his shoulder. He paced back to the door and craned his head to see his father.

He was standing with his shoulders back and his head straight. His discussion with the man seemed to be formal, perhaps unpleasant. Sonny strained his eyes to make out the man's features, but he could only see a thick mustache that seemed to cover most of the man's face. His father began to shake his head. Their voices began to rise. The other man stepped closer and moved his arms emphatically. Alonzo waved his hands.

Sonny, heart now stirring, made for the doorway. He wasn't sure what he would do, but figured his presence might defuse the situation.

He pushed back the door with the side of his hand and then stepped out.

His eyes widened as he saw the other man lift up his hand, a mutilated hand, a few nubs and a few fingers, covered in old scarred flesh. The man held his hand out in the reflection of his headlights, seeming to put it on display. Alonzo heard the creak of the door and turned to his boy. Before he could say anything, Sonny turned and ran back inside.

"Sonny!" his father said, calling out as the door slammed behind him. He hastened to the back of the shop, as far away from the door and the Hook Hand as he could get. He didn't know why the man had returned, but he didn't see any envelopes this time. Sonny didn't figure that any more good luck was about to befall them.

ALONZO

The silence blared in his ears. The darkness burned in his eyes.

They had been sitting in that old shack for what felt like an eternity, and Alonzo was beginning to wonder if they had made a mistake.

After the Armettas killed Uncle Umberto, he should have retaliated. He should have killed every last one of them. He should have filled up the cemeteries with every male relative of theirs in Sicily. Giuseppe had encouraged him to do just that. Young Turridru had promised he would do it himself. Old Ignazio had said that if he still had his sight, he would've shoved their corpses into barrels and they'd be halfway across the Atlantic by now.

But what was he supposed to do? Alonzo had three boys to look out for now. And the Armettas had proven how reckless they had become, how daring. They had also proven that they had no qualms about killing without honor. Using an automobile for a shooting and then scurrying away? Attacking at a baby's christening? Alonzo couldn't remember anything like this happening before. And as much as he wanted to avenge Uncle Umberto, he had his wife and children to think about. Rosa had always had a weak constitution when it came to the Borgata lifestyle, but after the attack, she was utterly shaken to her core. She looked at Alonzo with dark eyes that were filled with something he couldn't place. Apathy, perhaps? Anger? He didn't know. But something had to be done, or she might just drink herself into oblivion. Alonzo had told her to put down the flask a few times.

"Drinking that much while you're still breastfeeding the baby might not be good, Rosa." She looked at him blankly until he walked away. She blamed him for what had happened. She probably had the right to. But she blamed Piddu even more. Although the young man remained in their house, sleeping in their guest bed and eating their food, she wouldn't look or talk to him. It was as if he were not there.

Finally, the door creaked open. A beam of sunlight raced along the floors and up onto the walls, and dust stirred from the hay-covered barn floor. Alonzo and Giuseppe stood, and Ignazio struggled to do the same until Turridru helped him up.

"Are you armed?" Alonzo asked as his guests stepped into the darkness.

"No, we aren't armed. If we wanted you dead, you wouldn't leave this building," said Lupe, the patriarch of the Armettas, as he looked around the wooden shack.

"Was this really the only place we could meet?" one of his sons asked with a disapproving laugh.

"Didn't want it to be in public. In case you became trigger happy again," Giuseppe said, looking over each of the Armettas for anything suspicious.

Lupe pulled out a chair for the single table in the center of the room, and sat down deliberately. He removed his velvet hat and brushed his fingers over the peacock feather on its side.

"What is it you want to discuss?"

"What do you think?" Giuseppe asked.

"We want this bloodshed to end," Alonzo said, ignoring the grunt from Ignazio behind him.

"*Why would you wish to end a game you just started?*" Lupe said carelessly, munching on a cigar almost as long as his forearm, and lighting it with two matches.

"*We didn't start it,*" Alonzo replied.

Suddenly, Lupe's callous demeanor evaporated and he shifted in his chair. "*I seem to recall that three of my little cousins are now dead. And it was you who pulled the trigger.*"

"*We were avenging a slight. Blood demands blood. Those three men attacked and killed associates of mine. Not only did they kill the man but they killed his wife too. And they mutilated their son.*"

Lupe spun into a fit of rage and slammed his fist down on the table. "*Some sheep humping peasant family from Corleone or Palermo or wherever they came from! They come into this city, my city, and insult my relatives. They received what they deserved.*"

"*I should have been consulted. They were associates of mine, and I would have handled it.*"

"*Handled it like you're handling this now? With a conversation and a handshake? The coward's way wouldn't do,*" Lupe said, returning his focus to the tip of his cigar. Giuseppe stood with a stir, as did Lupe's sons.

"*Was the coward's way what I did in response? By killing the men who had wronged me and my family?*" Alonzo asked. Lupe ignored him.

"*What do you really want?*" Lupe asked sardonically. He made it clear that he was done talking.

"*The head of the man who killed my uncle. The man who attacked my family on the christening of my son.*"

Lupe laughed, and the men behind him shuffled uncomfortably. "*That man was my son,*" Lupe said. Alonzo noticed that, out of Lupe's four sons, the perpetrator was the only one not present.

"*I know. And Umberto was like a father to me, a grandfather to my boys. He would have killed more of us too, if he had better aim, and hadn't run off.*"

"*What makes you think I would give up my son?*"

"Justice. The men we killed were only those directly involved in the murders of my associates. We could have killed the proprietor of the restaurant; we could have retaliated on any number of your allies. But we didn't. We spilt the blood that needed to be spilt and left it there. But Umberto had nothing to do with all of this. He was an old man, sick and frail. You gained nothing from his death."

Lupe took a long drag on his cigar and pulled it away from his face. He leaned in and smirked. "Better for the old and weak to die than the young and strong." He winked.

"We want him dead, Lupe." Alonzo was unwavering on the outside. On the inside, he was about to fall apart. To his surprise, Lupe actually took a moment to think.

"You know I will never hand over my son to his death. So, why, I ask myself, would you come to me with this request?"

"If you can consider a suitable alternative, I'm open to hearing it. But as long as he is in Castellammare del Golfo, he will be marked for death. If I see him, I will kill him. And if I do, this war will continue, and neither of us can benefit from that."

"Perhaps we can send him off. He's nearly thirty now. Perhaps he could go to work in Milan, Naples, Syracuse... Is exile good enough for my son?"

"Yes."

"One thing I require"—Lupe held up a finger—"I want Piddu."

"Why?" Giuseppe asked, shocked and appalled. "He's just a boy."

"Let us be realistic, gentlemen. He has caused all of this. You, my son, your uncle...pawns in a game. It was Piddu and his family who started this, and my cousins who ended it. Now they are dead. Only one remains alive." Lupe puffed on his cigar and allowed the silence to linger. "He should be killed for the pain and hardship he has caused both of our families."

"That's ridiculous! How could you possibly pin all of this on a boy? He did nothing but come to me for aid." Alonzo couldn't imagine that a grown man could genuinely believe something so preposterous.

He must be angling for control. That's what Piddu's life was worth to him. Control, and nothing more.

"Only the boy needs to die."

"No," Alonzo said definitively. Turridru shot him a look of confusion, but he ignored it. He didn't want to hear what Ignazio had to say either.

"No? You tell me no after I promise to send my own son away to appease your gentle nature?" The veins in Lupe's neck and forehead began to bulge. He was starting to look like the pigheaded caricature he was sometimes known to be.

"The answer is no. The boy is under my protection, and I will not hand him over."

"As you've asked me to deliver up my own son?" Again, Lupe's fists smashed against the table.

"Perhaps we can send Piddu away as well."

"Not good enough. The boy needs to die. They should have never left him alive. There is nowhere in Sicily that I will not find him." He slammed his cigar down on the table, extinguishing the flame. "Even in your own home."

"Then we have nothing left to discuss."

Lupe stood and placed his hat back on his head.

"My son will remain here as long as Piddu is alive. If you want this war to end, that is what I require. As far as you and your dwindling little borgata, you are not worthy of my time. I have no more quarrel with you. Blood was shed, but it can end as soon as you would like. The boy is the only one who needs to die." Lupe and his sons left, the light from the door evaporating behind them.

ALONZO

Alonzo slid the deck of cards across the table to Sonny, and asked him to cut the deck. He had tried to pin down Enzo and Vico to play cards with them that summer evening, but, at eleven, they would rather spend time with other neighborhood kids than with their father and little brother.

"Oh, buddy, you better be scared. This is a good hand." Alonzo shook his head, his best attempt at dissuasion. Sonny stifled a grin and placed a few chips forward. He called his father's bluff, like he always did. Even at five years old, Sonny knew that, when his father actually had a good hand, he wouldn't say anything.

And he didn't. Alonzo pretended to be deliberating for some time, shuffling a few chips before throwing his cards on the table. "I fold."

Even in a game of cards with his son, Alonzo couldn't find much luck.

He thought that having his own place would fix his problems, turn everything around. That wasn't the case.

Along with a new business came many new expenses. He was earning an income, and his business was growing daily. But he could still see the look on his wife's face when he would count up his earnings and tell her that it was best if they didn't eat out that night. He still had to tell his boys that they couldn't afford new summer clothes, even though they were bursting at the seams in last year's attire.

"I think I'm getting better than you, Dad." Sonny giggled and swept the few chips into the center of the table to his holdings, as if it were all of King Midas's gold.

"Better than me? I'm just taking it easy on you."

Sonny looked away from their porch, down Mulberry Street toward the setting sun.

"What do you think it's like at home right now?"

"Home? We are home," Alonzo said, but he realized what Sonny meant before he finished speaking.

"In Sicily, Dad. Sometimes I don't remember it." Sonny struggled to shuffle the cards as his father had taught him.

Alonzo replied, "I bet it's hot. Hotter than it is here. You'd have to take a long dip in the water just to keep from melting."

Sonny grinned and shrugged his shoulders. "I like the heat. Vico says that there were bugs that would glow at night."

"Yes, lightning bugs. We have them here too, it's just hard to find them in the city."

"I haven't seen any." Alonzo looked up and nodded as some other tenement residents came and sat on the porch across from them. They ignored him, as most of the Italians did, and continued debating emphatically about something or another.

"Well, there's something we don't have in Sicily." Alonzo pointed to the young man walking up the rickety old steps to greet them.

"Antonello!" Sonny jumped to his feet, always excited to see his pal. His friend obviously didn't share his excitement. He stepped by Sonny, straight to Alonzo. He lowered his head and hid his eyes behind a ragged newsboy cap.

"Mr. Consentino, can I stay here for a few days?" He stifled a few sniffles.

"What's wrong, Antonello?" Alonzo asked, dusting off another chair beside him and patting for the boy to sit. Antonello pulled at his loose knickerbockers and kept his feet planted. "Antonello?" The boy began to cry more, and Alonzo stood.

Sonny ran inside, Alonzo figured to grab his mother. Alonzo noticed that Antonello was nursing one of his arms.

"Come here," he said firmly, but when he realized Sonny's friend wasn't going to move, he went to him instead. He unbuttoned the sleeve of Antonello's white shirt, the only one he ever seemed to wear, and rolled it up to reveal a large bruise. The wound followed the shape of a large hand. Alonzo tried to calm himself, but when Antonello finally looked up, he saw that the boy's lips were split and the skin around his left eye was puffy and purple.

"He was hitting my mamma, Mr. Consentino," the young man sobbed. "I tried to hit him with a candlestick." He finally made it to the seat Alonzo had offered him, plopping down in defeat.

"You can stay here, Antonello." He put a hand on the boy's shoulder.

"What was that?" Rosa said from the doorway, Sonny holding her hand. Alonzo now lamented that he'd let

Sonny go in to fetch Rosa. She was no fan of Antonello, who, at thirteen, was older than the twins yet liked to spend time with her five-year-old.

"I told this young man that he could stay with us for a while." Alonzo looked up at his wife, speaking firmly yet tenderly.

"Oh? Where will he stay? In the *two* beds our *three* boys share? Or should we sleep on the floor and let him take our bed? Perhaps he can share Maria's crib." She stepped forward, her voice containing the fire only a Sicilian can muster. Her anger was stunted when she saw the bruises, but only slightly.

"My pa kicked me out, Mrs. Consentino," Antonello said. "I don't know where else to go." He couldn't muster the courage to look at her.

Rosa wiped her hands on a pink dish towel hanging from her belt. "Dinner will be ready in half an hour. Make sure the twins are back. I want all you boys to wash your hands and face when you come in." She shot Alonzo a look that said she would relent this once but didn't appreciate him making these kinds of decisions without consulting her. Alonzo knew she wasn't really as hard as she pretended to be. He was an idealist and a fool, so he needed a pragmatist like Rosa, but he knew how soft and good her heart was. He knew she'd put up a fight, but she was never going to turn away a child in need.

"Come on, Antonello. We were playing some cards. We can deal you in." Alonzo tried to speak in English to the best of his ability, since it was Antonello's native language. He wanted to make him feel welcome.

"Mr. Consentino?"

"Yes?"

"It's my birthday."

"Well." Alonzo looked at Sonny and winked. He felt at

the change in his trouser pockets before continuing. "What are we doing?" He stood and headed for the stairs.

"Huh?" Antonello turned to him, showing the first bit of life since he had arrived.

"Come on, then. Ferrara is just down the road. We need to get some cannoli." Both of the boys leapt to their feet and chased after him. "Just don't tell your mother I let you have sweets before dinner."

"Yes, sir," they responded happily. As Alonzo led them down the sidewalk to their favorite pastry shop, he hoped they would come across that Antonello's deadbeat father. After Alonzo was done with him he wouldn't be hitting women and children anymore.

SONNY

Sonny followed his brothers up the stairs of their tenement fire escape. The twins bounded up a few stairs at a time with ease, but Sonny had to take one step at a time.

"Wait on me!" Sonny shouted, trying to pick up his pace. But he was weighted down by a few pillows under each arm and a deck of cards in his hand, and he was extremely cautious not to drop them.

They made it out onto the roof.

"Jesus, it's hot out here too!" Enzo shouted, sweat already darkening the back and underarms of his white shirt.

"Don't let Mamma here you say that, Enzo," Vico warned.

Sonny laughed at his brother and ignored the fact that he had taken the Lord's name in vain. Enzo was always hot, but on a night like this, no one could blame him. The heat was oppressive. It was thick, almost with a physical presence. Sonny thought the heat even seemed to have a smell, but perhaps it was just the rotting fruit and vegetables on the street carts below them.

It wasn't the first time, and probably wouldn't be the last, that their tenement was simply too hot to sleep in. On nights like this, Enzo would grumble and complain as Rosa instructed them to grab a few things and head to the roof.

Sonny enjoyed it, though. It was almost an adventure. And they all got to be together.

They nodded to the other tenants gathered there and found a spot by the edge of the roof to place their things.

"Who do you think that fella was?" Enzo asked, still reeling from seeing an important-looking gentleman in Alonzo's barbershop earlier that day. It was all he and Vico had been able to talk about since they'd gotten home.

"He sure did know how to dress," Vico said instead of replying.

"Did you see the money in his billfold? When he paid Papà he had a *roll* of dollar bills in there. He could have bought a lifetime of haircuts if he wanted to."

Sonny rolled his eyes and unrolled his sleeping bag, the one he'd be sleeping on top of tonight, rather than inside. He wasn't so impressed by the man. Sure, his chesterfield overcoat and hay-skimmer hat looked like they were fresh off a mannequin, and his watch had little diamonds set along the face, but he was rude. He'd skipped ahead of the other customers and hadn't waited his turn. Alonzo had cut his hair and remained courteous, but Sonny knew that, given the chance, his father would have used the moment to teach his sons about respect and treating others like you want to be treated, like the Bible said.

"That guy runs Little Italy. Did you see how everyone stood when he walked in?" Enzo said.

"You ever think Papà might be a big shot and just doesn't let us know?" Vico chimed in.

"I bet a nickel he is. He knows everybody in town."

"Papà said to stop talking about that man, Enzo," Sonny said, placing a few pillows down beside his for his mother and father.

"He isn't up here, is he? Mind your own potatoes."

Sonny didn't really understand what that meant, but he didn't say anything else. The twins were always bringing home funny sayings like this from school, to their mother's irritation.

"Any room for us?" Rosa asked from the door, balancing baby Maria on her hip, as Alonzo held it open for her.

"Yes, beside me!" Sonny scooted over and dusted off the spots he had designated for them.

Enzo and Vico rolled their eyes, but Sonny didn't mind, since both his mother and father approached and sat down beside him. "Can I hold Maria?" he asked.

Rosa had already been passing her along. Sonny prided himself on being a good little helper to his mother and father, who sometimes became too tired to take care of little Maria. Enzo and Vico said they had already helped with him, and they didn't want to again, but Sonny doubted how often they had been of any use.

He scooped up the baby girl and placed her in his lap, Rosa exhaling with relief beside him. She stretched, probably for the first time in hours, and laid her head on her knees.

"I'm tired, Sonny Boy," she said, and then pretended to snore.

"You're not asleep! Is she, Maria?" Sonny grinned.

His mother had recently taken a job working as a seamstress at a little old shop down the road. Sonny didn't know what she did, or why she had to work for so long, but she always came back exhausted and complaining about how bright everything was outdoors.

"No, I'm not sleeping yet, but I wish I were." Rosa continued to speak in Sicilian, as she always did.

"Not yet, Mamma! We have to count the stars," Sonny replied, dabbing at a glob of drool on Maria's chin.

It was tradition by this point. The first few times the tenement had become too sweltering to bear, everyone had been so irritable, they barely talked. Sonny's father, like always, wasn't going to allow his clan to pout. So he came up with a little game to cheer them up.

He said it was a game he played with his family back in Sicily, but Sonny decided his father was making it up on the spot, and he doubted that they had ever had to sleep on the roof back in Sicily. He didn't know much about their home back in Sicily, but he pictured it with luscious gardens, overflowing fountains, and spiral staircases.

"He's right, Rosa. We *have* to." Alonzo chuckled and gave his bride a wet kiss on the cheek. "You can start us off, Sonny. Where's the Big Dipper?"

Sonny flipped Maria around in his lap, and pretended to confer with her about the location.

"Right there!" Sonny used Maria's little hand to point it out.

"You got it. Boys, you going to join in?" Alonzo called out to the twins, who ignored him and continued to chat among themselves far enough way to avoid being over-heard. "Little Dipper?"

"I think that's it right there," Sonny said.

"That's right," Alonzo replied, but Sonny doubted the authenticity of his answer.

"Is it actually?"

Alonzo tilted his head and squinted his eyes until Rosa burst into laughter.

"He never really knows!" She slapped his knee.

"I think you're better than I am already, Sonny Boy," Alonzo said.

"You foolish man," Rosa said playfully.

"A fool for you." He leaned over to kiss her again, and this time, he waited until she offered her lips.

Sonny tried to think of something clever to say, or another constellation to test his father on, but when he turned again, both his parents were fast asleep in each other's arms.

Financial District, New York City—November 20, 1911

Laurel wreaths and garlands hung from the rooftops of every building on Wall Street. Everyone passing them by struggled underneath the weight of their Christmas gifts.- Sonny loved every minute of it. Everyone was cheerful. The general craze of Manhattan hadn't dissipated, but it was certainly different around the holidays. No one passing by called them "greaseballs," no one shot them disdainful glances or crossed the street when they saw the olive skin of the Consentino clan.

Cars sped by, their lights mixing in with the sparkling bulbs on the decorated trees lining the street. Sonny had to point out every single one.

"I want to find that Saint Nicholas fella. I want to check that out for myself," Enzo yelled to his family. He really just wanted to go to Times Square and visit the

Macy's store he had heard so much about. Alonzo had brought the whole family to the Financial District for a day trip, but there were limits to what he could spend.

"He's real. I heard Sammy Bacchiega say he saw him last year on Christmas Eve!" Antonello fought for Enzo's attention. He was still staying with them, and showed no signs of leaving. A month after Antonello had arrived at the Consentinos' tenement, his father had disappeared. "Up and left," his mother had said. Antonello continued to stay, to Sonny's delight, while his mother moved in with her sister's family and attempted to rebuild her life.

Everything seemed to be going well. The Hook Hand had made no more appearances, his father seemed less stressed, and his mother was cheerful when she could get a full night's rest, which Maria had been permitting a little more often after turning one year old that month.

Aside from the throng of women marching, signs in hand that said things like "Vote Dry" and "Let Us Vote," everyone seemed to be focused on nothing but the holiday season. People passed them by, ignoring the women's hymn, "Give to the Wind Thy Fears," and singing jollier tunes of their own.

"Dad, who are those men over there?" Sonny asked, pointing across the street at some men gathered together. They were dapper, dressed in fine suits, white gloves, and homburg hats. They were all talking loudly, some of them waving around rolled-up newspapers and shouting at one another in refined English.

"Those are Wall Street men. They work here," Alonzo said. His breath cut through the frigid air. "They work with something called 'the stock market.'"

"Like with babies?" Sonny asked, causing Enzo and Vico to burst into laughter.

"No, Sonny Boy, that's the stork. The stock market is

where… Well, they put money in big businesses, and if a company does well, they can make money in return."

"Businesses like the places we've been visiting?" Sonny's gaze remained fixed on the wealthy-looking men, the lights now slightly less dazzling.

"That's right. It's like playing cards. Legal gambling. It's mostly reserved for the whites," Alonzo said, disparagingly at first, before changing his tone. "What do you think about them?"

"I think they must be pretty smart to do that."

"Yes, I bet they are."

"I want to have clothes like those one day." Sonny finally broke his gaze, and, looking to his father, he found him smiling.

"I bet you're smarter than all of them combined. If you want to be one of those men, you can."

"Could I buy a car? And a house that isn't like ours?" Sonny bit his lips, feeling he may have offended his father.

"Absolutely. You can be anything you want. Remember that statue we passed on our way to America?"

"Of the lady?"

"Yes, that's the one. You were very young when you first saw her. But that's what I told you when we saw Lady Liberty. You can be whatever you want here."

"Can *you*?" Sonny asked. Alonzo thought for a moment and then scooped Sonny up in his arms, far slower than he had been able to just a few months prior.

"What? Of course, I can! I am already what I want to be. I am a barber. Don't ever be ashamed of what you are, Sonny Boy. You can be a barber, or a politician, or a soldier…anything. Just be proud of it." He flipped the brim of Sonny's wool newsboy cap playfully.

Sonny didn't laugh, though.

ALONZO

It was cool that evening, for the end of March in Sicily. Alonzo took advantage of the breeze at every opportunity. When the baby couldn't sleep, he would quietly take him out on the porch, allowing his exhausted wife to sleep. Sonny Boy seemed to like it, his frown generally turning into a smile. His father's powerful arms had that effect.

Alonzo installed himself in a rocking chair and looked out over his land, which he had inherited when his father had died three years before. He listened to the chorus of the insects and watched his freshly cut lawn shimmer in the moonlight.

He hadn't been able to sleep in days.

He blamed his weariness on the newborn in his arms, but in reality, it was just another excuse. He knew right from wrong, but he lacked clarity now more than ever. What was he to do about Piddu? A boy he barely knew, the son of a family that was now annihilated. What was one boy's life going to matter if the war with the Armettas continued? Much more blood would be spilt, and it would likely pour from those he loved the most, namely his sons and his wife.

He could hear his father's voice in his head. "The wicked High Priest Matthias claimed it was better to give up one than many, and it was Jesus who died for his crime." Devout Roman Catholic that he was, Alonzo's father and his platitudes continued to educate him, even from the grave.

Alonzo still couldn't make sense of it all when he heard a rustle through the barley in the distance.

He stood as gently as he could, so as to not wake the baby. He held his son in one arm, and reached for his pistol with his free hand. A figure materialized in the distance, coming quickly into focus as it grew closer .

Alonzo hunkered down behind the wooden pillar supporting the porch and held his weapon out in front of him.

"Lonz," Came the voice of his brother, Giuseppe.

"What the hell are you doing? I almost shot you!" Alonzo gritted his teeth.

"It's done." He looked a sight. Giuseppe's pant legs were torn, and blood was pouring from his knee. His face was covered in dirt and small cuts, his tie loosened and disheveled.

"What is done?"

"I killed him. I killed Lupo's son. I avenged Uncle Umberto." Alonzo was silent, his mouth agape. "Can I get some water, or wine… I feel like I just ran across half of Sicily."

"You killed him?"

"Yeah, he's dead. He was sleeping next to his wife. I shot him in the face." He noticed the look of horror on Alonzo's face. "No harm came to the woman. She rolled to the floor and took off screaming. But he's dead. Blood everywhere. Now, come on, about that wine."

Alonzo remembered the soundly sleeping baby in his arms and began to bounce him. He was reluctant to let his brother inside, and he didn't know why.

"You're sure he's dead?"

"Damn it, yes! And he isn't rising on the third day. He's gone, for

good. I would have checked his pulse if I could. I tried to get away quickly and cut my leg trying to get out the window."

"The Armettas aren't going to quit now."

"They never were going to quit, Lonz, you know better than that."

Alonzo rushed inside, moving quickly but attempting to remain light on his feet. He tucked Sonny back into his crib, then moved up the stairs, ignoring the creaking of the wood. Giuseppe followed close behind.

"Wake up. Wake up," Alonzo said, shaking Piddu. "Now." The young man shook the cobwebs from his eyes and looked at them in consternation.

"What's going on?" he asked with growing fear.

"You need to leave. You need to get out of this house. You need to leave now, and never come back." Alonzo was already gathering the few things Piddu had arrived with and throwing them into a burlap duffel. Giuseppe picked up the boy's day clothes and tossed them onto the bed.

"Why? What's going on?"

"The Armettas want you dead, and they'll be coming for you. You aren't safe here, and neither are my sons if you remain."

"I…don't understand." Piddu lifted his mangled hand, which was still wrapped up in bandages. "They already did this. Why would they want me dead now?"

"The men who orphaned and mutilated you are now dead," Giuseppe said in a semi-hushed tone, "and the ones who are still alive want to sink you in the Tyrrhenian."

Piddu finally swayed to his feet and slipped on his clothes half-heartedly.

"Go on, now." Giuseppe pointed him to the door once Piddu had slipped the bag over his shoulder.

"Where am I supposed to go?"

"You'll figure something out," Giuseppe said, but Alonzo had already turned toward the stairs. He raced into his bedroom, ignoring *the cries of his startled babe. Rosa sprang up from their bed like a catapult.*

"What is going on?" Her voice sounded worried but equally frustrated.

"Go back to bed, Rosa. You need your sleep," Alonzo replied. She generally argued with him on matters like this, but he spoke so firmly that she returned to her pillow and pulled the handmade quilt over her head.

Alonzo shuffled through his dresser drawers until he found an old lockbox. He reached above the bedroom doorframe for the key and opened the box. He grabbed the contents and ran back to the porch.

"Piddu!" he shouted, just in time to catch the boy before the stepped off the porch. "Take this." He shoved all of the money in his hands into the boy's bag. Piddu's words caught in his throat. "Make for Trapani," Alonzo said. "This should be more than enough to get you a ticket to America, and enough to sustain you until you can find a place to live."

Piddu shook his head, his eyes terrified.

"You must go. There is nowhere in Sicily that is safe for you." Alonzo recollected Lupo's words: "You can begin a new life for your-self over there."

"But—"

"No. Go and do not look back." He watched as the boy paced to the dirt path adjacent to Alonzo's garden, his heart still beating violently in his chest.

"We will have to rally all of our male relatives," Giuseppe said, lighting Alonzo's cigar with the same matches he had just used to light his own. "Cousin Calogero and Carlo in Siracusa, Pietro and Giovanni in Marsala, and Papà's old friend Tommaso would surely

come home to fight with us." Giuseppe picked bits of tobacco leaf from his teeth and thought deeply. "And Benedetto from—"

"No," Alonzo said and stepped toward his brother, shaking his head. "No more. No one else. We, me and you. We who started this will have to finish it. Our cousins and friends have all left Castellammare del Golfo for the very reason you wish to summon them home. You do not have sons, brother, but now I do. And I do not want them to live this life. I want them to get far away from here. And if they do, I will kill the man who tries to bring them back."

"Alonzo—"

"Giuseppe. I will not change my mind on this." Alonzo finally exhaled and placed a hand on his brother's shoulder. "We will finish this. Together." Giuseppe reluctantly nodded. They turned their gaze out to their father's fields, and wondered about what might lurk in the darkness.

PART 2

ENZO

Enzo fished through his hand-me-down overcoat for his cigarettes. At sixteen, he was old enough to make his own decisions, but he still didn't like to smoke in front of his parents. His mother had stopped smoking when she had given birth to Maria, and thereafter now considered the smell sickening. His father said cigarettes were effeminate when compared to a pipe or a cigar, the Sicilians' favored use of tobacco.

He took every advantage of his time away from his family to smoke, drink, and play the street tough. He might not be as smart as his little brother, Sonny, or as well-mannered as his twin, Vico, but he fancied himself the toughest brother, always ready for a fight.

Placing a Lucky Strike between his lips, he fumbled for a lighter and discovered in frustration that he had left it in his sock drawer back in Little Italy.

"Hey, you got a light, pal?" Enzo said to a man loading

a horse-drawn vegetable wagon, a cigarette dangling from his lips.

"Yeah, sure." The Sicilian shrugged and tossed him a book of matches.

That was why Enzo came to Williamsburg anytime he could. Everyone was like him. Everywhere he went, there were Sicilians. Little Italy just wasn't for him, he concluded. The Italians had warmed up to the Consentinos since they had arrived ten years before, but Enzo was less willing to mingle with them than his gregarious brothers were. Like his mother, he distrusted all Italians from the tip to the heel of the boot. Sicilians were the only ones he could trust, he had decided, remembering his great-uncle Giuseppe saying something like that back across the pond.

"Come on, don't use those. Here," another man said, coming closer to him, an expensive silver lighter in hand.

"Thanks." Enzo tossed the matches back to the worker and accepted the light, trying not to seem too impressed with the man's appearance. He was a well-built man in his early forties, wearing a freshly pressed gray suit with blue pinstripes, a fedora perched low on his head, and a snow-white pocket square in his overcoat. Enzo had arrived feeling like a prince in his new winter coat, but suddenly he felt underdressed. The man's floral tie looked more expensive than Enzo's entire wardrobe.

The trolley Enzo had been waiting on to take him to his friend's apartment pulled to a stop in front of him. He had planned on taking it, as he usually did with Vico when they visited Williamsburg, so they could circumvent the Jewish quarters that weren't always very friendly to Sicilian intruders.

Taking a second glance at the richly dressed man beside him, he decided he could catch the next trolley.

"What's your name? You aren't from around here," the man said, lighting a cigarette of his own. His voice was deep, manly, and guttural.

"I'm Enzo. You know everyone in Brooklyn?"

"In Williamsburg, yes," the man said, taking a step toward the wagon and the men who were loading it. "Be careful with those," he said to the workers. "Any of that spills, and you'll answer for it." They nodded anxiously. The expensively dressed man was clearly in charge.

"Well, I'm from Little Italy."

"You have a last name, Enzo from Little Italy?" The man stroked his neatly trimmed mustache with the back of his forefinger.

"Consentino," Enzo replied with a hint of pride, as usual, but he wasn't expecting the man to know the name. No one in Little Italy did.

"Consentino? You kin to Alonzo Consentino?" The man's interest was suddenly piqued.

"He's my old man."

"Really?" he asked, then returned his focus to his cigarette. Enzo almost began to walk away, thinking the man had nothing left to say. "I knew him back in Sicily."

"Oh yeah?"

"Yes. He was a fine man. Your grandfather was a mentor of mine in my early years. What is he doing in Little Italy? He doesn't want to be with his own people? The Castellammarese are all in Williamsburg, or in Buffalo, Chicago, Milwaukee."

Enzo shrugged. "We go where the opportunity is." The lie came easily to him.

"He can cut hair in Williamsburg. I hear that's all he is doing," the man said with a tinge of disapproval. "My name is Vito Bonventre. You can call me Mr. Bonventre."

"Nice to meet you, Mr. Bonventre. I'll let my old man know that I made your acquaintance."

"No point," the man said, now addressing him in Sicilian. "Your father knows where to find me if he wants my friendship. If you'd like to make more friends of your own kind, you know where to find me too."

"Yes, I do," Enzo replied in Sicilian as well. He had kept up on his native tongue because his mother refused to talk in any other language in the home.

"I could put you to work. Men like me can always use a strong, young Sicilian like yourself. Unless you want to be just a barber like your father." Enzo stared back, perplexed for a moment, not knowing what the man wanted to hear.

"I like spending my time with other Sicilians."

Bonventre nodded and slipped him a card. "This grocery is mine," he said, and motioned to the place behind him. "Come back tomorrow. I'll find some work for you."

"Carrying crates?" Enzo motioned to the men who were just now closing the wagon tailgate.

"No. I think we can find something more interesting for you, if you're tough enough."

"I am. Can I bring my brother?" Bonventre dropped his cigarette and stamped out the flame with his polished wing tips.

"Makes no difference to me. Just don't bring your father." Bonventre winked and headed back into the grocer.

VICO

"This is my kid brother, Mr. Bonventre," Enzo said as Vico extended his hand.

"I'm Vico. It's nice to meet you, sir," he said, declining to mention that they were twins. Mr. Bonventre accepted the handshake, his hands rough like mallets, and sized him up from head to toe. Vico shifted nervously and forced a smile.

"So what do you have for us to do?" Enzo said. Vico could tell his brother was nervous, but Enzo was smiling like he was the proudest man in the world.

"This is your brother?" Mr. Bonventre asked, turning to Vico.

"Yes, sir."

"You're fatter than him." It was Vico's turn to smile, but he lowered his face to hide it.

"Yeah, he never could eat his weight," Enzo said, but Bonventre already looked bored of talking.

"Come to the back." He turned and waved them on through the aisles of his little grocer. He unclipped a felt rope to the area behind the cash register and led them into a back room.

Vico squinted his eyes against the haze of smoke that drifted out to greet them. Within, several men were huddled around a table. The red cloth draped across it was covered in cigar ash and empty wineglasses.

"This is my cousin Stefano Magaddino." Bonventre pointed to one of the men, who had a cigarette clutched between his fingers.

"Nice to meet you, Stefano," Enzo said, and hurried across the room to greet him, hand extended. He prepared to give the man a kiss on either cheek, but Bonventre's younger cousin looked away with disinterest.

"What did I just hear come out of your mouth? Who is Stefano?" asked another man at the table. He stood up and glared back and forth between Enzo and Bonventre.

"Easy, Bartolo. These boys are new. They don't know the rules yet." Bonventre shot Enzo a look and clenched his jaw.

"You can call me Bartolo. You can call him Francesco. But that is Mr. Magaddino." The young man, not much older than Enzo and Vico, took a shot of whiskey and slammed the glass down on the table before returning to his seat.

"Right. Won't happen again," Enzo said and tried to readjust his shoulders. Ever since Enzo and Vico had left their tenement that morning, under the pretext of visiting friends in East Harlem, Enzo had been talking this meeting up. He'd described Mr. Bonventre like one might depict a friendly uncle, like his crew were old chums, and the two Consentino boys would walk in to an ovation. Vico was now ashamed that he had believed him.

"These are the boys we're taking with us?" Magaddino finally looked up from the table. He had a round, bovine face, and wild eyes. Vico figured he wasn't much older than thirty, but he was balding and had a touch of gray in his hair. He carried the same aura of experience and toughness that Bonventre did—similar to the one Vico had always sensed in his own father.

"Yes." Bonventre leaned across the table and filled three glasses of whiskey.

"Mr. Bonventre, what makes you think these two aren't some square johns who'll fold at the first sign of heat?" Bartolo said, not taking his eyes off Enzo. He placed a revolver on the red tablecloth, then returned his hand to a shot glass.

"That's none of your concern, Bartolo," Bonventre said.

"We aren't scared of the bulls," Enzo said, suddenly appearing every part the sixteen-year-old.

"Bushwa," the man identified as Francesco said from the opposite side of the table. Enzo looked at Mr. Bonventre in consternation. His mouth was open, and his eyes darted about rapidly.

"Bartolo." Mr. Bonventre stepped toward him and gestured for him to stand up. He lit a cigarette and came close to Bartolo's face. "I'm going to show you why they can be trusted."

"How?" Bartolo asked, his manner suddenly less imposing than before.

"I'll show you. Don't give me a reason to show you why you shouldn't question me." He turned then to Enzo and Vico. "Take off your shirts."

Vico looked to Enzo, suddenly wondering what he had gotten them into.

"Wh—" Enzo started to say, but stifled it. He began to

unbutton the shirt that had once belonged to his father. He turned to Vico and gestured for him to do the same.

"Get on your knees." Bonventre ashed his cigarette and then selected another from a gold cigarette holder.

"Did we do something wrong?" Enzo said, already hastening to do as he was told.

"Don't ask any questions." Magaddino reached across the table, grabbed the revolver, and began to clean its barrel with a handkerchief.

"There is something I learned back in Sicily. I actually learned it, believe it or not, from a Consentino, the grand-father of the two boys before you." Bonventre found himself a seat and gestured to Bartolo and Francesco. They stood up and slid off their belts. "Go ahead."

The two lined up behind Enzo and Vico. The first belt lash against Vico's back stung. The second hurt worse. As the third connected to his back and rib cage, he began to feel a numbing sensation. The fourth drove the wind from his lungs.

Bonventre watched with apathy, taking long drags of his cigarette.

The subsequent blows caused Vico's entire body to feel ice cold compared to the burning of his back.

"That's enough," Bonventre said. Vico looked up, now realizing how forced his breathing had become. He looked to Enzo, who was trying desperately to remain composed. "Now it's your turn," Bonventre said, his voice cold and definitive.

Behind them, Bartolo and Francesco began to unbutton their shirts, and plopped to their knees as well. They did so without pleasure, but Vico sensed it wasn't their first time receiving similar instructions. Enzo and Vico looked to each person in the room.

"Stand. And hit them harder than they hit you, twice

as hard. Twice as long." Bonventre's face was momentarily clouded by smoke.

They hesitated to stand, and assumed positions behind the two kneeling Sicilians.

Magaddino stood when he noticed their hesitation.

"Hey." He pointed, eyebrows raised and lips snarled. "Do it, or I'll give the second session myself."

Enzo and Vico began to do as instructed. Vico held back at first but, catching a glimpse of the men before them, continued again more violently.

"Enough." Bonventre stood after the blows had continued for a moment. In each hand, he clutched a glass of whiskey, which he handed to the twins. Returning to the table, he lifted a glass of his own. "It's one thing to say you'll be silent when things are silent, it is another entirely to remain silent when receiving a beating." He now spoke in Italian. Vico exhaled in relief and took his shot of whiskey with delight. His back now stung a little less.

They departed the grocer just after the sun had set.

"Do you know what you are to do?" Bonventre said, slipping on a fedora and brushing off his camel-hair polo coat.

"Yes, sir," Enzo and Vico said in unison. A car pulled to a stop along the curb. It was a Packard, Twin Six, if Vico guessed right. And when it came to cars, he usually did. A man exited the driver's seat and opened a door for Mr. Bonventre.

"I hope so. Francesco, I'll see you tomorrow. I expect my cut in an envelope in the morning." Francesco nodded as Mr. Bonventre and Magaddino entered the car.

"Let's go, then," Bartolo said, his thin frame already shivering from the cold. Enzo and Vico followed them down the street for less than a block. They came to a stop at a Ford Model T that was covered in a light dusting of snow.

"Ma and Papà will be worried about us." Vico spoke the concern that had been at the forefront of his mind since they had learned that this "job" would not take place until dark.

"We'll tell 'em we fell asleep at Tommy's. Don't worry about it." Enzo shrugged his shoulders, speaking in the Brooklyn accent that Bartolo and Francesco sported. Vico shook his head and blew hot air into his cupped hands.

"You two will be jigger men. Lookouts. When we break in, you're gonna stand outside, on either side of the road. You see a prowl car, come let us know," Francesco said, moving to the back of the automobile to crank-start it.

"Every bull in Williamsburg is a Mick, so they're probably drunk by now." Bartolo grinned. The thought of Irish policemen didn't comfort Vico at all. "You about finished?"

"The damn thing doesn't start when it's cold. Give me a damn minute," Francesco said. It was unclear whether or not his frustration came from Bartolo's impatience or his car.

"You know what the salesman tries to sell the guy with the Model T?" Bartolo said, addressing Enzo and Vico for the first time. They stuttered in confusion. "It's a joke," he said, frustrated.

"No, what's he tryin' to sell?" Enzo said.

"He tries to sell him a speedometer. But the guy says he don't need one. Why? He says it's 'cause when he goes five miles an hour, the fender rattles. When he goes ten miles an hour, his teeth rattle. When he goes fifteen miles an hour, the transmission drops out." Bartolo burst into laughter, with Enzo and Vico following his lead. Francesco looked up in frustration before returning his attention to the crankshaft. "Hey, I hear they are adding a magnet to the rear axle of the Ford."

"Oh yeah? What's the big idea?" Enzo asks, catching on.

"So it can pick up the parts that drop off the back." More forced laughter followed.

"Lay off it," Francesco said, the car finally rumbling to life. "Any of you have a car?" He waited. "Get in," he said when no one replied.

"You two have a piece?" Bartolo asked as Francesco shifted into first gear and the car rolled to a start.

"No," Vico said, his brother reluctant to do so.

"Here"—Bartolo tossed a revolver in the back seat— "you two can decide who keeps it. I've got two more of my own." Enzo reached for it and placed it in his lap. Vico didn't protest. He was beginning to think he had bitten off more than he could chew.

HEARINGS BEFORE THE
PERMANENT SUBCOMMITTEE ON INVESTIGATIONS
OF THE
COMMITTEE ON GOVERNMENT OPERATIONS
UNITED STATES SENATE
EIGHTY-EIGHTH CONGRESS
SECOND SESSION
PURSUANT TO SENATE RESOLUTION 17
SEPTEMBER 28, 1963

CHAIRMAN: Mr. Valachi, you mentioned that Enzo Consentino did not have a strong relationship with his father, Alonzo. Can you comment on this any further?

Mr. Valachi: I didn't know him until later on, probably mid- to late-nineteen twenties.

Chairman: Answer the question, Mr. Valachi.

Mr. Valachi: I heard that Alonzo was upset when he got connected. Enzo became involved, and his father didn't like it. Not one bit.

. . .

Chairman: Alonzo didn't approve when Enzo became involved in criminal activity?

Mr. Valachi: Correct, sir. That's about all I know. His father cut ties, and Enzo got more and more involved.

Chairman: Involved   with   Alonzo's associates?

Mr. Valachi: I don't know who Alonzo's associates were, or the associates of Enzo, for that matter. I wouldn't think so, though.

Chairman: You wouldn't think so. What leads you to this conclusion?

Mr. Valachi: If they were Alonzo's associates, they wouldn't have involved his family members if he didn't like it. He might have been a nobody in the States, but he still had powerful friends. I doubt anyone would have wanted to step on his toes.

Chairman: Step on his toes?

. . .

Mr. Valachi: Yeah. It would have been disrespectful to a Sicilian to involve his sons in the life without his say-so.

Chairman: Can you speculate about who these men might have been?
  (Mr. Valachi receives counsel from his attorney.)

Mr. Valachi: No. I didn't know them. I wasn't part of what the Sicilians did. I was still running with some Irish boys at the time. I don't have anything else to say on the matter.

Chairman: The board will decide which questions to ask, Mr. Valachi.

ALONZO

Alonzo was alone.

Less than a year after he had sent Piddu on his way, he'd sent his wife and three children to stay with Rosa's elderly father in Segesta. Anywhere was better and safer than Castellammare del Golfo, but Alonzo still worried.

After Giuseppe showed up at his doorstep saying that he had effectively guaranteed that this war of theirs would continue until the last man was standing, things had been silent. Alonzo hadn't left his property. Giuseppe had stayed with him most of the time, but he was restless, and he went to town whenever he could convince his brother to let him go, to "check on how things were."

Alonzo was restless in his own way too, but he wouldn't leave. Even in his own home, he expected to find a killer lurking behind every closed door. Still, unable to sit, he passed his time walking in the garden before his father's home, attempting to take in the sights of the beautiful coastline and the smell of budding grapefruit and lemons.

These held less meaning to him now than they had a few months prior.

He sat on his front porch, trying to calm his tapping foot as his brother had when his third son was being born. All the wine and cigars in Sicily couldn't seem to do the trick.

Giuseppe had only been gone two days, but the silence inside Alonzo's home was deafening. The quieter things became, the louder the voices in his head.

"Don Consentino?" a postal worker said from around the side of the house. Alonzo had seen him coming but had paid him no mind. His thoughts consumed him. A primitive state had taken control, and everything that was not perceived as a threat was ignored.

"Yes?"

"Delivery," the postal worker said as his young aide came forth. The boy struggled to manage the weight of a barrel.

"Who is it from?" Alonzo asked. He waited for a response, but both postal workers had turned and climbed back into their carriage without responding.

The lone barrel waited at the foot of the porch.

Alonzo approached it slowly. He was cautious—not frightened, but cautious. An Armetta hit man stowing away in a barrel? Unlikely. Still, he reached into the side of his coat and drew his pistol. There was nothing to gain in taking chances, but everything to lose.

As he arrived at the barrel, a repulsive stench attacked his nostrils. He pulled away for a moment before continuing. With his fingertips, he pried open the lid. Within was a body.

It looked like his brother.

Alonzo gasped and fell down beside the barrel.

Alonzo patted his face, trying to wake himself up. He felt his chest heaving, out of control. He moaned.

He couldn't help it, though, and leaned back over the barrel and lifted the lid.

It was his brother.

Giuseppe was stuffed into the barrel, his head hanging on by a single tendon, blood covering his face from unseen wounds. His eyes were wide open, and his face was still. At peace in death, but haunted by the last face he'd seen.

Alonzo moaned, and he fell on his back, the Sicilian sun burning his flooded eyes.

TURRIDRU

Turridru led his father by the hand, and held a bouquet of flowers in the other. He debated dropping them, and wasn't sure if the gesture would mean as much to Alonzo, as a month had passed since his brother's death.

"Slow down, boy," Ignazio said, and coughed. It was getting harder for him to travel all the time. Their donkey-drawn carriage had led them most of the way from the western part of the city, but Ignazio had demanded to walk the rest.

As Alonzo's renowned garden rounded into view, Turridru noticed that the grass had started to brow, and some of the vegetable stalks had begun to whither.

Alonzo was on the front porch, looking like he hadn't left that rocking chair in weeks. It very well might have been true. He certainly hadn't ventured into town since he had discovered his brother stuffed into a barrel like an old sack of grain.

"Hello, Don Consentino," Turridru said as he helped his father, step by step, up the porch.

"Thank you for coming." Alonzo's voice was barely audible. A creak sounded from the screened-in front door.

"Would you like something to drink?" It was Rosa. She and the boys had returned after receiving the news of Giuseppe's death. Alonzo had apparently tried to insist on them leaving again, but he could hardly talk, let alone put together a coherent argument.

"No, ma'am, I'm fine. Father, would you like anything?" Turridru asked.

"You make a mockery of death by wearing that, boy." Ignazio pointed to Alonzo's black suit and hat with his cane, ignoring the question.

"I am mourning the loss of my brother." Alonzo didn't look up, but it was clear he wasn't willing to submit on the matter.

"He's been dead over six months. It's time you moved on." Turridru considered trying to hush his father but couldn't bring himself to do it.

"Have a seat if you'd like." Alonzo gestured to the other chairs. Turridru helped his father into one and attempted to sit in another. The seat was suddenly blocked by Alonzo's foot. "Not that one. That was Giuseppe's." Alonzo looked up. His eyes were hazy, like he was drunk or had gone days without sleeping. Perhaps it was both. Turridru propped himself up on the porch railing instead, receiving a splinter in the palm.

"The question is, what are you going to do about this?" Ignazio asked. He was unwilling to make small talk in his old age.

"Wait," Alonzo said, and shrugged his shoulders.

"That isn't enough," Ignazio said, stirring. He was perturbed and didn't hesitate to make it known. Turridru shifted uncomfortably. Seeing the leader of their Borgata like this was unsettling enough, but seeing him chastised for it was worse still. "How old are you now, boy?" Ignazio asked, cupping a hand around his ear so he could hear the answer clearly.

Alonzo had to calculate for a moment. "Thirty."

"Thirty…" Ignazio considered the answer. "Not ten years a

man, with three boys of your own, and you're trying to lead this family in wartime." Ignazio shook his head. "I respected your father. I followed every order he ever gave, but he made a mistake when he placed you in charge after he died. It should have been someone else, someone older and wiser."

"I do not know why he wanted me to lead our Borgata. But here we are."

Ignazio slammed the butt of his cane into the wooden porch, and futilely attempted to make it to his feet.

"You've forgotten! You have forgotten!" he shouted, like an angry priest. Turridru looked over his shoulder at the garden and pretended he wasn't hearing any of this.

"I have forgotten nothing," Alonzo said with the first hint of life in his voice.

"But you have. Because of the work your grandfather and your father put in to give you all of this"—he gestured over Alonzo's land—"you have forgotten. You don't remember what it is like for the rest of Sicily, scraping and striving for every inch of land, clinging to what little bread they have left to feed their families. The land is arid and hard, the taxes rip everything out from under their feet. And yet you sit here, filling your belly and the bellies of your family with meats and cheeses. Look how tall they are becoming! And so, I say, you have forgotten that if you don't fight for it, you will lose it. You will lose all of this, and you'll become like the rest of us. Hungry, hard…with poverty and strife as a constant."

"You have not been so hungry. Not since my father brought you into this Borgata."

"Yes, and I earned that right by killing. By pulling the trigger. And now, even after all of that"—he finally made it to his feet—"we will lose that as well if we don't have someone to fight for us. A leader to protect us. And you don't have the ingredients, boy." Ignazio shook his head, his left eyelid, which had grown limp over the years, now twitching with anger.

"Here." Turridru attempted to hand Alonzo the flowers. Alonzo *let them fall from his lap to the porch. The wind scattered them, sending them across the porch and to the Sicilian soil beyond it.*

Turridru helped his father down the stairs, and gave Alonzo a glance over his shoulder. But Don Consentino wasn't looking. His eyes were fixed on the land before him, perhaps considering Ignazio's words.

SONNY

"Come on, Maria! You can do it," Sonny said, cheering her from their makeshift third base—the back tire of Mr. Bacchiega's Oldsmobile. The pitcher wound up and tossed it down the middle, Maria's bat whiffing long after it passed.

"I'm no good at baseball," Maria said, still shivering from the violent cold.

"Hey, how about you pitch it a little slower, fella. She's only six," Sonny suggested, tamping his frustration. Antonello waited anxiously in their "dugout," the light under the lamp post behind home plate. Being so much older than his playmates, he was dominant, and didn't care to show it. Ever since he had started living with the Consentinos, and had the ability to bathe and change his clothes a bit more often, some of the older boys began to tease him less. Still, he liked to spend time with Sonny. His loyalty was constantly on display, even when Enzo and Vico laughed at him for it.

The next pitch was underhand and slow, and the thin wooden bat, held out in front of Maria, smacked it back toward the pitcher. It didn't go very far, but the outfielders were good sports and allowed her to take first base without attempting to tag her out. Sonny didn't charge home plate to show his gratitude.

"Sonny," Maria said with a pouty lip from first base, "I want to go in." She held out her hands, allowing errant snowflakes to collect in the palms of the mittens her mother had sewn for her last winter.

"Okay, last hit," Sonny said, nodding to Antonello to take the base.

"No, Sonny, I want to go now," Maria said, her voice pleading.

Sonny sighed and stepped away from the Oldsmobile.

"Let's call it a tie game. We'll finish up tomorrow." Sonny put his arm around Maria and headed for home, which was just a few yards away.

"Maybe tomorrow we can leave the little girlies at home," Sammy Bacchiega said from the pitcher's mound, hocking a loogie.

"I think she's already better than you, Sam," Sonny jested.

"Yeah, says you. You don't know from nothing."

Sonny led Maria up the stairs, Antonello following behind. A tomboy by nature, Maria liked to tag along whenever Sonny would let her. He almost always did so, as his father had taught him to be especially good to Maria. Despite that, she did tend to get tired of playing most of the time.

Alonzo's voice carried through their tenement door:

"You break my heart." He spoke in Sicilian, and his voice was strained and fragile.

Sonny paused before the door, but Maria opened it and continued inside regardless.

Alonzo sat with the twins in dim candlelight. The lights on their first Christmas tree were not turned on. No music was playing in the background.

"I don't know what you want me to say," Enzo said. Sonny helped Maria take off her multiple layers, and hung them up on the coat hanger carefully.

"You suddenly show up with new coats, shiny black Oxford shoes... Did you not expect me to find out?" Alonzo continued to address the twins in Sicilian. It seemed he couldn't find the right words in English.

"And that makes you feel bad?" Enzo said, his voice bordering on disrespect. Sonny froze, shocked. It was rare to hear their father talked to like this—by anyone.

"You insult me. You insult my intelligence. You insult my ability to provide for our family."

"We got tired of wearing your old saddle shoes." Enzo exhaled.

Silence crept into the empty space of their small abode, and Sonny decided to try and make it to his room, leading Maria by the hand. He refrained from looking into the living room, not wanting to provoke a conversation with his father or brothers. He did, however, peer into the kitchen, where his mother hovered over the kitchen sink scrubbing the dishes, her knuckles white from clutching the sponge so tightly. She looked over her shoulder at them, her eyes bloodshot. Tears stained her cheeks.

"Mamma, what's wrong?" Maria asked, her voice not as quiet as she thought.

"Go to your room, Maria." Rosa sniffled.

"And you do all this while living in my home?" Alonzo's voice carried from the living room.

"I'm sorry, Papà," Vico said, but Alonzo continued.

"I have given you everything you could have ever needed. You have betrayed me! My heart is broken." He increased his volume even further. "You bring this illegal money into my home, in front of your brother and your little sister?" Sonny, leading Maria to her room, reluctantly stole a glance into the living room. Enzo and Vico were seated beside each other on the couch, Alonzo looming over them like a policeman in an investigation. In his hand, he clutched a wad of money. It was clear he had found it somewhere in the home. "People talk. And I can hear them snickering behind my back, like I don't know that my boys are criminals."

"Dad, we didn't mean to hurt you, or Ma, or the kids. We're just trying to make our way, like you did," Enzo said. Alonzo hid his face. Sonny looked on, unable to peel his eyes away, like when he stepped on a bug and had to check the extent of the carnage.

In the dull living room light, Alonzo did not look his forty years. He looked more like sixty. The flesh of his face hung, and centered in bags under his faded-blue eyes. The hair on his head was swept over to hide his growing baldness, but there was nothing he could do to hide the gray developing around his ears. His fragility in this moment shocked Sonny as much as the argument.

"You say to me, 'we're sorry,' and yet you will not say you will quit what you are doing. So, if you want to be on the streets, you can live on the streets. I want you out by the morning." Alonzo's voice was now barely audible.

"Pa, it's freezing out there," Vico said, pleading, fear in his voice.

"You have friends now. If they care for you as much as

you attest, they will surely have a place for you to stay. Also"—he turned for the hallway, noticing Sonny for the first time—"you have all this." He tossed the wad of dollar bills onto the couch.

Alonzo passed by Sonny and paused in the kitchen. He looked at his wife for a moment, his hands akimbo on his hips, wet streaks staining his face. He turned to Sonny, blinking tears from his eyes. The look told Sonny something like: "You don't ever do this to me."

Sonny struggled to swallow, and finally found the courage to walk to his room.

He nestled onto the floor, in between the two twin beds he had shared with Enzo and Vico. He didn't know if they would be coming in tonight—or ever again, for that matter. But he wanted to leave their beds open, just in case.

During the night, Enzo and Vico came in and began packing a few of their things. Sonny pretended to be asleep until he felt one of the twins hovering over him.

"I love you, Sonny Boy," Enzo said, and kissed him on the cheek. It was the first time the brothers had ever used the term. Sonny found himself being hoisted into the air, in Vico's arms. His brother laid him on the bed and tucked him in. They knew he wasn't a very sound sleeper, but Sonny pretended to still be dozing regardless.

"Come on," Enzo said from the doorway, and the twins left. Sonny wished he had the right words to say, but he couldn't find them.

ENZO

"Bring us some more brown," Enzo shouted to the barkeep. They were regulars at the Olympic Club now, and therefore had earned the right to make orders like this. Enzo delighted in it, and he thought Vico enjoyed it more than he let on.

They had begun attending with Bartolo and Francesco, but now spent most of their afternoons there, taking part in the "free lunch" deal painted on the window. The fact that the bartender never asked where their parents were didn't hurt. A pint of beer or a glass of whiskey was perpetually in hand.

"Ante up, boys," Bartolo managed to say from one side of his lips, a ten-cent cigar dangling from the other. They tossed a few chips on the table. Gambling was illegal, or so they had been told, but no one seemed to care in Williamsburg.

Enzo remembered how his father had taught them to

play cards. Not like this, he thought. A saloon, booze, smokes: this is where men were men.

"I see that smile, Francesco. It's a dead tell." Vico folded. He had been gloomy lately, and it had brought Enzo down. They had spent Christmas alone, for the first time in their lives, and Vico seemed to be unhappy with their new living quarters on the corner of Grand Street and Sixth Avenue. But he had an affinity for cards. Maybe it reminded him of home and their little brother.

The bartender placed four drinks on the table in front of them, spilling some over their shoulders.

"Easy, old boy," Bartolo said, wiping some of it off.

"Say, Francesco, who was that dame you've been keeping company with? She was a real looker," Enzo asked, finally feeling on equal terms enough to jest with them. The Consentino boys might still be outsiders, but they were outsiders on the inside. The new guys, but *guys* none the less.

"Mind your own potatoes," Francesco said, then analyzed his cards and placed the first bet.

"Oh, I've seen her too," Bartolo, picking up on it, continued. "She's a real bug-eyed Betty. Do you roll her over when you're makin' whoopee?"

"My car, my girl…you're just looking for something." The bet came back to Francesco, and he threw his cards on the table. "The only Jane this guy has is Rosy Palm and her five sisters." He grinned triumphantly, wiggling the fingers of his own hand. Enzo laughed and slapped the table.

"You kidding me? I chase more skirt than all of youse three combined," Bartolo said, only slightly offended that the joke had bounced back on him.

A burst of sunlight spilled into the saloon, followed by a stampede of footsteps.

Enzo instinctively grabbed the piece he had recently purchased, but turning to see that all of the men had gold badges on their chests, he slid it back into his belt.

"No one move a muscle," one of the policemen said, pushing through the other bar patrons.

"Is there something wrong, Officer?" the bartender asked.

"Just shut up," the policeman replied, a distilled Irish accent in his voice. His eyes surveyed the room and finally settled on their table. "Enzo and Vico Consentino?" he asked. His uniform was buttoned so tight, and so high, it looked like it would cut off his circulation.

"What of it?" Enzo asked, undisturbed.

"You're both under arrest for the robbery of Burnett's Clothing Store." He materialized a warrant from his jacket pocket. Several of the other policemen rushed forward and pushed the brothers against the table, restraining their arms behind them.

Enzo looked across the table at Bartolo and Francesco, who were silent, mouths agape. Bartolo shook his head as slowly as possible, as if to say, "Don't say a word."

"Don't worry, Vico, these bulls don't have shit," Enzo said, eating the felt of the tablecloth. The policemen were rough, and tugged his arms farther up his back into a chicken wing. "You hear me? You stupid Micks!" Enzo shouted. A billy club crashed against his head, and the lights went out.

VICO

The only thing in the courtroom older than Chief Justice Hiscock was the wood floor. The judge lowered his bifocals and seemed to be analyzing a few papers. Enzo and Vico had been in there for what felt like days, but was really more like hours.

Vico's heart hadn't stopped racing, and when called upon, he struggled just to summon the strength to project his voice. He knew Enzo was afraid too, but he held his head in such a way that made Vico think he was proud. Not proud of the theft, or proud of being arrested, but proud that they had kept their mouths shut. They could have probably walked away free if they had sung like canaries, but they'd decided beforehand to keep quiet.

They weren't even the perpetrators of the crime, after all, but simply lookouts. Enzo had said in their holding cell that if they kept quiet, they would be lauded as heroes when they got back. As always, Vico believed him.

The benches behind them were mostly empty, but Vico kept looking over his shoulder to see if his mother and father had come. Each time, he was relieved but also saddened. The trial was decided from the beginning. They were guaranteed to be sentenced. But the child in him felt like Alonzo could explain to the judge that they were simply misguided youths, and then Chief Hiscock might just let them off the hook.

"This is your first offense, boys," the judge said, tapping his lips and sitting back in his chair. Vico thought his wardrobe looked ridiculous. "That makes me want to give you another option. You have stolen from your countrymen in a time of hardship, in a time of war. Do you understand that?"

Vico had to clear his throat before he could answer. "Ye-yes, Your Honor."

"Acts like this make it hard for Americans to trust your people when they come over. You make it more difficult for everyone. But this is your first offense. I will allow either or both of you to join the United States Army, for the duration of the war"—Vico lost his breath—"or I hereby sentence you to two years in Sing Sing penitentiary. I believe you can return from either as decent members of society, but currently you are unfit for that freedom."

The county-assigned attorney stood and gestured for both the twins to do the same.

"So, what do you decide?"

"I'll go to prison," was Enzo's only reply. Vico imagined the elongated response as something like, "the Kaiser never did me no wrong. Besides, we can do time in Sing Sing standin' on our heads. No big deal."

"And do you wish to go to jail with your brother?" the judge asked, all eyes suddenly falling on Vico. He shuffled nervously when he realized how long he had been standing silently.

"I'll go—" he tried to say.

"Speak up."

"I'll go to war." Vico did his best to ignore his brother's shocked response. It was the first time the two of them would ever be away from one another. And that's precisely why Vico had decided to go.

SONNY

The smell of tomato, ricotta salata, basil, and eggplant filled the restaurant. It was quaint, warm from the food, and had good music playing in the background. Being only a few blocks away from their doorstep, Sonny was surprised his father had never brought him here before.

"How is it?" Alonzo said, his mouth open to cool his first bite.

"Excellent, Papà." Sonny's favorite dish had always been *pasta alla Norma*, but it was usually when his mother made it. This little restaurant on Prince Street made him reconsider, though.

"Good, well, eat up. Your mother says you haven't been eating enough." It was true. Ever since the twins had left, Sonny had felt sick at his stomach. Some of the boys had spread rumors that his brothers had gone to jail or to war, but when Sonny would ask about it, his parents would reply that they didn't want to talk about it.

Ever since Enzo and Vico's departure, Alonzo had doubled down on his desire to spend one-on-one time with Sonny. He had always fashioned himself Alonzo's favorite, but now the two seemed inseparable. His father looked at him in a way that unnerved him, as if his father were worried. Always worried.

His father seemed to be afraid that Sonny was unraveling. He wasn't, but he didn't mind the extra attention. He wasn't unraveling, but he was confused. About a lot of things.

"How is it, *paisano*?" The Hook Hand approached, a wily grin on his face. Sonny was now twelve, and neither the Hook Hand nor his deformity unnerved him as much as they once had. He simply did not like him. He didn't like how his father stiffened when he drew near. Perhaps this was why Alonzo had never brought him here.

"Delicious." Alonzo leaned back and kissed the man on the cheek. "Have you met my son?" The Hook Hand turned to Sonny, and they locked eyes for the first time. They were gray and piercing. Sonny wanted to look away, but couldn't.

"Nice to meet you." The Hook Hand extended his hand. Mercifully, it was his good one. "I'm Giuseppe Morello." Sonny gave a curt nod, but hoped he would walk away.

"He doesn't talk much to strangers. Come on, Sonny, tell him your name," Alonzo said, but Sonny could sense that his father was uncomfortable too.

"My name is Vincente. Everyone calls me Sonny."

"Sonny? Well, if we are going to use nicknames, then you can call me Piddu. It's what your father used to call me in Sicily." Morello patted Alonzo's shoulder with his deformed hand and squeezed it with his few fingers.

"Thank you for letting us eat here," Alonzo said, mercifully drawing Morello's attention away from Sonny.

"Of course. You are always welcome here. Make sure you get a few cannoli before you leave. Tell them Mr. Morello ordered it." He stepped away, and both Consentinos let out sighs of relief.

"You knew him in Sicily?" Sonny asked, twirling his fork around in his pasta. His appetite had dissipated.

"I did. He was a good man…*is* a good man," Alonzo said. Sonny wasn't buying it, and his father seemed to notice. "Things are just different now. I came here to show my respect."

They finished their food in relative silence. Every so often, Alonzo would ask him about his schooling, or attempt to engage him about sports, but Sonny responded the way he typically did to everyone else: with short, stinted responses.

After their cannoli arrived, wrapped up in a scarlet cloth, Alonzo paid the bill and they exited out onto the cold streets of Little Italy.

Car tires squealed around the corner a block or so down, and two black cars raced forward. Gold stars were painted on their sides. They pulled to a stop beside Alonzo and Sonny, the latter paralyzed with fear. They policemen jumped out and rushed passed them, though, into Morello's spaghetti restaurant.

"Walk faster, Sonny." Alonzo wrapped his arms around Sonny's shoulders and quickened their pace.

A tumult sounded from the restaurant, and shouts rang out. Alonzo walked faster still.

"Dad?" Sonny said, not knowing what he expected to hear.

"Faster," Alonzo said, breaking into a jog. "I told you

once that there would always be good men to protect us, right?"

"Yeah."

"Do you remember?"

"I remember."

"Men who fight the bad guys. Those good men are still out there." Alonzo led Sonny up the steps to their tenement.

"And Piddu is one of the bad guys?" Sonny asked, but Alonzo continued to walk.

"I don't know, Sonny Boy," he said at length. "That's for those policemen to decide."

ENZO

Serving time in a federal penitentiary wasn't a walk in a park, but it wasn't all the bad either. Enzo had heard stories about how things were a few years before. "Hell" was an understatement.

But now they had baseball teams, for crying out loud. Sure, he spent most of his time smashing rocks and going crazy in his cell, but it was still better than marching around in the mud in France, shooting at a bunch of Krauts who had never done him wrong and didn't owe him any money. Vico was the one who had made the wrong decision.

They even had access to education at Sing Sing. Sure, Enzo had already gone through a few years of school, but he had nothing better to do. He still couldn't read worth a damn, but at least he'd be able to make out the street signs once he got out.

And that's what he kept counting down to. The day he

got out. Maybe Sing Sing would have been hell if he had to stay there long. But two years was nothing; he could do that standing on his head.

Enzo spit on a rag and wiped vigorously at his black boots. Since everything he wore was assigned, he didn't have any way to differentiate himself from the other bums in the pin. And Enzo didn't like that. He had become used to wearing nice clothes and showing up his peers. Sing Sing's white-and-black-striped uniforms didn't cut it. The least he could do was make sure he had the shiniest boots.

It had been over a year since he had come to Sing Sing, or "come up the river," a term Enzo had carefully adapted after he'd heard the other inmates say it, and he was counting down the days to his exit.

Luckily, an Italian was really in charge of Sing Sing. Sure, the warden came by every few days to strut around and get intoxicated on his power, but he didn't really run things. The real control belonged to Alessandro Vollero. He was unabashedly Neapolitan, and hated Sicilians, but he kept the bulls at bay, so even guys like Enzo had a bit more freedom.

Enzo finished polishing his boots and inspected them. He was a bit disappointed that he couldn't make them look any better. Perhaps he could trade a pack of cigarettes for some polish from one of the penitentiary fences. But he probably wouldn't do that. The occasional drag of a cigarette helped him get through this shit more than anything else.

"Hey there, fat boy," a voice sounded from the entrance to his cell. Enzo jolted with fright, which the intruders laughed at.

"You must have snuck up on cat's paws. I didn't see you there," Enzo said, pretending that he wasn't embarrassed.

He knew these guys. They were Italians, and they were

trouble. He saw them looking at him from across the chow hall occasionally, but he hadn't yet approached him. And he wasn't pleased that they were doing so now.

One of the Italians began to sniff audibly at the air.

"Smell that? I think he shit himself."

"Come on."

"The john's over there," another said between snorts of laughter.

"What the hell do you fellas want?" Enzo pounced to his feet, already puffing out his chest and chin before he could think better of it. The three of them together could punish him far worse than the Sing Sing guards could, and they could give a pretty thorough beating.

"Oh, you're a tough guy now?" one of them said, his brows furrowing. The Italians stepped inside the cell. It was clear why they had swung by for this visit.

"You got a problem with me?" Enzo asked, maintaining the tough-guy act, although he feared his voice had wavered.

"You bet we got a problem with you." One of the burlier Italians wrapped his bulky arms around Enzo's head and threw him out of the cell into the common area. Before Enzo could scurry to his feet, several inmates had gathered to watch.

"The hell did I do to you boys?" Enzo said, trying to decide whether to pounce or run. He was unable to do either.

"We know why you're in here. We heard about your brother," one of them said as the three of them circled around him. "You must have eaten the lion's share of the meals. I heard he wasn't as fat as you."

"Go chase yourself." Enzo flicked his hand under his chin.

"That's not very nice."

"We want to make sure you understand the rules. You're only in here for a little while. When you get out, you better be a good boy." One of them reached across with a surprisingly long wingspan to pat Enzo's face. Enzo quickly batted the hand away, to their amusement. His head kept swiveling, keeping an eye on each of them as they closed in on him like sharks.

"Go peddle your papers, boys. I don't have any trouble with you," Enzo said.

"But we have a problem with you. I think you're a four-flushing piece of shit. You walk around this place like you're a big shot. Like you're better than the rest of us because you'll get out sooner. You think you're special because you have friends on the outside? Our friends could bury yours."

Enzo's heart rate and breathing quickened. They were closer now.

"Bully for you, then," Enzo said, fists clenching in preparation.

Enzo shot a quick look to the far end of the cellblock, where the guard was looking away and whistling a happy tune. He didn't mind making it clear that he was paid for his compliance.

"Let's do it, then."

They stepped in closer and raised their fists. That's what they had been waiting for.

"Whoa, now." The voice came from a man who stepped into their midst, his hands raised. "Let's not be hasty now, boys."

"What's it to you?" one of the Italian boys said, more irritated than anything else.

"What's *he* to you?" another asked, rolling up his sleeves.

"Nothing in particular," the man said, and shrugged

his shoulders. Enzo recognized him as Dominick Petrelli. He had never approached the man, for obvious reasons. Petrelli was a big shot. His term in Sing Sing was a vacation, and everyone knew it. The minute he was released, he would return to ruling New York's streets. Enzo eyed him with more curiosity than he had the three assailants.

"Then why don't you get the hell out of our way?"

"I'd rather not." Petrelli shot them a smile. He oozed charisma. And these Italian morons didn't know how to respond.

"Come on, fella. Get out of the way. We have orders just like you do," the smallest of the three said with a shake of the head.

"I'm not going to."

"Three of us, two of you. We'll crush you," the largest —and clearly the dumbest—of them said.

"You know how to count. Impressive. But you failed to consider my associate." Petrelli nodded behind him. Enzo followed his gaze to a man behind them, who stood with his arms folded, tapping a shiv against his massive biceps.

The three assailants backed off.

"You got lucky, fat boy," the apparent ringleader said as they departed for their own cellblocks.

"Go futz your mother," Enzo shouted after them, feeling a bit more confident. When he turned to Petrelli, he found the man smiling at him jollier than Santa Claus. "I guess I owe you a token of appreciation." He lowered his head out of respect.

The other inmates shrugged and returned to their cots, disappointed that there hadn't been a fight.

"No need for that. Do you know who those gentlemen were?" Petrelli said.

"Italians?" Enzo asked, feeling for the first time like he

hadn't learned as much in Sing Sing as he had believed. Petrelli and his associate both laughed.

"Well, yes, they are Italian. They're Joe Masseria's boys. You know who Joe Masseria is?"

Enzo considered whether or not he should answer honestly.

"Maybe I have," he said, deciding on taking the middle ground.

"He runs New York City, buddy," Petrelli's muscular friend said, stepping forward.

"Masseria's guys are sloppy, so they get locked up in droves. There's a lot of them to begin with too, so you're going to see a lot more of them than you're going to see guys like us."

Enzo swelled with pride for a split second, but tamped it down.

"'Guys like us,' Mr. Petrelli?"

Petrelli smiled and wrapped an arm around Enzo's shoulder, leading him away from the gawking eyes.

"Call me 'the Gap.' Everyone does. I fought it at first, but now it's a persona. This is Joe Cargo." He gestured to his associate.

"How do you do?" Enzo shook the man's meaty palm.

"We've heard about you, Mr. Consentino," the Gap interrupted.

"Enzo the Thief," he corrected. If everyone else had a moniker, he should too.

"Enzo the Thief, then. We've heard about you. We know the heat was on you and your brother, and you stood tall and didn't sing about any of your associates. We can always use guys like that in our crew."

"Your crew?"

"That's right. I have a lot of connections back home.

Maybe I could make an introduction?" Petrelli eyed him with curiosity.

Enzo thought about it. He did have Bonventre and Magaddino back home, but those were the same fellas who'd allowed him to get locked up without saying a word.

"I'm intrigued." Enzo tried to appear more intelligent than he was, and for a moment, he feared this was apparent. But the Gap wrapped an arm around his shoulders and patted him on the chest.

"As long as you're there for us if any problem with Masseria's boys come to fruition, I'm sure we'll get along just fine."

ALONZO

Alonzo hadn't talked in days.

He had been silent for so long that Rosa had all but given up on trying to communicate with him. At first, it was a sort of defiance, a protest against the way the world really is. After a month or so of near silence, it was becoming a way of life. He spoke only to himself, and he was concocting a plan.

When he arose from a spiteful sleep that morning, he experienced the same hesitation he had been dealing with for weeks, but eventually decided today was as good as any.

He left as the sun was just appearing over the green ocean in the distance, and stuck to the side roads, headed west to Via Segesta. It was hot out, but he wore an overcoat regardless, with the collar up to hide his jaw. A straw fedora was perched on his head, and bent low, almost covering his eyes.

He entered Pietro's eatery a little before nine and ordered a cup of coffee. He sat in a corner that gave him a clear view of the entire room.

Less than an hour later, the Armettas arrived. Lupe and three sons, the fourth having been buried a few months prior.

"Morning, Don Armetta," the proprietor said as they entered.

"Pietro, how's your old woman treating you?" Lupe asked. One of Lupe's sons pulled out a chair for him, and he sat happily. Food was rushed out, apparently prepared in advance. Alonzo hid his face behind a menu, but he was beginning to receive strange glances from Pietro. He had been there for too long to have not ordered something to eat.

As if reading his mind, Pietro approached.

"Have you decided what you'll be having? Or will coffee do it for today?"

"Just give me whatever they're having." Alonzo nodded to the Armettas across the room. "It looks very good."

Pietro hesitated before writing down the order. "You got it."

Alonzo bade his time. Luckily, Pietro and the woman cooking with him took their time in preparing his order. Lupe ate his fill, and then some more, before loosening his belt and leaning back in his chair.

"I'm going to go push." Lupe stood and walked to the back of the restaurant to the bathroom. Alonzo counted down in his head, and once a few moments had passed, he stood and followed Lupe. Armetta's sons were too preoccupied with their desserts to notice him. They probably wouldn't have recognized him anyway. He hadn't shaved his mourning beard for as long as he'd been silent.

As he entered the bathroom, he heard the grunting of an old man trying to defecate. He experienced some sort of resistance, believing somewhere that it might be dishonorable to kill his enemy while he was on the commode. Before he was forced to decide, Lupe opened the stall door. His face lit up as he recognized Alonzo, who pounced.

He slammed Lupe into the stall door, and the two slipped on the wet linoleum floor. Lupe's head smacked against the toilet he had just filled, but his grip continued to tighten on Alonzo's throat.

"You—" Lupe said, spitting the word at the man holding him down, but he couldn't get out much else. Alonzo tried to hold him

steady, a hand placed over his mouth to keep him quiet. With his free hand, he reached back to his boot, where a dagger was hidden in its sheath. Before he could retrieve it, his head jolted to the left on the other side of Lupe's fist. He fell off of him, and tried to regain his composure.

Lupe scurried to his feet like a man half his age, and broke for the door. Alonzo stretched out and grabbed his foot. Lupe fell again, crashing hard against the ground.

If his sons had any sense, they would be coming soon. Alonzo crawled onto Lupe's back and wrapped his forearm across the man's throat. He cracked the back of Lupe's head with an elbow.

Lupe forced himself onto his stomach, pushing Alonzo off. Blood was dripping from his lips and forehead, and he no longer bore any arrogance in his eyes. Instead, he wore the look of a cornered animal.

Lupe punched Alonzo twice, once to the eye, once to the mouth.

Lupe reared his head back and tried to shout. Alonzo slammed his hand onto Lupe's mouth just before he could.

The old man was beginning to tire, and Alonzo reached back and pulled the dagger from his boot. He held it up and plunged it toward Lupe's chest. Lupe caught Alonzo's hand and forced it back with the second wind of a fish nearly brought to shore. With a final burst of energy, he headbutted Alonzo, who had leaned too close. Lupe took advantage of Alonzo's distraction, and sent the dagger spiraling across the bathroom floor.

Alonzo moved off of him, and now it was his turn to be pursued. Lupe clutched to Alonzo's leg, and kept him in place. He lurched on top of him and placed his thumbs over Alonzo's eyes. Lupe could have called for help now, but he clearly intended to finish this himself.

Alonzo grunted as his eyes threatened to burst within his skull. Then, in his own final push, he pulled his father's razor from his pocket and, in one swift motion, sliced at Lupe's throat. Both of Lupe's hands left Alonzo's eyes and clutched desperately to the wound. Alonzo struggled to his feet, panting.

He stepped over Lupe, and stomped on his chest. Then, he leaned *down and forced Lupe's hands away, strength now flowing back through his veins. Alonzo's eyes were puffy and swollen, but he fumbled until his father's razor was on Lupe's jugular. Then he cut deep. He dug in farther, grinding it through flesh and sinew, up against the bone.*

Lupe's face contorted, and he gargled, blood bubbling and spewing from his lips. His head shook violently back and forth, as if disagreeing with the death that was upon him. Alonzo, undeterred, sliced the edge of the razor deeper and deeper, until Lupe's eyes rolled back in his head, his blood-soaked tongue puffing out and falling over his lips.

Alonzo cleaned the razor on Lupe's coat, then adjusted his own. He picked his fedora up off the floor and popped it back atop his head.

He took one last moment to look at the lifeless corpse. For a man who had killed so many of Alonzo's loved ones, he now looked as harmless as any dead thing. Alonzo opened the door, relieved that his sons hadn't heard a thing, and he would never have to see any of them again.

Castellammare del Golfo—July 22, 1907

"Come on, get your things," Alonzo said, bursting through the front door.

"Now you want to talk? And you give a command? It's been a month since you offered a single word to me, Lonz." Rosa's eyes were wet but not without the anger only attainable by a Sicilian woman.

"Don't fight me on this, Rosa. Get everything you can. I've got a horse and cart prepared." The baby stirred in his crib and began to cry.

"And where are we going?"

"Trapani."

"Oh, are you going to send us off like you did Piddu?" she said, that famous anger rising.

"No. I'm going with you." A violent knock sounded on the door. Alonzo froze and looked out, but noticing it was only Turridru, he relaxed. *"It's unlocked,"* he shouted.

"Did you hear? I just heard," Turridru said, teeming with excitement.

"Yes, I've heard." Alonzo continued to move around the dining area, gathering up the few things he considered essentials.

"Heard what?" Rosa asked, to no response. *"Heard what, Alonzo?"* Her anger dissipated and was replaced by fear.

"Just get your things, Rosa."

"Get your things? Why?" Turridru asked.

"We're leaving," Alonzo said, shooting off to the bedroom, not stopping to see the baby.

"Leaving?" Turridru laughed in confusion. *"Lupe is dead. Why would you leave?"*

"What? Who? Lupe Armetta is dead?" Rosa said after gasping. Then she began to follow Alonzo's orders.

"Yes, and that is why we are leaving." Alonzo tried to catch his breath, his eyes still darting around the room. *"Go get the twins, Rosa. Tell them to pack a single bag each with anything they need."*

"Don Consentino, why are you doing this?" Turridru tried to be respectful, but his irritation and shock were not disguised.

"I'm done fighting, Turridru. I'm done toiling to keep my family safe, and I'm done burying my loved ones." He didn't want to explain himself any further, but Turridru refused to relent so easily.

Alonzo ran up the stairs, his young companion following close behind.

"The Armettas will take over the city! Your entire Borgata will be at risk," Turridru pleaded.

"I don't have a Borgata anymore."

"*What about us, then? Don Consentino, I beg you to reconsider! What will become of us?*" Alonzo planted on his feet and turned to Turridru like an angry bull. He swept him up by the collar of his shirt and looked him in the eyes.

"*I have to look after my family. Do you think I want to leave? This is my home, the only place I've ever loved. But this has gone too far. Too many have died. Now the deaths of my people have been avenged. And I am leaving before more blood is spilt.*"

"*Don—*"

"*I will hear no more of it. We're leaving. You could come with us, if you'd like?*" Alonzo turned and continued his ascent of the stairs. Turridru paused and looked at the ground.

"*My father will never leave Sicily.*"

"*No. He won't. And he'll likely call me a coward.*" Alonzo finally stopped and looked back down the stairs at Turridru. "*This is the only way. You must see that. If I am gone, the Armettas will have no one left to kill. This war can end.*" Turridru said nothing else. "*Come on, boys, hurry up,*" Alonzo said as he entered their bedroom. "*We're leaving and we aren't coming back.*"

ALONZO

It was probably two a.m. Alonzo was exhausted, but he wasn't going to bed until his sweetheart was prepared to go with him. But she was still drinking.

And, for once, he drank with her.

Enzo and Vico weren't there, and hadn't been for some time. He knew where both of them were, but tried to forget it as much as possible. Vico was done with the war, he was sure, but Alonzo didn't expect him to come calling when he got home. Enzo was probably out of jail too, but it didn't matter. Alonzo wasn't sure how he'd react if either of them did show up.

He blocked the thought from his mind and turned up the radio.

"Turn that down!" Rosa cried as she swirled her wine around in her glass.

Alonzo had spent far more than was responsible on that little radio, so he had no intention of doing so.

"On your feet, *mio tesoro*."

She rolled her eyes and feigned irritation until she laughed.

"That's my sweet girl, I knew you were still there. Come, then, on your feet." He bowed his head and extended his hand farther. He delighted in her laughter until she drained her wine and accepted his hand.

Alonzo pulled her close to him, drinking in the smell of her hair.

"Do you remember how angry my father was when he first saw us dancing?" she asked.

"We were just children. If he wasn't scared of my father, the welts he would have caused would still be on my back, I'm certain."

"Maybe he was right," she said, but he could feel her smile against his cheek.

"All the belts in the world couldn't have stopped me from loving you." He pulled her in until she was close enough to feel his excitement.

And he could sense a hunger in her too, one that had never really left but one she hadn't allowed to emerge since they were young and without children.

Something about the New Year's spirit, perhaps, or at least New York's.

Alonzo reached an arm behind them to turn the radio up. Helen Kane's "I Want to Be Bad" was on, and he was hoping it might give his wife some ideas.

She was far too intelligent to be fooled by his subliminal tricks.

"I can see what you're doing, Lonz," she said.

"Your eyes are closed, dear."

"I can feel it. On my leg." She laughed, and he laughed with her, but didn't stop dancing.

But then she did. The demeanor of the room shifted so

drastically that he paused and almost sobered up in an instant.

"What is it? I was only toying with you, dove."

"What do you think the boys are doing tonight?"

He knew instantly what she meant. He'd hoped she wouldn't mention it. It had been a long time since she last had. She wasn't talking about Sonny and Antonello, as they both knew they were asleep in their room.

"I don't know, dear," he said, meeting her eyes.

"Do you think they're happy?" she asked, displaying far more vulnerability than she normally would. He wanted to believe it was just the wine talking, but he knew better. It was another of the decisions he had made without her permission. At the time, he'd believed his wife would want to be spared the pain of having to make such a decision. And she had accepted what happened as dutifully as any Sicilian wife could. But it wasn't resentment in her eyes now. It was simply fear.

The same fear that was in Alonzo's eyes.

"I hope so, love," Alonzo said. He tried to think of some way to apologize, or offer some sort of condolences, but he could never find the words.

They continued to dance, but much more slowly now. And there was no longer any hunger.

ENZO

Little Italy, Manhattan—February 22, 1919

There was just something about being a twin. Enzo felt like a part of him was missing the entire time he was locked up in Sing Sing, and it had nothing to do with the outside. Even after two years, he didn't feel right without his brother there.

At times, he'd wake up at night with bad dreams and cold sweats, and wondered if Vico was safe across the pond. That gut feeling used to be as reliable as if he had seen Vico suffering with his own eyes, but that connection had been diluted.

He was even beginning to worry that Vico wouldn't show.

Enzo had been at the Spring Street station for half an hour, and had watched a dozen doughboys arrive and leave with their loved ones amid outbursts of tears and kisses. Enzo waited as calmly as he could, but patience had never been a virtue of his. He couldn't help but check his watch, only to find that the hands had hardly budged.

Every time a train arrived, Enzo would stand as tall as he could and shout his brother's name over the din of the crowd, ignoring the looks he received.

Vico's letter said he would be there. At 3:30. Enzo had waited so long, and at 3:43, he didn't want to wait any longer.

"Don't you recognize your baby brother?"

Enzo started, then recognized the voice from across the parkway. "Vico." He hiked up his trousers and ran across the rainy street to his brother. "*Madonna mia,* you really made it home." Enzo felt himself choking up.

"What, you weren't betting against me, were ya?" Enzo wrapped Vico up in a big hug and shook him.

"Just look at you," Enzo said, but wished he hadn't. He was suddenly aware that Vico had grown several inches taller than him, and while his brother's chest and forearms had doubled in size, the only part of Enzo that had grown was his midsection. "What in the hell were they feeding you over there?" Enzo laughed, squeezing Vico's bicep.

"What in the hell were they feeding you in the pen?" Vico patted Enzo's belly, and they both smiled. Enzo noticed his brother's dialect had been diluted since they had last seen each other at the New York County Supreme Court two years before.

"Come on, doughboy, let's get you home and get some brown in your hand."

"I'd settle for a fag if you got one," Vico said as Enzo hurried to give him a Lucky Strike and a lighter. "Look at this lighter. It's got your initials and everything. Sing Sing must not have treated you so bad."

Enzo led him to a nearby tram that was headed for

Brooklyn. "I made some friends on the inside. I'll tell you all about 'em when we get to Williamsburg," Enzo said as Vico stopped walking behind him.

"You don't want to stop by Mulberry? See if the family is in for the evening?" Vico said, readjusting the strap of the army kit bag on his shoulder.

Enzo looked down.

"They don't want to see us, Vico." They spent a moment in shared sorrow, without saying anything.

"You think?" Vico finally said, tapping his cigarette out on the sole of his boot. "Alright, well, lead the way, then."

They boarded the tram, squeezing in between a few old Yiddish men and a German who reeked of sauerkraut.

"So how was your sleepover in the clink?" Vico asked.

"Eh, could of done it standing on my head," Enzo boasted proudly. "I heard a bunch of horror stories on my way there about working in stone quarries and all kinds of bullshit. But if you play your cards right, and you make the right friends, life in Sing Sing ain't so bad."

"Papà always made sure we knew how to play our cards," Vico said. Both men smiled, but those smiles quickly faded.

After their trolley arrived in Williamsburg, Enzo rushed Vico along to Sixth Street.

"This looks a little familiar," Vico said.

"You betcha. I got us a place a story down from the place we were at before we got pinched. It's perfect." Enzo led the way to their old apartment complex and fumbled through his keys. "Here she is. I'm telling you, Vico, this one's even better than the last. It doesn't face the river, so you don't gotta deal with that smell. And we even got a radio now, if I can get the damn thing to work." He noticed that Vico had paused in the doorway and was analyzing the room from top to bottom. "Everything alright?"

"Yeah, yeah." Vico remembered himself and stepped into their new domain, shrugging his bag off and stretching.

"Just like the old place, huh? We can pick up right where we left off. But even better," Enzo said, and Vico nodded. "And we got this too. How could I forget?" Enzo hurried to the refrigerator, and pulled out two bottles of beer, gesturing to them like a street salesman. "A toast to the war hero!" He slapped his brother's rock-solid shoulders.

"*Salute*," Vico said, and Enzo echoed the cheers as their bottles clinked.

"So, tell me, brother, how bad did you give it to those Krauts?"

"We just did what we were supposed to," Vico said, and shrugged.

"Bushwa! Level with me, Vico. Did you get your hands dirty? Scalp any of those bastards?" Enzo grinned, but stopped when he realized that Vico wasn't doing the same.

"Everybody got their hands pretty dirty."

"Well, take a load off." Enzo gestured to the sofa he had purchased just a week before. "You meet any of our guys over there? Those Jerries wouldn't know what to do against a battalion of Sicilian men of honor."

"No, not too many." Vico shrugged. "Not many guys like us were ready to lead the charge. I met one. He's from Chicago."

Enzo eventually gave up talking about the war. The

past was the past, he concluded. Time to look toward the future, and it was bright.

"I gotta introduce you to these boys in Harlem. They aren't like Bonventre's crew. They wouldn't leave us out to dry the way Bartolo and Francesco did."

"You met them in Sing Sing?"

"You better believe it. Lots of our guys in there. It's like a paid vacation." Enzo laughed, ignoring the memories of solitary confinement as best he could. "They have lots of work for us. They're on the up-and-up too. Part of a big crew, really going places. And—"

Vico cut him off. "I don't want any part of it, Enzo."

"What? Don't want any part of what?"

"Any of it. I'm done with all that."

Enzo was at a loss for words.

"Yeah, you need some rest. I understand."

"No, Enzo. I mean ever. I'm not doing any of that again."

"You…you haven't even met my guys. They aren't gonna send you to another war, Vico."

"Enzo"—Vico's eyes were weary and strained—"I know what it's like to kill. And I know what it's like to think you're gonna die. I'm not doing it again." Vico lowered his head and ruffled up his army haircut.

Enzo clenched his jaw. His brother had never told him no before. Not in their entire lives. Before, Vico would have followed him blindly into the gates of hell if asked. Enzo felt like the soldier beside him was a stranger.

"Hey," Enzo said, waiting for Vico to look up, "was it worth it? Going to war, I mean. Was it worth it?"

Vico thought and scratched at his temple. His Adam's apple began to bounce like a yo-yo, and his chest heaved. Vico buried his face in his hands and wept.

Enzo froze for a moment, but then leaned over and put

a hand on his brother's shoulder. It was all he could do. For the first time in their lives, Enzo didn't know what Vico had been through, what he was thinking, or what he planned to do.

SONNY

It had been over two years since Alonzo had kicked the twins out, but there wasn't a day that passed that Sonny didn't think about it. As the rumors continued to spread, Alonzo and Rosa were eventually forced to sit Sonny and Maria down and explain to them everything that had happened.

Enzo had gone to jail. Vico had gone to war. They were both likely back home now, if they were still alive. But they hadn't visited.

It was all Sonny could think about when he was at A.C. Barbers and things slowed down.

"Sonny, I'm talking to you," Alonzo said. "Go to the back and grab some more hot lather, I'm running short." Sonny put down the broom and dustpan and hurried off, his thoughts about Enzo and Vico unrelenting.

"Here ya go," Sonny said, handing his father a bottle of Johnson's shaving cream, his father's favorite.

"Thanks, Sonny Boy," Alonzo said, patting his shoulder. He seemed older every day, but Sonny, now fourteen, was growing enough to keep up with him. Sonny had been working in the barbershop every day after school for years now, and was beginning to feel he was a peer to his father and his customers.

Sonny was sweeping up hair and Alonzo was focused on his razor blade when a man entered. Everyone stood. Sonny wheeled around, confused about what was happening. Even Oscar's client, half shaved and half lathered, stood up, hair falling all over his shoes.

Alonzo was the last to notice.

"Don Consentino," the man said in Sicilian, the words smooth and confident.

Alonzo turned and stared for some time.

"*Madonna mia.*" Alonzo was in shock as he gave the man a hug and a kiss on either cheek, careful not to soil the man's fine blue pinstripe suit with any hair products. They lingered for a moment.

"It is good to see you."

"You too." Alonzo spoke in Sicilian as well, and it seemed less labored than when he spoke it at home. "I guess I should call you Don Maranzano now," he said, and nodded.

"It has been a long time."

"Are you here for a trim?" Alonzo asked, the man in his chair already stepping away to offer his spot if Maranzano would like to go first.

"That won't be necessary. I just wanted to see you. I have just arrived in the States, but I plan to stay for a while. Some friends of mine are driving me around New York. It's quite a circus, isn't it?" He smiled, his teeth perfect and white. Sonny couldn't take his eyes off of this Don Maranzano. He had a magnetic presence, and everyone else was paying him just as much attention. Most of the important men who had been visiting A.C. Barbers were identified by their fine jewelry and loud sack suits. This man wore nothing shiny but a watch and a wedding ring, but his demeanor identified him as someone to be listened to.

"Do you have somewhere to stay?" Alonzo asked, and seemed to blush.

"I do. I have an apartment in the East Village—on Second Avenue, to be exact." Uncomfortable silence grew as Alonzo searched for what to say, but Maranzano seemed content enough.

"Here, meet my son," Alonzo finally said, and gestured for Sonny to step forward. He was both horrified and delighted to earn the man's attention.

"Is this Vico or Enzo?" The man stuck out his hand and leaned down to Sonny's level. "Surely, this isn't little Vincente?"

"Yes, sir," Sonny replied in Italian.

"And what a strong young Sicilian this boy is." He looked up at Alonzo, who was full of pride. "Do you listen to your father, Vincente?"

"Yes, sir." He didn't want to tell him that he only went by Sonny. His full name, Vincente, seemed more appropriate from this man.

"Good. Do you read your Bible?" he asked with a furtive grin. Sonny felt a smile split across his own lips as well.

"Yes, sir."

"He's a very good reader. Smarter than most of the boys his age," Alonzo said.

"Smarter than most of us too," Oscar said from across the barbershop, although not in Sicilian.

"Of course, he is. He's a Consentino." Don Maranzano stood back up. "It was a pleasure to meet you,

Vincente." His voice had an entrancing echo-like quality. Sonny accepted a handshake, feeling about five feet taller. "And it was good to see you again, Don Consentino"—he kissed Alonzo again—"and perhaps we will cross paths again." He tipped his homburg, and left, the room suddenly more alive than before his arrival.

SONNY

Sonny flipped another card. A Three of Hearts. He tossed it aside and continued. A few months prior, Antonello had finally gotten a job in Brooklyn and had moved out. He visited often, but when he didn't, Sonny spent most of his time at the barbershop or on the stoop, looking at cards. It was a little bit like tarot card reading, except he got to make the rules and decipher the meanings. He didn't believe in it much, but it was a way to pass the time. He used to look forward to the weekends, but now he dreaded them.

He knew Alonzo and Rosa worried about him.

He had graduated high school two years prior, and was now a full-time employee at A.C. Barbers. He didn't have many friends, and he didn't do much for fun, but he always reminded his parents that he had Antonello whenever they came to him with that concerned look only parents can have. He had Maria also, whose life he had taken an active role in, almost like an uncle or a third parent.

Jack of Spades.

It wasn't the life he had wanted, sure. He had once told his father that he wanted to be a Wall Street man, someone important and knowledgeable. He had kept up with the stock market since he was a little boy, and had borrowed at least a dozen books on investing from the library just north of Little Italy. But the thought of being a businessman, with nice suits and expensive cars, was about as lofty as being the first Sicilian president of the United States.

Four of Diamonds.

He had all but given up on that. He certainly never talked about it. It was more important to him to simply be a good helper to his father, and a caring older brother to Maria.

"Sonny Boy." Alonzo walked up behind him and plopped down in a chair.

"Hey, Dad. Want to play a hand?" Sonny perked up some. Rosa's rule of only speaking Sicilian in the house had long since been abandoned.

"Not right now, Sonny. But I have something to tell you." Alonzo leaned back and crossed his legs. He rubbed the stubble on his chin and looked contemplative.

"Come on, Dad, are you going to tell me or not?" Sonny said, not sure why his heart rate was increasing.

"I'm sending you to college, Sonny Boy." Sonny jolted to his feet, the chair falling down behind him.

"What!" he shouted.

"Calm down! Calm down," Alonzo said, and laughed.

"How? Where did you get the money?"

Alonzo looked down and his smile faded. "I've been saving for a long time, Sonny Boy. I always wanted you to go, and I know you did too... There were times when you and the others had to go without certain things because I was saving this. So it's only right that you use it now." Alonzo revealed an envelope and put it down on their favorite card table. Alonzo snatched it back when Sonny reached for it. "Ah-ah, not so fast. I'll hold on to this, old boy. But it's going straight to your schooling."

"How much is it?" Sonny was at a loss for words.

"A few thousand." Alonzo waved down Sonny's excitement. "Come on, it's not that much." Sonny ran through the numbers in his head. It would have taken a long time saving up a barber's pay to have a few spare thousand dollars lying around.

"That's a lot of scratch, Dad."

"Well, it's just enough to put you through four years at Columbia." Sonny had to bite his knuckles. He lowered his head, embarrassed by how giddy he was becoming.

"Dad…"

"I knew it was where you always wanted to go."

"Think I'll get in?"

"With your grades, it's guaranteed. Come here." He gestured for a hug and gave Sonny a kiss on the cheek.

"How did you do this? How do you have this much?"

Alonzo thought for a moment before responding, and turned his gaze out to Mulberry Street before them. "That's why it took me so long to get it for you. I didn't know how or what I was going to do for a while. But I would do anything for my family, so I figured it out." Sonny looked on, still wondering if this might be a dream. "Anything, Sonny Boy. Don't you worry about it."

RACHEL

"Oh, turn that up! This is my favorite song," Rachel shouted to one of her friends, and then took a sip of her gin and lime through a straw.

Another Friday night, another party her mother would be ashamed of her attending. Of course, Rachel's mother also still said that women shouldn't be allowed to, or want to, vote. She wasn't the most modern woman.

"Is that better?" Allison cupped her hands around her mouth and shouted over "You're the Cream in My Coffee" and the clopping feet of the dancers.

"Now I just need to find someone to dance with," Rachel said, moving her hips to the music, feeling the effects of the booze come over her like a current.

It wasn't exactly a petting party, but everyone knew why they were there. Guys and gals were huddled in every corner of the dance hall, necking.

"I'm you guy, Mamma," a member of Sigma Phi

Epsilon said, stepping into view and placing a hand on her hip. Rachel had already seen him dancing with a few other girls that evening, and the stale smell of cigarettes was so rank on his breath that she had to step away.

"Who's that fellow over there?" Rachel asked Allison, effectively ignoring the fraternity boy. The student in her eyesight was an awkward-looking chap, clearly not used to such social gatherings. He leaned up against the wall and nursed his drink, tapping his foot to the music but not moving another muscle. The tall green socks, plaid knickerbockers, and worn newsboy cap didn't paint a very attractive picture, but Rachel could see natural muscles under those rags and the etching of a strong jaw.

"I've never seen him before," Allison said. Rachel maintained her gaze.

The fraternity brother stepped back into her line of sight and continued to plead his case. "You don't want to dance with him. He's a barb." It was true that the boy across the dance hall wasn't in a fraternity himself; otherwise, he'd have a pin on his lapel, and he would certainly be out on the dance floor. "And he's a Sicilian. Can't you smell the grease from here? A Jewish dame like yourself needs to dance with someone with a bit more class." The fraternity boy swayed back and forth from the alcohol, not exactly the picture of class to Rachel.

She took his hand and pulled it away from her side a bit more forcefully this time.

"Think I could get a dance with him?" Rachel asked her friend.

"You can get a dance with anyone in here," Allison replied, and topped off her gin.

The fraternity brother threw up his hands and transferred his attention to Allison.

"What about you? You sure are a bear cat."

"Go peddle your papers somewhere else," Allison said with a flick of the wrist as Rachel started across the hall.

It was a bit surprising that Rachel found her chest tightening as she approached the boy. She was a real charmer, and she knew it. She knew the outcome of approaching any other guy there, but it was different with a wallflower. He would be a bit unpredictable, which was perhaps why she was interested in the first place.

"You could be the cream in *my* coffee," she said, startling him.

"Oh, I didn't see you there." He fidgeted uncomfortably and looked down at the drink in his hand. He was clearly Sicilian, but Rachel was surprised to find his English refined and his words carefully pronounced. She liked that.

"New around here?" she asked.

He nodded at length and eventually worked up the courage to meet her gaze.

"I'm a freshman."

"And how!" she exclaimed.

His face twisted in confusion.

"What?"

"It means something like…indeed."

"Oh. And how." He smiled, which made Rachel find him more charming than all the well-dressed, oil-haired sheiks in there.

"What's your name?" She stepped forward and placed a deliberate hand on his forearm.

"I'm Vincente…" He paused and seemed to rethink his answer. "Everyone calls me Sonny, though." She nodded and waited for him to ask her name, which he forgot to do for an awkward moment. "And your name?"

"I'm Rachel Katz," she replied proudly. She figured he might know her father, a renowned physician in the area.

His face didn't convey that he was familiar with the last name.

"It's a pretty name," he said with a forced grin.

The more he looked at her, the more his feet tapped.

She tightened the grip around his arm. Her chest wasn't tight anymore. She knew where to take things from here.

"Would you like to dance?"

Sonny's mouth opened to respond, but then he looked around the room.

"Boy, you all sure move quick. I don't really know how to dance like that."

"Finish your drink, daddy. I'll show you how."

He deliberated for a moment but clearly couldn't see a way out. So he finished his drink, winced, and allowed Rachel to lead him by the hand out onto the dance floor.

She took both of his hands in hers and placed them on her hips.

He didn't seem to notice how flushed his face was.

"It's called the black bottom. Just bounce on your feet a little, and I'll do the rest."

The music picked up at just the right time.

"Okay, now when I kick one of my feet out, you do it too, right beside mine." She tried to lock her eyes with his, but his gaze was fixed on her T-strap heels to see what her feet were doing. He did his best, but he was woefully uncoordinated. A few fraternity brothers were laughing nearby; she wondered if they were laughing at him, but she didn't care. That look of intense focus was endearing, in an odd way. And when he dipped her, his grip was so firm and strong, she wanted him to hold her like that all night.

"Now watch this." The alcohol was making her confident, so she took a few steps back and began to shimmy, throwing her arms around and shooting him the most tantalizing eyes she could.

"It looks like you're gyrating!" he said, but she saw his eyes follow the movement of her chest.

"You don't like it?"

"No, I think I do."

She fell back into his arms.

"You ever kissed a girl?" Her voice rose over the music.

"Sure, I have!" He seemed a little embarrassed, and flushed.

"Want to kiss another?" She pushed out her chin up to him.

"C-can I?" he stammered.

She pulled away again and placed her hands on her hips.

"Well, you better make me another drink, then!"

"Oh. Certainly. Gin and lime?"

"How'd you know?" she asked with a grin.

"I saw you drinking it before." He rubbed at the back of his neck and then hurried off to get it for her.

She had him now. And if it was up to her, it wouldn't be their last dance together.

ALONZO

"Forgive me, Father, for I have sinned." Alonzo shifted in the confession booth.

"How long has it been since your last confession?" The ominous voice of the priest carried from the other side.

"Depends on how you reckon it."

"By your reckoning."

Alonzo calculated before responding. "I have come to Old St. Patrick's for confession every Tuesday since I arrived in America. Twenty-some years ago. But I have never been able to talk." He found it difficult to do so now.

"I have been present for many of these occasions. I can tell that something has been troubling you. What do you need to confess, child?"

Alonzo pulled out a handkerchief and dabbed at his nose. "It's been so long…" Tears welled up in his eyes.

"Sins, no matter how old, must be repented. Christ is faithful to wash you clean, if you will allow him."

"I've done bad things, Father. I have killed. I have done very bad things."

"How long ago, my child?"

"A lifetime ago. Sometimes it feels like yesterday."

"Have you remained sinless since then?" Alonzo assumed the question was rhetorical. He felt an onslaught of guilt come over him.

"Better than before, Father."

"And the sins of your past have haunted you enough that you have been unable to truly attend confession all this time?"

"Yes, Father. That is true."

"Then why are you here now? Has the Holy Spirit finally led you to repentance?" Alonzo leaned over, stifling his sobs in the sleeve of his jacket.

"Because I am afraid, Father."

"What are you afraid of, child? The wrath of God?" The priest waited patiently as Alonzo tried to catch his breath.

"I am afraid for my children. I am afraid that my sins will haunt them..."

"Go on," the priest said. Alonzo tried.

"I am afraid they will suffer because of the things I have done."

"In the Gospel of John, Chapter 9, Verses 2 and 3, the disciples ask Jesus if a blind man was cursed by God for his sins, or that of his father. Jesus replied that neither the father nor the son had sinned, but the man was afflicted so that the works of God might be displayed in him."

"I do not want my children to suffer at all, Father."

"It isn't about what you want, child. It is about the will of the Father, and the free will he endowed us with."

"I would give all that I have to spare them."

"God abhors your sacrifices, my child. He only desires

a broken and contrite heart." The priest continued as Alonzo sobbed. "Have your children yet been afflicted because of your sins?"

"I don't know, Father. My…my two eldest…they began to commit sins of their own. And I left them to their own devices."

"How do you feel about this decision?"

Alonzo looked through the small framed window, hoping to see a comforting face on the other side. He could make nothing out but the silhouette of the priest, and the cross that lay atop his robes.

"I have been haunted by it for years. I have no idea where they are now. One went into the war… The other…"

"And what of the children that remained with you? You said that these two were only your eldest."

"Yes, Father. One has gone to college." Alonzo instantly regretted saying this. The priest surely knew who he was now. Sonny was the only boy within half a mile that had left for school. No reason to hold back now. "And my daughter, she will graduate school this month. She turns eighteen in November. I am very proud of them both."

"Are you afraid that your two youngest will follow in your footsteps? As your two eldest have?"

"I don't know what I am afraid of, Father."

"Lay your fears down at the cross, child. Leave them with Jesus Christ, the Son of the Living God, who promises to overcome this world."

"I will, Father."

"Are you ready to confess your sins?"

Alonzo was silent for a moment. "And if I sin again?"

"Christ will only accept true repentance. If sin remains in your heart, he cannot cleanse you."

Alonzo stood and opened the confessional booth door, his tears finally subsided.

RACHEL

It had been three years since their first dance, and Rachel was still going steady with Sonny. It hadn't been easy at first. Her girlfriends had given her a hard time, of course. He had no social standing at the school, but she considered this a project and made him a bit more popular each day. She also taught him how to dress more stylish, and they had practiced their dance moves alone in his dorm enough that, by his junior year, Sonny was as smooth a dancer as anyone at Columbia. Perhaps he still seemed a bit out of place, but he had proven time and again that he was willing to go anywhere for her.

He was a novice; she was experienced. Rachel was his teacher, in more ways than one, educating him on everything he needed to know about being with a woman.

It was difficult for Rachel to be tied down too. Her friends said she was a prom-trotter by any standard, and it was probably true, but she eventually had decided to restrain herself for Sonny. All the other fellows brashly asked her to come home with them, or to go out and neck. But Sonny had waited patiently for her permission, in all things, displaying at all times that he was grateful and perhaps surprised that she had given him her affections.

And that made her want him. Want him enough to spend three years of her collegiate career to being only with him.

"Wake up, sleepy boy." She nudged him off of her shoulder.

"Right. Right. What were we on?" He wiped the cobwebs from his eyes and tried to focus again on the textbook in his lap. He had only been in school for three years, but had quickly caught up with Rachel in terms of credits. He studied harder than anyone else at the university, and only went out when Rachel made him. They'd both be in cap and gown that May.

"Maybe I just need to wake you up a bit." She placed a hand on his thigh.

"Come on, Rach. I have to finish studying first." A grin creased his lips, and she could tell he was tempted, but no boy she had ever met could resist a temptation like Sonny Consentino.

The most difficult hurdle for their romance was the way her parents felt about it. When her father heard she was dating a Sicilian, he pitched a fit and threatened to stop paying for her tuition. She knew that wasn't going to happen, though; she could charm her father like any other fellow. Her mother, on the other hand, immediately set about compiling a list of a dozen or so eligible Jewish bachelors. In time, though, Sonny had won them over by the considerate way he tended to Rachel, and the mature manner in which he could carry on a conversation with her father about the intricacies of finance.

"Fine." She pouted and leaned back on the bed, pushing away her own textbook with the bottom of her bare foot.

A knock sounded on the door, and her brother, Alfred, entered without waiting for permission.

He cocked an eyebrow when he saw Sonny in bed beside his sister.

"Well, hello, old boy. I wasn't expecting to see you here this time of evening."

"The resident assistant knows and said she'd tell me if anyone in the faculty comes snooping," Rachel replied for him. She didn't like it when Alfred came around Sonny. He made all kinds of sideways comments meant to belittle him and his ethnicity. Sonny accepted it all with patience, but Rachel knew there had to be a limit to what he could endure. The repressed strength she knew was within her sheik was something that enthralled her, but she hoped it wouldn't be her brother who would get the brunt of his aggression if Sonny ever unleashed it.

"No matter. Actually, you're just the fellow I wanted to talk to. Some of the other law students and I were planning a little function to celebrate the new semester. Do you think you could get us some…you know?" He leaned in and lowered his voice, needlessly cryptic.

"No, what?" Sonny replied, sitting up in bed and distancing himself from Rachel slightly.

"Hooch."

"Umm"—Sonny smiled but furrowed his brows—"no, I don't think I could get you any. Why would I be able to do that?"

"Well, you know." Alfred leaned back, grinned, and shrugged. "You know what they say about Italians."

"No, what do they say?"

"Alfred, stop!" Rachel gritted her teeth and shot him a look he knew the meaning of.

"What? I just mean you often have relatives in the trade of alcohol!"

"Get out, Al! That's enough."

He laughed and shook his head. Sonny said nothing but clenched his jaw.

"Who salted your undies? You know it's true."

"I'm not Italian. I'm Sicilian."

Alfred shot them both a look of confusion.

"What's the difference?"

"He can't get you any drink, Alfred. Any other reason for your social call?" Rachel rolled her eyes. This was just like him. It wasn't simply that he was rude, but he delighted in how much it bothered her.

"So you really can't get us anything? We might even let you two lovebirds come if you—"

"No! He can't."

"Fine. Well, if you talk to any of your cousins, and something changes, just let me know." Alfred tipped his hat and left the room, whistling on his way out.

"Sonny, I'm so sorry…" She closed her eyes and placed a hand on her forehead. It was one thing to have backward parents, but why did her brother have to be the biggest jerk on campus?

"No, don't worry about it. He's right, you know… A lot of the men back on Mulberry sell alcohol. They don't even hide it."

"But…none of your family members, right?" she asked, and immediately regretted it. She should have added that it didn't matter to her either way.

Sonny considered his answer.

"I don't know, honestly. My father paid for my tuition, and I'm not sure how he could have on a barber's budget.

And then there's always my brothers… No one knows what they're doing, but they've been in trouble before."

"Hush. It doesn't matter. My brother is an intolerable ass." She swung a leg over his waist and unbuttoned the top of her blouse. "Now, put that textbook down. I'm not asking this time."

"Yes, ma'am." He shoved the book off his lap and leaned back.

Talking about his family was always painful for Sonny. Luckily, she knew just how to get his mind off the subject.

HEARINGS BEFORE THE
PERMANENT SUBCOMMITTEE ON INVESTIGATIONS
OF THE
COMMITTEE ON GOVERNMENT OPERATIONS
UNITED STATES SENATE
EIGHTY-EIGHTH CONGRESS
THIRD SESSION
PURSUANT TO SENATE RESOLUTION 17
SEPTEMBER 29, 1963

CHAIRMAN: Mr. Valachi, this committee is trying to collect as much information as we can on Vincente Consentino and his associates. There are many crimes from the late nineteen twenties and early nineteen thirties that have been associated with him. Can you tell the committee exactly when you believe he became involved in organized crime?

Mr. Valachi: I can't give an exact date. No.

Chairman: Your best approximation will do, then. Was he involved in organized crime before attending Columbia University? Or during his time there?

. . .

Mr. Valachi: Maybe, but I don't think so. He was known as a square john until late in the twenties.

Chairman: A "square john"? Explain to the committee what that means.

Mr. Valachi: Yeah, a law-abiding citizen.

Chairman: Did Vincente "Sonny" Consentino ever discuss how he was able to pay for his education?

Mr. Valachi: His father paid.

Chairman: Alonzo Consentino? The barber?

Mr. Valachi: We all thought the same thing as well.

Chairman: If Vincente Consentino was a law-abiding citizen up until this time, what do you suspect led him to be connected with a series of murders beginning in 1930? There are missing persons cases from that time that are still open.

. . .

Mr. Valachi: Most of us believed it was after what happened to his father.

Chairman: What do you mean, exactly?

Mr. Valachi: After they found his father the way they did, Sonny changed. He became one of us.

SONNY

Sonny stopped and fixed his tie in the mirror. He was quite pleased with himself. He was no Joe Brooks, but at the behest of his friends, he had saved up for a porkpie hat and some more fashionable knickerbockers. After what felt like a thousand requests, he had finally attempted dancing. He couldn't get the hang of the Charleston, not one bit, but after hours of practice in solitude, he was beginning to be just fine at the fox-trot.

He hadn't been out dancing yet, and he knew it would please the girl he had been keeping company with.

He was still the same Sonny, he told himself. Still quiet and reserved, much like his father, but there was something about that that appealed to the other college students at Columbia, and the baby vamps at the all-female Barnard College just down the road.

"Wow, look at you," Rachel said from the doorway. Sonny jolted with surprise, causing Rachel to laugh at him.

"What are you doing in here? No girls in the dormitory."

"I wanted to say hello before we left. You sure you aren't coming?" She wrapped her arms around him from behind. Sonny admired her in the mirror, but pretended to be adjusting his tie. How he had landed a girl like Rachel was beyond him. With a girlish bob, and a thin chemise that came down only to her knees, she was the most beautiful girl he had ever seen. She powdered her nose and wore an enchanting fragrance. She even wore lipstick in the beesting fashion, which Professor Clark had called "poisonous scarlet." But Sonny liked it just fine. He had been concerned about introducing her to his mother, of course, but assumed that her natural charm would eventually win his folks over.

"No, I can't go. I told you, it's my sister's birthday!"

"But you look so nice tonight." She pouted her lips and batted her eyelashes. She could convince him to do just about anything, but missing his sister's eighteenth birthday dinner was the exception.

"Wish I could. Think any of the fellas will try to dance with you tonight?" Sonny asked bashfully.

"I don't think so." She pointed to the fraternity pin he had given her, now attached to her lapel. At Columbia University, it was as binding as a wedding ring.

"Let me know if they do. I'll rough 'em up."

"So I'll have to dance all alone?" She pouted again, but then smiled and stepped away.

They heard footsteps running down the hall, and Rachel vanished behind his drapes.

"We see you, Sheba," Sonny's fraternity brother, who went by his last name, Johnson, said, peering into the room. A few of his other brothers followed behind.

"Shucks." She came out from behind her hiding place.

"Look at this guy!" the brothers said as they came into the room, teasing Sonny.

"You must be headed to a petting party, all dressed up like that," Johnson said, patting him on the back.

"No. It's the first time I'm seeing my folks in a while. Just want to look nice." In all honesty, he wanted to ensure he was sharply dressed if Enzo and Vico happened to show up. But he forced the thought from his mind.

"Wait, so you aren't coming?" said another brother, who was called Catfish for his habit of "bottom-feeding" on the less than attractive girls.

"I can't. I told you fellas that."

"You're all wet, Sonny! Some girl from Barnard said she knows someone who knows someone, and they're bringing a case of hooch. You really aren't coming?"

"No use in trying, boys," Rachel said, touching Sonny on the arm with her gloved hands. "I've tried everything and can't get him to crack." They shook their heads at him and went off to bother someone else. "What are you all going to do?"

"We're going to get Maria a cannoli at Ferrara in Little Italy, maybe eat something first. I'd still love to have you come along, Rachel," Sonny said, but didn't plan on attempting to convince her. She was just as stubborn as he was.

"Well, maybe we can take her to a talkie afterward? She's eighteen now, after all, and I heard *The Singing Fool* is a riot."

"My pa might even let her. He's still on cloud nine after the Yankees swept the World Series. We'll see."

"Well, I'll let you get ready, then." She leaned on her tiptoes to kiss his cheek, leaving a smear of scarlet.

"Vincente?" a voice came from the door. Sonny looked, finding his resident assistant. To Sonny's horror, the RA had already seen a girl in the dorm, which meant trouble.

"Yeah?" No point in hiding now. The short RA looked at him through glasses that magnified his eyes threefold, and they seemed serious. He didn't even seem to mind Rachel. "Yeah, what is it?"

"Somebody rang for you. We have the call on hold in the lobby."

"Well, who is it?" Sonny popped on his hat.

"Sounds serious." He scurried off. Rachel clutched his hands between her own, and they hurried downstairs.

Little Italy, Manhattan—November 11, 1928

Sonny had left the moment he'd picked up the phone, leaving Rachel standing in the lobby.

He didn't believe it.

He wouldn't believe it. It wasn't true.

He hopped in a taxicab and told the man he'd pay him everything he had in his wallet to get him back to Little Italy as quickly as he could.

The voice on the other end of the line was his little sister's. After the receptionist had told him that, he'd picked up the phone, beginning to recite "Happy Birthday" to the best of his ability. When he heard the sobs coming from the other end of the line, he paused.

He heard what she said, but she was hysterical. She must have been wrong. Or he must have misunderstood.

Sonny left immediately, without offering an explanation to Rachel or anyone else.

He jumped out of the taxi before it came to a full stop, following the growing crowd to A.C. Barbers.

He pushed through the crowd, shoulder checking anyone who stood in his way.

"Hold it. Stop. Stop!" The policemen baring the entrance tried to restrain him.

"He's my dad!" Sonny's voice was hoarse. He pushed through.

There on the floor of his barbershop was Alonzo. Rosa was on top of him, her hands covered in blood, and her face distorted into a perpetual scream, although no noise was omitted.

"Papà!" Sonny rushed to him. But was forced to take a step back. Alonzo's eyes, still opened, stared off at the ceiling. He expected them to blink, but instead, Alonzo remained indifferent to the world around him.

Sonny spotted the single bullet hole in his father's head. Dark blood pooled up beneath his head and at the hem of his chesterfield overcoat.

Sonny moaned and fell to his knees beside his mother.

Rosa looked at him and lifted her frail, blood-covered hands, perplexed.

Sonny couldn't breathe. Everything melted but his father before him, mangled and lifeless. He felt strong arms wrap around him and pull him to his feet.

"No...no..." Drool spilled from his lips, and his vision was distorted through the lens of his tears. "No...no." The policemen removed him from the building, as gently as they could. His father faded from view and into the darkness.

PART 3

MARIA

"Blessed are those who mourn, for they shall be comforted," the father said as the coffin was laid down atop its grave. Maria couldn't bear to look. She looked to her mother, whose face was covered by a black veil. Still, it couldn't hide her tears. "Blessed are the meek, for they shall inherit the kingdom of God."

The pallbearers, Sonny, Enzo, Vico, and Oscar found their seats in the front row. Sonny let his tears roll without covering them. His face was still, calm, but his eyes were full of torment. Enzo and Vico were also crying. It was the first time Maria had seen them since Alonzo had ushered them out of the tenement, but they always wore their emotions on their sleeve. It was easy to tell that they were struggling as much as the rest of them. Perhaps their guilt over the past compounded the pain as well.

The coffin began to lower. Rosa let out a moan, and fell over against Vico, who held her in his arms.

Several of Little Italy's residents had come to pay their respects. Some of them were the Italians who hadn't been very friendly at the offset but whom Alonzo had eventually won over with cordiality and good haircuts.

"Blessed are those who hunger and thirst for right-eousness, for they shall be filled," the father continued.

Others had come too. Several men Maria had never met were present, and their cars were lined up along Mott Street with chauffeurs waiting outside the doors.

When the coffin found its resting place, the father said his final verse. Those gathered bowed their heads to pray. Maria at first closed her eyes, but then looked at those in attendance. Sonny's head was raised, his eyes fixed on the coffin.

"Amen," the priest said. Everyone rose from their seats and began the procession away from the gravesite. Rosa could hardly walk. The twins stabilized her, but they could still take only a few steps at a time. Perhaps that was the one solace in this tragedy: the family had been brought back together, as if Alonzo was the one thing that had been keeping them apart.

Rosa had not been well. After they had discovered Alonzo's body, she had refused to clean the blood from her hands, saying she wouldn't "wash away her husband." She hadn't eaten, and had barely talked.

Sonny rested on the arm of his young dame, Rachel, their hands interlocked. Maria had become exceedingly fond of her, not only for her marvelous sense of fashion but also for the way she had been a bedrock for Sonny throughout this time. She hadn't left his side, which was apparent in this moment, as she seemed to be the only thing keeping Sonny on his feet.

As worried as Maria had been about her mother, she was just as frightened for her brother. Sonny lived by his father's word. They had always been best friends, even during his time at Columbia.

"Maria?" said a gentle voice from behind her. She turned to find a young man she did not know. He wore a slicked-back undercut, and had a handsome face. She could tell by the way he held himself that he was a soldier. She stopped and waited for him to continue, but he struggled to find his words. "I met your father before he passed. I could tell that he loved you very much. He was a good man." Maria hadn't expected this, and she began to sob.

He materialized a handkerchief and held it out to her.

"Thanks for coming, Domingo," Vico said, patting the man on his back.

"You know my brother?" Maria managed to say.

"We served together in France."

"Did you come all this way just for the funeral?"

Domingo smiled, and then sadness flashed across his face. "Well, I've been back from France for ten years. My people are out West, though. I just moved to New York recently." She handed the handkerchief back to him. "No, keep it," he said.

"Thank you. And thank you for your kind words," Maria said with a sad smile.

"I wish you all the best." He touched her hand and joined the rest of the procession.

SONNY

Sonny tapped his feet as he waited in the gymnasium of the New York City Police Department at 240 Centre Street. The rest of the room was filled with convicts waiting in line for their mug shots.

He was quite aware that there was a luxurious lobby available for waiting visitors, and wondered if his ethnicity had anything to do with the clerk's decision to have him wait with the convicts.

That lobby was conspicuously luxurious too, especially since the police department was primarily tasked with looking after the poor districts surrounding it.

And they say crime doesn't pay. Well, it clearly pays for someone.

Sonny wondered if his brothers were right. Enzo and Vico had said the bulls wouldn't be of any use; they didn't give a damn about dagos. Rosa had said nothing as he'd put on his best coat and left for Centre Street.

"Mr. Consentino?" A pretty girl with curly hair and gray rayon stockings approached from his side.

"Yeah, that's me." Sonny stood and flipped the brim of the hat in his hands.

"The detective is ready to see you. If you'll follow me." She led the way from the gymnasium, careful to stay away from the convicts who gazed at her hips like they were peaches at a Mulberry Bend fruit stand.

"Have a seat, kid," the detective mumbled, tapping out his cigar, as the secretary opened the door for Sonny.

"Thank you for seeing me, Detective."

"Just sit down." The detective was a typical New York cop, tall and bulky, Irish, with a nose that wheezed from being broken a few too many times.

He picked at the leftover bits of his lunch and chewed with his mouth open.

"So, your father. Tell me about him."

"What do you want to know?"

"Did he like daisies or roses?" The detective cracked a smile, revealing a missing incisor. "Did he have any enemies?" he asked when he realized Sonny had been oblivious to the joke.

"Not that I know of. He got along with pretty with much anyone."

"Not everyone." The detective formed a gun with his fingers and pulled the thumb trigger, aiming at his head.

"Maybe it wasn't personal…"

"Nothing was reported stolen."

"There was a car. No one's seen it since my father's… murder." It was still hard to say out loud.

"A car? We looked into it. No record of purchase."

"I talked to him a few days before. He'd just bought it for my sister."

"Sorry, kid. Maybe he hadn't picked it up yet." The

detective obviously didn't realize what an honest man
Alonzo had been. He wouldn't have claimed to have something unless he actually did.

"So there's no chance he was killed for the car?"

"He had cash in his wallet. There was an expensive
gramophone in the back. Neither were taken. It doesn't fit
the bill." The detective flashed the first bit of sympathy
since Sonny had walked in, and then he picked up the
smooshed cigar and attempted to relight it. "I need you to
be honest with me here, kid. I need you to think hard. Was
there anyone you think might have wanted your father
gone?" He leaned forward and placed his elbows on the
cluttered desk between them.

"I really don't know. I've been away at university for a
few years... Everyone seemed to respect and like him."
Sonny regretted saying "respect" immediately, as he saw
something shift in the detective's eyes.

"No old feuds?" The detective finally got the cigar lit,
the smoke stinging Sonny's nose.

Sonny remembered his childhood fear of the Hook
Hand, but decided not to mention it. He had seen the man
get arrested. And, anyway, he had no reason to assume
anything bad about the man aside from foolish childhood
fears.

"Maybe someone from the old country," Sonny said
after a delay.

"That's what I'm looking for. Who from across the
pond might want your father dead?"

"I don't know... Occasionally, my brothers said they
thought there was some kind of feud back in Sicily... I
don't know, Detective. Maybe some other family that didn't
like him." Sonny fidgeted nervously. He didn't like talking
about it. It was the same reason he had never inquired
further. "That's not who my father was anymore. He was a

good, decent, hardworking man." Sonny felt as if he were pleading. If only the detective knew what his father was like, he wouldn't assume the worst.

"People don't ever really change, though, do they? You work my beat for twenty-three years, and you'll realize that."

Sonny stood, the chair scraping against the linoleum.

"I should have known. Thank you for your time, Detective. It's true what they say, though. The police don't care about the Italians."

The detective leaned back in his chair and clicked his tongue.

"If we didn't care about the Italians, we wouldn't care about anyone in this neighborhood. I'm not saying I'd invite you over for a mug of ale, but we want justice for you too. Sit back down."

Sonny contemplated leaving but finally returned to his seat.

"I'm just asking you to be reasonable here, kid. Even if he did have new wheels, did he afford that by shaving grocers and shop clerks?"

Sonny lowered his head and stared at his wing tips. The same thought, especially about the money for college, had eaten away at him for years.

"If your father was involved in any illicit activities, we need to know. That won't keep us from searching for his killers. It'll give us more leads, lad. That's it."

Sonny nodded and inhaled deeply.

"There was a guy who used to come around sometimes. When I was a kid."

"Alright." The detective smiled triumphantly and pushed aside his papers to find a legal pad to take notes.

"Sometimes he'd give me dad an envelope. And then we could afford...I don't know. Good things occasionally happened afterward." Sonny felt ashamed as he spoke, as if speaking life into that fact brought dishonor upon his father. He could only imagine his mother's judgment if she knew.

"What did he look like?"

"Bushy mustache. He wore a black overcoat sometimes. Sicilians don't really wear black, it brings bad spirits, so I found that odd... I don't know. It's been a long time. Maybe I'm misremembering."

"Trust yourself, lad. What else?" The detective scribbled everything down as quickly as Sonny could speak it.

Sonny looked up and locked eyes with the detective. He waited for him to stop writing.

"He had a mutilated hand."

The detective lit up briefly and tapped the tip of his pen on his chin.

"Now, that's what I'm looking for. Not many stump hands running around Little Italy."

"Detective, I really don't know if this fellow had anything to do with this. He might have—"

"Kid, relax. We're not gonna send a guy to the chair just because you tell us he used to visit your dad when you were a babe. We're just looking for leads."

"Alright. What else can I do to help?"

"I think that's it, boyo. We'll do our job and keep you informed." He nodded his head toward the door.

"That's it? There's nothing else I can do?"

"I'll call on you when I need you."

Sonny stood and slipped the fedora back onto his head. He left the police department no more confident that his father's murderer would be brought to justice than he was when he'd entered.

VICO

Ever since he had started boxing in '21, Vico he had been drinking more. Sometimes he drank to dull the pain of his perpetually broken nose; sometimes he drank because he was mad that no one wanted to talk about his fights, choosing instead to talk about the Long Count Fight between the "college kid" Gene Tunney and the "champ" Jack Dempsey.

Tonight, Vico drank because he couldn't sleep. Weeks had passed since his father's death, and Vico still couldn't sleep. So he took long pulls directly from his bottle of rotgut and tried to close his eyes.

The booze usually helped him shut down his thoughts, but tonight, they seemed to continue in a haze. He should have been there. Enzo too. They could have done something. He should have made things right with his parents, should have begged Alonzo to forgive him after he'd returned from the war.

He tried to open his eyes wide enough to find his cigarettes. He lit another, already on to his third pack since that morning. His lungs felt sunburned.

The door opened and closed, and he heard Enzo's footsteps approaching. Vico leaned up over the couch and peered into the kitchen to ensure that he had cleaned the remains of his vomit in the sink.

"Hey, champ. How was the fight?" Enzo asked, more reserved than usual. Vico rolled his eyes and threw up his hands. "*Madonna mia*, you look horrible." It was true that Vico's nose was once again cut and swollen, his eyes hidden behind purple knots. But Vico could feel himself sweating and assumed it wasn't just his battle wounds that Enzo was talking about.

"I got my ass kicked," Vico said, then rolled to a seated position and took another pull, using his shirtsleeve to dab away at the excess that poured over his chin.

"You can't win 'em all. There are more pebbles on the beach."

"No, I can't fight no more. I'm sloppy. Getting hit too much." Vico felt for the ice pack beside him on the couch, which was now melted.

"You're fighting twice a week now, brother. You need to give yourself some rest."

Enzo set the keys to his new Packard down on the kitchen table and took off his coat.

"Gotta make money somehow. I'm not sitting pretty like you," Vico said.

Enzo plopped down on the couch beside him and put an arm around his shoulders. Vico could tell by Enzo's hesitation that he considered offering him work, but he had long since given up. To ask Vico to join him in his criminal activity would insult him.

"Go on, just say it," Vico said, wincing at the burn of his whiskey.

"I'll say this: you've had enough to drink. Put that shit down before you end up in the hospital." Enzo tried to wrench it from his hands, but, even drunk, Vico's grip was too strong for him to do so.

"My big gangster brother telling me when to stop drinking. Your friends are the ones selling it. Just say it, Enzo. Say I'm a stupid two-bit punk and I should just give up fighting. Say I should come work with you boys in Harlem."

"Come on."

"No, I'm serious. Say it. I make eight dollars when I win and four dollars when I don't. I'm a loser, Enzo."

"You're doing what you think you're supposed to, Vico." Enzo's voice was far more consoling and tender than usual, and something about it concerned Vico.

"What? What's wrong?" he asked. Enzo stood and turned his back to his brother.

"Nothin'. We'll talk about it tomorrow."

"Leaving already? Tell me." Enzo had moved to East Harlem a few years back to be closer to his new associates, but he still visited whenever he could.

"We shouldn't talk about it when you're like this."

"Like what? Come on, Enzo. I'm not a kid anymore." Vico was a head taller than Enzo by now, and carried more strength in his pinky finger than most did in their arms.

"You're drunk, Vico."

"Tell me," Vico said firmly. He composed himself long enough to make it clear he wasn't giving up.

"I heard a guy talking about the old man today."

"What?" Vico managed to get to his feet.

"Yeah. They said Papà got knocked off by a gangster. I

tried to ask who, but they said they didn't know. Said they know someone who does."

"Did you go find him?" Vico was suddenly sober and alert.

"No, it's not that simple. They told me it was better I didn't know. Over my head."

Vico breathed heavily through his broken nose, a whistle following each exhale.

"Tell me who. I'll go find 'em."

"Vico, come on."

"Tell me."

"Vico, it's complicated. They don't share that stuff with just anyone. You got to be one of them."

"Like you?"

"No, not like me. I'm just a button guy. A nobody." Enzo waved his hands. He had become known as "Enzo the Thief," a title that meant that he was good at his job, but one he didn't have a particular affinity for.

"What do you have to do to get in? I'll do it. If it means we can find out who killed Dad, I'll do anything." Enzo refused to turn around, so Vico pulled his shoulder forcefully. "What do you have to do?"

"You wait until you're called, Vico." Enzo freed himself and stepped away. "It's complicated. You have to earn their trust. I heard one guy say you have to kill someone. I'm no killer. I just earn the way I have to."

"Tell them you know someone who can kill," Vico said. Enzo turned and regarded him for a moment. He seemed afraid of Vico's sudden coldness.

"I thought you didn't want to get wrapped up in all this."

"I have nothing left to lose. I used to be afraid to lose my life."

"You still should be."

Vico threw his bottle against the wall. Glass splintered and shot off around the room.

"I died in France. I just didn't know it. Tell me who to kill, and I'll kill. As long as I find the guy who widowed our mother."

Enzo gathered his coat and began to put it on.

"You're crazy. I'll talk to you tomorrow." Vico barred the exit before he could leave.

"You tell them tomorrow. Tell 'em you know a guy who knows his potatoes. Can pull his weight. Tell 'em I'm a veteran." Vico was amazed that Enzo hadn't lost his patience. Instead, he stood quietly, mulling it over.

"They aren't going to tell you shit as long as they know you're a Consentino. They'll know you're out for revenge, and that's bad for business."

"I'll use my ring name. You'll have to pretend we aren't brothers." Vico had been going by "Bobby Doyle" since he'd started boxing. No one wanted to see a guinea fight, so he'd assumed the identity of a dark-skinned Irishman.

"There is no turning back if you do this, baby brother."

"I don't want to come back." Vico looked around the barren apartment. He hated it. It could burn down, for all he cared. It was just a reminder that he hadn't been there for his father, that he had made mistakes all those years ago.

Enzo kissed him on the cheek and slowly opened the door. "I'll call you tomorrow." He patted Vico's swollen cheeks and smiled. "Try to sober up before then."

HEARINGS BEFORE THE
PERMANENT SUBCOMMITTEE ON INVESTIGATIONS
OF THE
COMMITTEE ON GOVERNMENT OPERATIONS
UNITED STATES SENATE
EIGHTY-EIGHTH CONGRESS
THIRD SESSION
PURSUANT TO SENATE RESOLUTION 17
SEPTEMBER 29, 1963

CHAIRMAN: Mr. Valachi, did Sonny Consentino ever say who he believed had killed his father?

Mr. Valachi: Not with certainty, no. He kept most of that to himself. But we all knew he was searching for answers.

Chairman: Is it true that he left school after his father was killed?

Mr. Valachi: Yes. That is true. We all called him "College Boy" because he went, but as far as I know, he never graduated. He quit after his father got hit, so he could provide for his family.

. . .

Chairman: Did Alonzo leave his family with much after his death?

Mr. Valachi: I always assumed they weren't left with very much. That's why Sonny and his brothers done what they did.

MARIA

"Make sure it's not too hot before you take a sip, dear," Maria said as she sat down at the table beside Sonny's girl.

"Oh, it's just perfect," Rachel said, taking the whiff of the hot tea. Maria had become close to Rachel over the three years she had been dating Sonny, but especially since Alonzo's death. Sometimes Sonny and Rachel would pick her up to go to a talkie or out on the town, but rarely did Rachel stop by alone.

Maria waited patiently to hear what the purpose of the visit was. Perhaps she was just checking in on Maria and her mother, but the look in her eyes revealed it might be something else.

"Hey, Mamma, could you turn that down please?" Maria asked in Sicilian. Rosa sat in the living room with a half-stitched quilt across her lap. She had stopped working on it when her husband was murdered, and hadn't yet deigned to finish it. A radio show was blaring, but Rosa only stared at the floor. At length, she reached across and adjusted the volume.

"I hope it's okay. Maybe I didn't let it steep long enough," Maria said, sipping from her own cup.

"It's perfect, doll. I love your cloche." She pointed to Maria's cap. Rachel was the sharpest dresser she knew, so Maria took this as quite a compliment.

"You look concerned, Rach." Maria decided to cut to the nub of it.

"It's your brother," Rachel said, all too happy to explain why she had come. "I'm worried about him."

"I know…Sonny Boy has really been having a time with it, hasn't he? He and Papà were so close."

Rachel hid her face behind her cup of tea for a moment.

"It's something more. He's just been…obsessed. It's all he can talk about. He's all but ignored his studies. He's been going to the library to read public records everyday… hoping he'll find something in them." Rachel looked down, and her eyes glistened with tears. "I know it's only natural… I know he's struggling, but…"

"It's okay, girl." Maria reached forward and took Rachel's gloved hands between her own.

"I'm trying to be there for him, trying to be supportive. But it's like he doesn't even hear me, like I'm not even there." Even weeping, Rachel was beautiful. Her lipstick was drawn on in the beesting fashion, and the powder on her cheeks was perfection. She was an it girl if there ever was one, and Sonny was a fool if he let his father's death ruin it.

"You don't need to explain, Rachel. I know how he is…and I know how hard this has been on him. But if he won't let you be there for him, who will he?"

"Well, Antonello has been coming around more. I

thought, at first, it was because they both grew up with Alonzo and were simply mourning together. But, I don't know. Now it's just like they…talk quietly together and don't want me there." Rachel stared at the table and dabbed at her eye with a handkerchief.

"What do you mean?" Maria asked, slightly concerned.

"I don't know. But I don't like it," Rachel replied, and declined to continue.

"Well, I'll talk to him for you—"

"No, don't! Excuse me, I'm sorry. But you don't need to say anything. I just wanted to ask how I might be better for him right now. Or what I can do. Or how to make him happy… I think I love him, Maria." Her lips began to quiver, and another tear streamed from under her eyelid as her fingers trembled around a handkerchief.

"Here, sweetie." Maria scooted her chair to the other side of the table, closer to Rachel, and put an arm around her shoulders.

"What a fright I must look! How silly." Rachel laughed even as the tears continued to fall. "Here you are, just having lost your father, and you're comforting me."

"Look at me, Rachel." Maria gently pulled at Rachel's chin until those big, wet eyes met hers. "Sonny is good. He has a lot of our father in him. He won't throw away everything good in his life because of this. Just give him some time. And maybe knock some sense into him if you have to." The two laughed and wept together. They finished their tea.

When Rachel left in a taxicab back for Columbia University, Maria was left to wonder if anything she had said was true.

VICO

They wore all black, and hid their faces with red bandannas.

"I look like a cowboy in the pictures," Enzo had said, but Vico didn't laugh.

Enzo was good on his promise, and he'd gotten a job for Vico.

The twins followed a man introduced as Joe Cargo through the back alleys of Midtown.

"This is it," Cargo said, nodding to a green door with chipped paint and Yiddish words painted across it. "Jimmy the lock, Enzo," Cargo said, and pointed to where he wanted the lookout to stand.

With expert precision, Enzo opened the door with the skeleton key they had received from a shylock in Harlem.

"Alright, we gotta hurry up," Cargo said, straining his eyes to make out the clothing store in the darkness. "Enzo, hit the cash register."

"I'm gonna check the back. These Jews like to keep their scratch locked up." Vico moved with cautious haste to the back, ducking clotheslines like he'd dodged barbwire and bullets in France.

The door to the back room was locked. Deferring to wait for a key, Vico kicked the door with all the strength he could muster, the wood splintering.

Splinters ripped through his shin, but he couldn't feel anything but adrenaline. Vico wedged his foot loose and reached through the hole to unlock it.

"Stop dress shopping, Cargo! We gotta hurry. The stoplights are running all night now, so if the bulls are tailing us, we won't get away," Enzo said, shoving stacks of small bills into a burlap sack.

"I gotta find a size twelve. It's what my girl, May, wears."

Vico ignored them and entered the office, pushing over shelves and shuffling through papers. Fumbling in the dark, he felt a metal lockbox beneath the owner's desk. He slid a knife from its hostler around his ankle and bent the flimsy lock until he could pry open the box.

No one- or two-dollar notes were present, only the big bills. He scooped up the whole box and returned to the main store.

"Come on, I got it." Vico paced to the door, declining to take anything for himself, unconcerned with the small hay Enzo was collecting.

Cargo took a look over Vico's shoulder as he passed by.

"Look at that, Doyle," he said with a toothy grin, "that greedy kike won't know what hit him."

They followed Vico out the door, and tapped the lookout boy on the shoulder.

"Move, move," Cargo said like a sergeant on the front line. They stuck to the buildings, avoiding the streetlights as best they could. Cargo's car was parked around the corner; the driver should be ready to peel out when he saw them.

A siren sounded in the distance. They continued running, but tried to measure how close the police were.

"Futz. I told you, Cargo." Enzo picked up his pace.

"Now what?" Vico stopped running.

"What are you doing, Doyle? Come on," Cargo shouted, keeping up his speed.

"Take this." Vico held out the lockbox.

"What?" Enzo finally stopped, bouncing on his feet.

"Take this. Tell the driver to take Eighth Street—I'll throw them off the scent."

Cargo finally stopped, allowing the lookout to shoot past him. "That war must have messed you up, Doyle. You don't want to end up in Sing Sing. Let's go."

Vico approached and shoved the lockbox into Cargo's arms.

"Go on," he said, "now. I'll find my way back to Harlem."

Enzo looked at him, pleading, but finally turned and followed Cargo. The getaway car rumbled to a start, shooting beams of light across the street.

Vico stood, surprised to find himself completely composed.

The sirens were approaching.

He caught sight of a fire hydrant and approached it.

He took a knee and ran his fingers over the jagged edges of the hydrant.

This was going to hurt, but not as much as nine rounds with Rocco Milone on Friday-night fights.

He slammed his forehead into the fire hydrant, his brain bouncing off his skull. He saw stars. Vico waited to compose himself before doing it again, this time dragging his face across a sharp edge. He grunted as he felt the skin split, warm blood pouring over his eyebrows.

He stumbled back and groaned.

The blue-and-red lights of the police car rounded the corner. Two bulls bounced out, hands on the pistols in their holsters.

"The bastards clocked me, man!" Vico shouted, the blood on his lips spewing.

"You the guy that called it in?"

"Yeah," Vico said. "I tried to stall 'em, but one whipped me with his gun, and I blacked out."

"Which way did they go?"

Vico pointed in the opposite direction of the getaway car's path. "East. They're in a black Ford."

The bulls nodded to each other and hopped back into the patrol car.

"Thanks." The Irish cop tipped his cap.

"Just doing my part." Vico smiled, bloody teeth shining in the headlights as the cops sped off.

East Harlem, Manhattan—December 7, 1928

"You ready?" Cargo asked the twins as they stood under the neon lights of the Rainbow Gardens.

"I hope so. These guys are big shots." Cargo blew hot air into his hands and bounced on his toes. He was a short man, built like a bull, with a crew cut and a clean-shaven face. He was perceptibly nervous as he opened the door, but he appeared to be nervous doing anything other than breaking and entering.

"The Gap is a good guy," Enzo said quietly to Vico as they entered into the warmth and smoky haze of the bar. "He went up the river to Sing Sing just a while before me. That's where me, Cargo, and him met up. He'll do right by you."

"Can't wait," Vico said. The self-inflicted wounds to his forehead still throbbed, and he was anxious to numb them with a drink.

"Look who it is," came a shout from across the room. The man stood, tossing aside the waitress who had been sitting on his lap. "Good to see ya." He gave Enzo a hug and Cargo the same. His clothing was made of fine fabrics, but his suit top was absent and his vest was unbuttoned, his shirtsleeves rolled to the elbow.

"Who's this?" he asked, grinning to reveal a missing incisor. Now Vico understood why they called him "the Gap."

"This is Bobby Doyle." Cargo made the introduction, and Vico accepted the Gap's hand.

"Good to meet you."

"Any pal of Cargo and 'the Thief' is a friend of mine. I'm Dominick Petrelli"—he looked at Enzo and Cargo—"but I bet these two have already told you my nickname. World's worst-kept secret." He smiled like a dental patient.

"I could hardly notice." Vico shrugged.

"Yeah? Well, you're as crazy as Cargo told me you are." He slapped Vico's shoulder and sized him up. His eyes fixed on Vico's poorly stitched forehead. "True you did that to yourself?"

"It made more sense at the time. Had to throw the bulls off the scent."

The Gap looked impressed.

"You boys done good. You got out with the loot. That's all that matters." He looked over his shoulder and received a nod from a man at the table he had previously been sitting at. "Somebody wants to meet you."

"The big man?" Cargo said, visibly nervous again.

"Yeah. He wants to meet him." He pointed to Vico. "Word about Bobby Doyle has been spreading. The boss wants to meet you." Enzo and Cargo looked deflated. "You boys get some drinks, chase some skirt. He just wants to ask some questions."

"Go on." Enzo patted Vico's arm, a tinge of jealousy in his voice. As far as Vico knew, Enzo had never met the leaders of the organization, despite working for them for nearly ten years.

Vico followed the Gap across the room. "You, the Thief, and Cargo fall under me. So be on your best behavior, capisce?"

Vico nodded the affirmative, and approached the table.

He already knew the men sitting there. He had done his research. He had found pictures of their old mug shots and newspaper clippings at the library. Regardless, he could have identified them by their easy presence of command.

"Mr. Gagliano, Mr. Reina, this is Bobby Doyle."

They looked him up and down, and then glanced at one another.

"Scram, kid," Gagliano said to the waitress kissing at his neck. Once the girls had left the table, Vico was invited to sit.

"My name is Gaetano Reina." Vico accepted a handshake before sitting down across from him. "Dominick tells me you've made a name for yourself. What you did in Midtown was impressive." He spoke in a low, calculated tone.

"Not many of our boys would have gone to such lengths," Gagliano said, his voice even deeper than

Reina's. He appeared like a candidate for political office, or a commodities broker. A giant of a man, even seated at the table, he was the perfect second-in-command. Vico had learned that both men were businessmen to their core, cold and impartial, but good people to have on your side, and good people to serve.

"I did what I felt I had to," Vico said, and shrugged.

"Just like you did in the war?" Reina leaned across the table, extending a gold cigarette case, one separated from the rest, just for Vico.

"I did a lot worse than that over there." He didn't smile, nor did the others.

"That is precisely why we wanted to talk," Reina said, just a trace of an Italian accent in his refined English. "Did you kill in France?"

"I killed a lot in France."

"For your country?"

"For my pals." Vico accepted the drink offered to him by a waitress, who winked at him and touched his shoulder as she left.

"Would you raise a gun again? Would you pull the trigger to protect your new friends?" Gagliano gestured to the table.

"Would you do the same for me?"

After a moment, Reina nodded.

"Then, yes, I would."

"You're a good shot?"

"The best in the Fighting 69th," Vico said, although Buster had always been a better sharpshooter.

"We may need your services. Most of these guys talk like tough guys, but they fall apart when it comes down to it." Gagliano pointed to some of the other men seated around the room.

"We have a problem." Reina leaned across the table.

"There are other organizations like ours in New York. We have existed peacefully for a long time. My interests in Manhattan are limited—to Harlem, in fact. My business is done in the Bronx. Most of the other families stay in Manhattan and Brooklyn. But, one of the other families is causing trouble."

"Masseria," Vico said confidently. He had done his research. And most importantly, he kept his ears pinned back. The "boss of bosses," Joe Masseria had made a name for himself.

"Yes, Masseria," Gagliano said with distaste as he threw back a glass of whiskey.

"You've heard of him?" Reina asked, measuring him.

"Yeah. I've heard of him."

"We've never had any quarrel with Masseria's people. I leave the bootlegging and the gambling and the loan-sharking in Manhattan to his people. All I want is my ice," Reina said, taking a sip of his drink.

"Your ice?" Vico asked.

"There isn't a block of ice sold in New York City that I don't get a cut of. I own it all. And everyone needs ice. This allows me to avoid the troubles of bootlegging. Keep my nose clean."

"I see." Vico already knew this but nodded like he didn't.

"Masseria wants a cut now. He wants to muscle in on us. He feels he is entitled to a piece of everything." Gagliano lit a cigar.

"You want me to take care of Masseria?"

Reina gave a faint smile.

"If only it were that simple. That would cause a war. A war we wouldn't win," Reina said.

"He's also pretty good at dodging bullets," Gagliano said.

"I don't miss." Vico took a sip of his drink.

"We don't need Masseria. He can continue to roll in his hay and shove Italian cuisine down his gullet. I want the guy he is pushing on us. His name is Giosue LaDuca."

"Tell me where he is." Vico knew better than to ask questions. Reina and Gagliano shared a look of approval.

"You can find that fat bastard in the Bronx," Reina said. Gagliano wrote down the address and slid it across the table to Vico.

"That's his office. Most of the time he'll be there trying to steal from us. He is spineless, so he might run."

"I won't give him the chance."

"Take Cargo and Enzo with you. They can help, but you'll be the point man," Reina said.

"I'll get it done."

"You do this, you'll have an extra merry Christmas," Gagliano said.

"There is actually something specific I would ask in return," Vico said. He hoped he wasn't revealing his hand too early, but he couldn't help himself.

"What's that?" Gagliano asked.

"A friend of mine was killed in Little Italy. His name was Alonzo Consentino. I want the guy who killed him." The Gap, who had been silent up until then, stood and walked away. Gagliano deferred to Reina, who took a moment before replying.

"He was a 'friend' of yours? He was a great deal older than you," Reina said.

"He was the best barber in Manhattan." Vico pointed to his hair. "Can't get that good of a cut for double the price."

"What did you say your name was again?" Gagliano asked, eyes narrow. "Your real name?"

"Girolamo. Girolamo Santuccio." The name belonged

to a friend of Vico's in the army who had died at the beginning of the Argonne Forest offensive, but the name appeared to him, and Vico went with it.

"You can find a new barber," Reina said.

"If I kill LaDuca, can you tell me who killed Alonzo?" Vico made it clear he wasn't budging.

"If you kill LaDuca, you will have earned our trust. And our gratitude. We can work something out."

"It was a pleasure to meet you."

"Doyle," Reina said, pulling a cigarette away from his lips. "Don't bother coming back here if the fat bastard isn't dead." Vico nodded. Killing LaDuca was the least of his concerns.

SONNY

"Ouch!" Sonny shouted as one of the crates landed on his index finger. Some of the other workers laughed.

"It's just picking up and putting down crates, kid. It doesn't take a college degree," one of them said.

When Oscar had said he didn't need any help at the barbershop, Sonny had headed to the Staten Island Ferry to work, where he carried crates on and off freighters for two dollars a day. It wasn't much, but it would keep food on his mother's table.

A bell tolled in the distance, and a few birds squawked overhead. Sonny picked up another crate.

"Vincente?" came a voice from behind him. Sonny tried to locate the source but couldn't see over the box.

"Yeah, that's me."

"It's Detective Gallagher."

Sonny set the crate down where he stood and turned to the detective with fresh vigor.

"How are you, sir? What do you have for me?"

Both Gallagher and the deputy beside him wore long faces.

"You're a hard man to find, lad. Your mother and sister have no idea where you are," Gallagher said, munching on the cigar hanging from the corner of his mouth.

"It doesn't matter as long as I bring home a few dollars, right?" The officers looked around at the dock behind him, probably considering how little he was being paid here.

"We found the guy you mentioned. The club hand. It wasn't him."

"How do you know?"

"He just got out of jail a few years ago. He's been clean ever since, as far as we can tell."

Sonny shook his head and wondered if they were joking.

"You mean, he just hasn't been caught. You can't be serious?"

"Serious as polio. We keep an eye on the guy. There's no chance this guy could have arranged the murder of a respected barber in the middle of the city without us knowing about it," the deputy replied.

"Well *someone* did."

"From everything we've looked into, the man was an associate of your father's in Sicily. They connected a few times when they both arrived here in the States, and then went their own ways," the detective said, tapping the tip of his cigar on the bottom of his boot.

Sonny took a moment to digest the information. He was nervous to hear the answer to his next question.

"So what's our next lead?"

"We don't have one," Gallagher said firmly but not without a hint of shame.

"There has to be someone. Have you talked to

witnesses? Someone who might have seen the guy going in?"

"You know your onions, kid, so I'm going to be upfront with you. The department is stretched thin as it is, what with all these gangland killings. We're under a strict mandate: if something looks like it has something to do with the illegal booze trade, it *does have* something to do with the illegal booze trade. And we can only devote so many resources to the investigation. Sorry, kid."

"What makes you think this had anything to do with alcohol? My father's olive skin and greasy hair?" Sonny's voice rose, and he clenched his fists.

"We had an officer at the funeral, boyo. Half the biggest bootleggers in Manhattan were in attendance," the deputy said, stepping forward, his thumbs in his belt loops.

Sonny started to stammer out a response, shocked by the revelation, but Gallagher put a hand on his shoulder to stop him.

"There's nothing else we can do, kid. Now, if you find something more substantial, you know where to find me. I'll look into it on my own time." Gallagher patted Sonny's shoulder a few times and then turned to leave with the deputy.

They were almost back to the patrol car when Sonny shouted after them: "My brothers and I will keep looking. And when we do, we'll take care of it ourselves."

Gallagher did an about-face and approached Sonny, the empathy drained from his face entirely.

"Alright. You do that, kid. Then you'll die, and we won't be able to find your killers either." He threw his cigar to the pavement and stomped it out. "I just feel bad for Sicilian women. They're the ones always left to spoon up your guts."

Sonny's eyelids twitched, and he thought about

throwing a punch. Luckily, the two policemen turned and entered the car before he'd made up his mind.

He picked up his crate again, far more aggressively than before.

Columbia University, Manhattan—December 16, 1928

Sonny took his time ascending the steps of the Columbia dormitory to his room. He dreaded seeing anyone.

He didn't want to hear their condolences. He didn't want to hear that he would be in their prayers, and he certainly didn't want to answer their questions. They had been interested in his Italian culture, and its tendency to act outside the realm of the law. How much more would they be interested in now that his father had been killed in cold blood? Was his father just another fatality in a long string of gangland killings that dated back to the inauguration of Prohibition? Perhaps the detective was right.

His Columbia University friendships now seemed shallow, fake.

He ducked into his room and, to his relief, found that his roommate, Ralphie, wasn't present. He was probably at another dance, finding some easy girl to neck with. Sonny didn't want any more of it.

He grabbed a shoebox beneath his bed and began sweeping a few things into it. The Bible from his nightstand, a deck of playing cards from his dresser, a pair of black oxford shoes from his closet.

There in the closet hung his new suit and his porkpie hat. The outfit had cost him half of what he earned in an entire semester, and he had been proud of it. He felt nothing but disgust now.

He pulled the suit from the hanger and the porkpie hat from the shelf, then threw both of them at the wall.

They were reminders that he hadn't been there. He should have been there.

They were reminders that things would never go back to how they were.

He should have been at A.C. Barbers. He should have been with his dad. Nothing would have happened then.

He shut the box and hurried out of the room.

"Whoa, where are you headed, sailor?" Rachel said, meeting him as he exited the building. "I was just coming to see if you were home."

"What?"

"I wanted to see you tonight." Her eyes traced down to the box in his hands. "What's that?"

"I'm leaving, Rach."

"What?" Her face twisted in confusion and fear.

"Yeah. I need to be with my family." He stepped toward her, hoping she would embrace him.

"There is nothing you can do now, Sonny."

"I don't know. But my mind is made up," he said.

"You're going to graduate in May, Sonny. Don't do this." She placed both hands on his shoulders, and attempted to shake him until he met her eyes.

"I've already missed a few of my finals. I'm going to have to repeat the semester."

"Next year, then. Alonzo would want you to finish your schooling."

He tensed at the mention of his father.

"I have to earn for my family."

"And how well will you be able to do that without finishing your degree, Sonny? What about finance?"

Sonny looked away.

"I'll come back and finish."

She removed her hands from his shoulders and stepped back.

"Let's just call the kettle black, Sonny. You aren't leaving for money! I know what you're doing. You're going to do something stupid."

He looked off at the bell tower in the distance.

"I just need to be with my family."

"He isn't coming back, Sonny. I wish he was. I wish I could do something about it, but I can't. You can't either. Sonny, please don't do this. Let me help you." She reached forward and put her arms around him. She buried her head in his chest.

The smell of her hair almost made him reconsider, but his mind was already made up. For the past three years, he had comforted her over every trivial little thing that accompanied life on campus. The sound of her weeping made it hard for him to breathe. But there was nothing he could do about it, not anymore.

He stepped away from her.

"It's just something I have to do, Rach."

She shook her head.

"No. You don't. You just want to." She reached inside her dress and pulled the necklace with his class ring off and handed it to him.

"Why are you giving this to me?" he asked. It was pretty obviously, he thought, but he didn't want it back.

"Maybe another dame will come along and save you, Sonny. But I don't deserve to be your girlfriend if I can't keep you from destroying your life." Bitter tears ripped from the side of her eyes and flowed with her mascara down her cheeks.

She turned and walked away.

Sonny thought about chasing her down, saying that he loved her and that one day he would make things right and they could be together again. But it was no use. He kept his feet planted until she ascended the steps into the female dormitory.

He let the class ring slip from his fingers, and then stepped past it.

Little Italy, Manhattan—December 23, 1928

Sonny held his father's rosary beneath the table, rubbing the beads with the tips of his thumbs.

"You have to eat your food, Ma," he said, tamping down his frustration. She looked at him with displeasure and pushed the plate away. The police had given the rosary and a few other items to Sonny after they were finished analyzing Alonzo's body. He had asked where his father's ivory-handled razor was, but apparently it had never turned up. He searched the barbershop himself, to no avail. The rosary would make a nice consolation prize. It hadn't left him since.

"It's good, Ma. I worked hard on it," Maria said. It wasn't good, Sonny thought, but he couldn't blame his sister much. Rosa had been the cook of the house until Alonzo's death. Afterward, she showed disinterest in eating altogether.

A knock sounded on the door.

"I'll get it," Sonny said, standing from his chair.

"No, allow me," Maria said, just as anxious to get away from their sulking mother.

Sonny made it to the door first, finding a man he didn't recognize on the other side.

"Hello," the man said, a grin appearing and then disappearing just as fast.

"Can we help you?" Sonny asked. The man extended a bouquet of flowers and a brown bag.

"Mr. Domingo?" Maria said, craning to see over Sonny's shoulder.

"Yeah. Well, just call me Buster. Here, I brought you some flowers." He handed them to Maria, and gave the brown bag to Sonny. "That's rigatoni. My family's favorite dish. That's for Mrs. Consentino."

"Thanks," Sonny said, and began to shut the door.

"Thank you, Buster. She'll love it," Maria said. Sonny knew Rosa wouldn't eat it, and assumed Maria did too.

Buster tipped his hat and turned to leave. Maria pushed by her big brother and followed Buster. Sonny started to close the door, but then left the door open a crack to watch them.

"Why did you come?" Her voice was more gentle than questioning.

Buster lit a cigarette and leaned up against the wall.

"I don't know. I haven't been able to sleep," he said, trying to explain himself by talking with his hands, but he still couldn't find a way to express what he meant. "Thinking about you all without your father on Christmas. Your brother meant a lot to me in France, and I just…" He couldn't make eye contact. "I better go."

"Wait," Maria said, following him down the steps, "what are you doing for the holidays?"

He shrugged. "I don't know. My family is all in Chicago. I guess nothing."

"You should join us."

"No, I couldn't. I don't want to impose." He leaned down the stairs like he was trying to get away.

"Please do. Maybe you can convince Vico to come. We'd love to see both the twins. And you as well."

Buster hesitated, and seemed to search for more excuses. "Okay. I'll be here. I'll make sure Vico is here too. We may be out of uniform, but he'll still follow an order." He gave Maria a boyish grin and then descended down the steps.

Maria walked back into their tenement, her cheeks rosy.

"You should of asked Ma first, Maria." Sonny was suspicious, like any big brother might have been.

"Maybe he can cheer her up. He cheers me up," she said, scurrying into the kitchen.

"Yeah, I bet."

MARIA

The tree was adorned with garlands and several ornaments, but it still felt bare. Perhaps it was the lack of presents beneath it.

Empty stockings hung from nails in the wall. They didn't have a fireplace, but Sonny had bought some extra wood for a nickel on Christmas Eve, and he loaded it into the kitchen furnace to simulate one, like they usually did. "O Come, All Ye Faithful" played from a little radio Alonzo had saved up for the year prior.

Regardless of recent events, Maria was excited for Christmas dinner. It was nice to have everyone in one place for the evening, and she had longed to see Buster again since he'd visited a few days before.

"Hey, Ma," Enzo said as he, Vico, Buster arrived. He leaned down and kissed Rosa on the head, followed by Vico, and Buster gave her a kiss on the hand. Maria found herself anxious, hoping that they could have a pleasant evening. It was the first time the entire family had been together in years without a death as the cause for the reunion.

"Hey, Sonny Boy." Vico gave his brother a hug. His American Sicilian accent, once fairly thick, had dissipated during his time in France. Enzo's had noticeably deepened as a result of the company he had kept in Sing Sing penitentiary.

"Hey, Maria," Buster said with a nervous grin, "food smells delicious."

"Well, let's hope it tastes just as good. We've been laboring since we first woke up," Maria said, throwing a dish towel over her shoulder and giving Buster a lingering hug.

The door opened and closed again. The sound was followed by loud footsteps. Everyone knew who it was.

"You didn't think you could have a Christmas dinner without me, did you?" Antonello Balducci entered the room with a low bow, as if he were the honored guest. A smile split across Sonny's face as they embraced. Even after Sonny had left for college, Antonello had continued to come around, and even visited his boyhood friend at Columbia for some of their most interesting parties.

Tall, thin, and handsome, he had matured from the underfed awkward youth to a brash and loud young man.

"Merry Christmas, Ma!" He bent and gave Rosa a big hug. He had taken to calling her that some years ago after living with the Consentinos, partially in jest.

"Antonello, you should be with your own mother on Christmas," Rosa said with a furrowed brow. Maria was thankful just to hear her voice.

"I've been with her all day. She likes to hit the hay early these days. Plus, I had to come get some of your famous cooking."

"I was the cook today, actually," Maria said with pride.

"Of course. And I bet it'll be a masterpiece." Antonello gave her a forceful hug, embarrassing her.

"Well, let's dig in. I'm starvin'," Enzo said, patting his growing midsection.

They settled in around the table, and after a brief pause, Sonny assumed the seat once reserved for their father.

Rosa materialized a flask and poured a bit into the coffee Maria had just prepared for her. Her kids exchanged a glance but didn't dare say a word. She had never much obeyed the laws of Prohibition, calling it an Anglo-Saxon attack on their "foreigners' ways." But since Alonzo's death, she had remained saturated in alcohol most evenings.

"Mind if I get a pull, Ma?" Enzo said playfully, trying to lighten the mood. Maria frowned at him, and he shrugged. "*Madonna mia*, that's the real McCoy, Ma," Enzo said, wincing after his first taste. "You must know somebody good."

"Can we just say the blessing?" Maria asked, hoping to get to more pleasant conversation. She was interested to hear Buster speak more. They bowed their heads, and Sonny led the Lord's Prayer, the others murmuring along quietly with him.

They ate their fill, and some more. Enzo and Antonello entertained them with stories, and kept the table laughing, leading the charge themselves.

"Come on, soldier boys, tell us a war story," Enzo said when he had run through all of his fresh material. Vico looked to Buster, who spun his fork through the remaining *pesce spada* on the plate.

"Not much to tell, really. Long time ago now."

"Vico told me you gave the Kaiser a right ass kicking in those woods." Antonello winked.

"Nothing we couldn't handle." Buster set his fork down, making it clear he didn't want to discuss the war any further.

"You boys want some dessert?" Maria asked, already standing.

"Her custard is the cat's pajamas," Sonny said, kissing the tips of his fingers. Modern phrases like these always seemed awkward coming from him, and he seemed to know it.

"I couldn't. The war might have been a long time ago, but us soldiers are still easily sated." Buster stood and folded his napkin. "Anything I can do to help clean up?"

"No, no, we'll take care of that," Maria said, really wanting to ask him to stay longer. "Coffee?"

"No, I better get going. The papers say the roads might get fairly icy. Better get home before long." He thanked Rosa with a kiss on the cheek, and shook the hands of the men, one by one. "Maria, thank you for a delightful meal."

After he had left, Maria noticed a pair of gloves beside a table in the entryway. "Oh, I think he forgot his gloves."

"The brown ones are mine," Antonello said, and craned his head to see if they were his.

"I'll just run and ask him." She hurried out the door, hoping she could still catch him. "Buster," she said after descending the three flights of the stairs to the front of the tenement. Chasing him outside was becoming a reoccurring pattern.

"Yeah?" he replied, not surprised by her presence.

"These your gloves?"

"Oh no. Don't own any, actually."

"Oh," she said, feeling a bit foolish. Before he could leave, she said, "There's a talkie I've been wanting to see."

"Really?" He seemed interested. "What is it?"

"Yeah, a Charlie Chaplin. My girlfriends say it's the best they've seen."

"Sounds nifty."

"I want you to take me." She pretended she wasn't nervous.

"Oh...okay. Next week, then?" He couldn't hide his flushed cheeks.

"Thursday works." She pulled nervously on the hemline of her dress and began ascending the stairs, only smiling once he was out of view.

BUSTER

Maria fingered the leather of Buster's car seats as she watched the city lights pass them by.

"Did you enjoy the nickelodeon?" he asked, realizing he had been watching her more carefully than the road.

"You know I always wanted one of these?" she said, distracted.

"Wanted what?"

"A Ford Model A. It was my dream. I used to draw pictures of them in class. I even wanted the same color—Niagara Blue."

"I guess it was good luck you and I met, then."

Maria smiled. "Don't take me home yet," she said, becoming more forthright every moment they spent together.

"Where else did you want to go?"

"I want to see your apartment."

Buster found himself blushing.

"Why? Not much to see, really. I'm not much of a decorator."

"I want to see where you live, what it's like."

"Your mother will worry."

"I bet you keep it as clean as your car."

"Fine," he assented, "but I'll have to sneak you in. Your brothers share a place down the street. No telling what they would think if they saw you coming over at this hour." She leaned forward in her seat in anticipation.

She had never been so charming. She wore a cloche hat, pulled over her forehead and covering her eyes mysteriously, a brooch hanging atop it. Her fitted dress was pulled up around her knees, revealing taupe stockings and unfastened galoshes.

Buster's heart rate picked up every time he looked at her. The longer she kept her eyes from him, the more his were drawn to her. He had to summon all his willpower to keep his eyes on the busy city streets ahead of them.

It took them some time to make it to the Williamsburg neighborhood of Brooklyn, but Maria didn't seem to mind. As time passed, she leaned back in her seat and put her feet on the dashboard. At first, he was nervous that it might leave a scuff mark, but the sight was so damned enticing, he couldn't bring himself to say anything.

"Here we are. I'm on the first floor." He hurried out of the car to open her door.

"It's not as crowded as Little Italy," she said as she looked around the neighborhood.

"Come on, before someone sees you." He threw his overcoat around her shoulders and walked her to the door. As they walked, she reached out and took his hand. After a moment, she interlaced her fingers with his.

"So this is it," Buster said, locking the door behind them. She looked around as if she were visiting a fine museum. She analyzed everything from the texture of the furniture to the light fixtures on the ceiling. "Don't keep me waiting, say something!"

"You're cleaner than any man I've ever met." She continued her inspection. "Very…Spartan." He was a bit embarrassed. It was true. He didn't have a single accent piece in the entire place. Utility was the byword for his little domain. "You're a perfectionist, aren't you?" she asked.

"I don't know if I'd say that."

She peered into his bedroom down the hall. "Not a woman in the house, and your bed is made up like that? I'm impressed, I'll admit."

"You seen what you came for? Did I pass the test?"

She didn't reply but continued to administer the exam. She spotted a piano in the corner of the room, and her face lit up with excitement. Buster sighed as she ran across the room and sat down.

"Can you play? You can't play?" She looked at him in disbelief.

"As a matter of fact, I can. I'm a teacher."

"A teacher?"

"That's what I do. I give music lessons to kids. Done it ever since I got back from France." She broke into laughter, and Buster flushed with embarrassment.

"No, no, I like it! I'm just surprised, is all." She had noticed that she had embarrassed him, so she reached out for his hand. "With rough hands like these, I just figured it would be something different."

He pulled his hand away and rolled up his sleeves.

"Got those in the war. Music…calms me."

"Play something for me." She patted the bench beside her.

"Come on, really?"

When she wasn't to be dissuaded, he sat down and spread his hands. He played a few notes, but he felt his hands trembling like they had when he had a Kraut in his sights in the Argonne.

"Buster." He stopped and looked at her. "Why have you not kissed me yet?" Her face was so serious, so intent, that he had to smile.

He began stammering and tried to explain himself.

"Stop that, and just kiss me," she said. She draped her hands around his neck and pulled him close. He stood and leaned over her, against the piano, accidentally hitting a few keys as he did so.

He had been waiting a long time to do this. He didn't know if it was right. It probably wasn't. But he couldn't help it.

She slid his suspenders over his shoulders, and he unbuttoned the back of her dress.

He led her to the bedroom, and she lay down on top of his made-up bed, which had hospital corners like he had learned to make in the army.

They struggled to get his shirt off as he kissed her neck. He had completely lost control of his senses. She had him mesmerized.

Suddenly, she stopped, his dog tags dangling on her bare chest.

"Sorry…" He paused and then began to pull them off. "I can't ever seem to get away from them."

"No." She ran her fingers over the words and numbers imprinted onto them, inspecting them as she had his home. "I like them. Leave them on." He did so, and leaned in for another kiss.

ENZO

Enzo, Vico, and Cargo had trailed LuDuca for over a month.

He wasn't a very hard man to find, prone to pageantry and excess, but he had a cortege of bodyguards around him most of the time.

After a few days, they were able to determine his exact schedule. He was a creature of habit, and creatures of habit can become easy prey.

On Tuesday nights, he threw a high-stakes poker game at a speakeasy on Murray Street. Every Thursday afternoon, he enjoyed a lunch on Coney Island that could have fed a small family. He faithfully returned to the Chelsea neighborhood of Manhattan to have dinner with his wife and two boys. On Sunday mornings, he was sure to be present at Mass at St. Peter's Church in the Financial District with the rest of New York's players.

On Monday evenings, though, he stayed at his office in

the Bronx. After all his workers left, he would stick around for a few hours. At first, Enzo, Vico, and Cargo had assumed that he was catching up on the work he neglected the rest of the week. It didn't take long to figure out that this was his favorite time to screw.

Most connected guys had *goomahs* on the side. He wouldn't have been judged by his peers for infidelity, but his penchant for underage women would have been shunned.

"Even a guy like Masseria wouldn't want to associate with a scumbag like that," Cargo said, assuming the boss of bosses didn't know.

For Enzo and Vico, the fat bastard's deviancy made the thought of killing him even more desirable.

Every Monday when a girl walked out to the prearranged taxicab, sore and deflated of life, Enzo thought of new ways to make LaDuca suffer.

After three weeks of watching his weekly infidelities, they knew exactly when they could strike.

One guard, who LaDuca called "Charlie," protected the entrance until nine p.m., when the guard was changed and a new man would appear. Charlie was out of shape like his employer, and obviously less aware of his surroundings than the unknown second guard, so they determined eight o'clock was their prime time. After everyone left but before anyone else could arrive.

Cargo pulled the car to a stop a block away from the fat bastard's command station.

"I'll take care of Charlie," Vico said as they ensured their pistols were loaded. Enzo was relieved to hear him say that. The close-quarters stuff made him squeamish, even if he wouldn't admit it.

They crept in the darkness as they had during their heists.

Charlie was propped up beside the entrance eating a hoagie wrapped up in a paper bag.

"He makes any noise, you gotta come help me shut him up," Vico whispered, and then stepped off without waiting for confirmation.

Enzo strained his eyes in the darkness, feeling for the first time like he was in a war zone like Vico had been. His twin brother was clearly in his element, moving swiftly but on feet as silent as cat's paws.

Vico propped himself behind the building, around the corner from LaDuca's guard. Enzo saw him fiddling with something in the dirt. Finally, he realized Vico had picked up a glass bottle, and he launched it past the guard.

"Hey," Charlie said, jerking to attention. He stepped away from the wall and craned his head to make out something in the darkness.

Vico rushed forward and wrapped a cord around the guard's neck. They struggled to the dirt, and Charlie pushed his feet into the ground, leveraging his weight on Vico.

Cargo and Enzo shot off as quickly as they could, terrified that some noise might escape the victim.

When they arrived, they helped restrain the guard, but Vico seemed to have it under control. Charlie's face was swollen and purple, his eyes darting around rapidly like a trapped animal's.

Vico was calm, breathing only a little harder than usual.

"It's too late. You're gonna die," Vico whispered into his ear. "Shh, shh."

Charlie's legs squirmed against the dirt as his hands swatted at Vico behind him and tried to pull the cord away, but his strength was waning. A thin stream of blood escaped from under the cord where it had begun to dig into his throat.

Vico rolled the bodyguard over onto his stomach and mounted his back, straining until Charlie's body fell still.

"Let's go get this fat bastard," Vico said, and brushed the dirt off his suit.

They entered the building silently, Vico leading the way. Their pistols were drawn, fingers already on the triggers.

LaDuca was straight ahead. He was facing away from them, his hairy back glistening with sweat as he humped like a donkey in heat. It was a wonder a fat man like that could even get it in, Enzo thought.

They took a few steps forward, but Cargo got spooked. His pistol barked. A scream erupted from the girl bent over on LaDuca's desk as the bullet ripped through the fat bastard's excess flesh. He collapsed to the floor, and the girl shot off running, her screams echoing behind her.

Vico shot Cargo a look of irritation.

"Trying to be a hero or something?"

"He was gonna hear us, Bobby." Cargo shrugged, still shaking.

Vico rolled his eyes.

"What about the girl?" Enzo asked.

"What about her? She isn't gonna talk. She isn't gonna say shit about this to anyone. And neither will that bitch mother who brings her here for a few bucks." Vico picked up his pace to LaDuca, who was clawing at his desk, trying to get to his feet. "See, this...this is why you get caught." Vico stepped over LaDuca and sat him up.

The bullet had entered above his kidneys and somehow managed to exit through his rotund belly. Blood was bubbling from his lips, and his eyes wept in fear.

"You get caught 'cause you're sloppy." Vico tugged at

LaDuca's hair, forcing the fat bastard to look at the other two assailants. "Man is a hard animal to kill, see. When you go to pull the trigger, your finger twitches, your hand shakes, your eyes lie to you... You watching, Enzo?" he said, looking up at his brother. He waited for confirmation.

"Yeah, I'm watching, Bobby," Enzo said after gulping. The look in Vico's eye unnerved him.

"You gotta put the barrel right up to 'em like this. You gotta see the flesh billow up next to it. I mean, you gotta..." He looked up. "Cargo?"

"Yeah."

"You gotta be close enough to get cuts from the bits of skull you're about to send flyin'." Vico buried the pistol in the flesh of LaDuca's forehead, and moved it around in circles to make his point.

The shot ignited, and the fat bastard collapsed against Vico like a sack of potatoes.

Vico stood up. And started to step away.

"Let's go," Cargo said, his voice shaky.

Vico turned around and emptied the rest of the clip into the fat man's chest and stomach.

He tossed the weapon across the room and turned to leave, adjusting his suit as he did so.

"Was that necessary?" Enzo asked.

"Gotta make a point. No one is gonna mess with Reina again. I'd say the next fat pervert whose got squirrel fever for kids will look over his shoulder too."

Vico paced past them and led the way to the car.

Cargo got behind the wheel and started it up. Enzo looked at Vico in the front seat, and wanted to hurl. Blood was spattered across his face, and he didn't seem to mind. He seemed as calm as a parishioner on Sunday morning.

Vico turned and noticed the look on Enzo's face.

"It ain't like it is in the pictures, huh? This is what you wanted, Enzo," he said, to which he received no response.

When they arrived at the Rainbow Gardens, Vico wiped away the majority of the blood at Enzo's request.

"Happy now?" Vico asked as he stepped out of the car. They walked in without hesitation.

Gagliano was waiting by the entrance. They had sent word that today might just be the day.

"How's that fat bastard doing?" Gagliano asked, a smile already creasing his face as he noticed a few stray drops of blood on Vico's lapel.

"We bought him a cement overcoat," Cargo said, anxious for his share of the credit. Gagliano nodded, impressed.

"I'll tell the ice man."

"He'll tell me what I want to know?"

Gagliano squinted and looked away, drawing on his cigarette.

"He'll call you."

Vico nodded. Cargo sat down for a drink, pleased with their night's work, but Vico turned to leave.

"All I care about is that phone call," he said as he passed by Enzo, who stood still beside the door, unsure who to follow.

SONNY

Sonny tried to keep his feet still, but they tapped against his wishes. He tried to pray the rosary, as his father had taught him, but after eight job interviews in as many days, he was becoming more nervous with each one.

Each day, he put on his only suit and set out for Wall Street. Each time, he was turned away, most of the time before actually sitting down with anyone. Then, he would hurry home, take off his suit, and either head to A.C. Barbers to help Oscar, or to the Staten Island Ferry to load more crates, neither of which paid very much.

"Mr. Consentino?" the rosy-cheeked receptionist said.

"Yes, ma'am. That's me."

"Mr. Wallingford will see you now." She ushered him into the boss's office on the third floor of the Eagle Corporation Building.

"Hello." Sonny extended his hand, which was only

accepted after Mr. Wallingford peeled his eyes away from the documents before him.

"So you're here for a job?" Mr. Wallingford leaned back and gnawed on the butt of an unlit cigar.

"Yes, sir. I think I would be a good fit, and have plenty to bring to the table."

The man lowered his spectacles to the tip of his nose, and chuckled condescendingly.

"You do? And what makes you think that?"

Sonny dried his palms on the hem of his britches and tried to clear his throat.

"I didn't graduate, but I have three years of education at Columbia University studying business and econo—"

"Let me stop you right there." Mr. Wallingford waved him to silence. "Why in God's name do you think I would want to hire a greaseball like you?" He leaned forward in his giant office chair, feigned sympathy etched across his face.

Sonny tried to offer a retort but was again silenced.

"Look, my clients don't want to work with a dago. Plain and simple."

"I can bring my own clients," Sonny said, avoiding eye contact. He felt himself stiffen when the man began to laugh.

"You mean other Italians? They don't have any money. What little they do have, they probably took from good, hardworking Americans."

"I know Italians with money." He now made eye contact, and held it. He actually didn't know any Italians with money, but he was convinced he could find them.

"Go tell it to Sweeney, kid." Mr. Wallingford pointed to the door. Sonny began to stand and then sat back down.

"You're a businessman, Mr. Wallingford. Am I correct to assume that you're a fan of Dale Carnegie?"

The man exhaled in frustration. "Yes, I am. What's your point?"

"Mr. Carnegie says a good businessman should never turn down an opportunity. And this is quite an opportunity. You can get a sharp, smart young salesman with a college education before any of your competitors have a chance." He noticed that Mr. Wallingford was finally intrigued, so he continued. "And I'll do it for less."

"You're damned right you will. Half the commission of the rest of my employees. That's for the damage hiring a dago will do to my reputation." He shook his head, as if surprised at himself.

"So we have a deal?" Sonny said, more wishful than confident.

Mr. Wallingford continued to chew on his cigar.

"You'll start your training next Monday." Sonny stood, shook his hand, and turned to leave. "And if you can, borrow a suit from somebody else. Looks like you just raided your old man's closet. You're not going to sell shit looking like that."

Williamsburg, Brooklyn—May 30, 1929

Sonny knew every word he was about to say, but he still choked on them more often than not. He had rehearsed his sales pitch every morning in the mirror, and recounted it in his mind as he rode the tram each day. It wasn't what he had expected. Sonny wanted to be one of the Wall Street gurus who sat behind a big desk, following the stock tape and making important decisions. He had never been much for talking, especially with strangers. He was also aware that he wasn't very good at it. But, due to the sheer number of people he had seen, he was leading the company in sales for the month of May.

He forced himself to knock on the door before him, the fourth house he had visited that morning on Roebling Street. He had started out visiting tenements much like the one he was raised in, but he knew the money was going to be in these houses.

A young woman answered the door. She was below average height, with a plump face and a toothy smile. It was gentle and unassuming, unlike the faces of most he visited.

"Good day, ma'am." He shifted his briefcase to his left hand and shook hers with his right. He kicked himself for forgetting to lead with his name, as the script ordained.

"Good morning to you. What can I do for you?"

"My name is Vincente, and I work with Goldberg Funds. I would like the chance to talk with your father or husband about some excellent opportunities we have right now."

"Yes, that seems like something my husband would be more interested in hearing. Joseph," she said, calling into the house while gesturing for him to take a step inside. This was a rare gesture indeed.

"Good morning, old boy, what can I do for you?" the man said with a wide grin as he approached. He appeared to just be getting ready for the day, but was wearing the finest suit Sonny had seen in Brooklyn. Black, with fine gray pinstripes, and a snow-white pocket square. His head was large, with large eyebrows and a Roman nose. He looked like royalty.

"It's nice to meet you, sir. I was just introducing myself to your wife." He extended his hand and hoped that it wasn't too clammy. "My name is Vincente, and I work for Goldberg Funds. We have some excellent opportunities right now for a savvy businessman like yourself, if you'd like to hear about them." Sonny felt his chances were good, since he was already past the door of their home, but the man hesitated.

"I'm involved in so many ventures right now..." He shook his head. "Perhaps another time?"

"Oh." Sonny's heart sank. Every time he received a rejection, he thought about the bills that were piling up around his mother's tenement. "Absolutely. Thank you for your time." He was instructed to schedule a revisit after such rejections, but he just didn't feel up to it.

"What did you say your name was, old boy?"

"Vincente. Vincente Consentino." The man's face lit up, and he popped his forehead as if embarrassed.

"Your English was so fine, I didn't recognize you as one of ours. I should have known you were a paisano!" He now addressed him in Italian. "Come, sit. I don't mind to hear about these opportunities, I just choose to only work with Sicilians." He nodded at Sonny, as if he expected him to understand.

"Absolutely, sir," Sonny said, following him into the kitchen.

"Please, call me Joe. And this is my wife, Fay."

"It's a pleasure to meet you both. You keep a lovely house, Fay." Sonny was still no good at talking to strangers, but his comfort was growing due to the amiability of his hosts. He set his briefcase down on their table and began to search for some of his sales materials.

"Tell me about these opportunities of yours," Joe said, sitting down beside him. Fay brought them two cups of coffee, cubes of sugar, and some stirring spoons. Even though Sonny couldn't remember much about Sicily, Joe and Fay's home reminded them of his early years across the pond. The entire place was decorated like they were Sicilian royalty, if such a thing existed.

"I would love to," he said, and laid out some of his sales materials and directed him to the drawing of a pyramid. "This is the financial planning pyramid. We have to start with the base, which is protecting you against all the things that can go wrong"—he moved his pen up the pyramid—"so that we might have the opportunity to plan for everything that can go right." Joe pulled out a pair of round bifocals and put them on. The married couple was probably only a handful of years older than Sonny, but he felt like a boy in their presence. They were leagues ahead of him, and he hoped that they didn't notice it as much as he did.

"I like that. Protect against what can go wrong." Joe looked across the kitchen to Fay.

"And once we get the base covered with our affordable life insurance and disability policies, we can begin to invest in the stock market."

"I've seen a few articles about the stock market in the paper. The skies seem pretty bright for you Wall Street fellas."

"Yes, sir. That's right. And you can share in that profit." Sonny began to settle in. "You know what they say: there are two ways to make money." A smile creased Joe's face when Sonny mentioned money.

"What are the two ways, Mr. Consentino?"

"Man at work, and money at work. You can put on your boots every day and go to work… And what do you do, sir?"

"I'm an…importer." Joe shrugged.

"An importer. You can work each day importing goods,

or you can put the money you've already earned to work for you. Money making money."

Joe leaned back in his chair, listening to Sonny with one eyebrow raised. "Money making money, I like that."

"Yes, sir."

"That simple?"

"For you, yes, sir. We take care of everything else. I'll be your personal representative, and take care of all the boring paperwork and trades. You can just sit back and watch the jack roll in."

"Well"—Joe took off his spectacles and twirled them in between his fingers—"in my line of work, I value discretion. You know how it is for us Sicilians. We are inclined to do business with our own. I'm always cautious of having America's Uncle Sam looking over our shoulders. But we can't keep this quiet, can we? I'm sure your team will see everything you do?"

Sonny thought for a moment. His training had not given him any instructions for how to handle such a question. "You'll be working with me directly, Mr…?"

"Bonanno."

"Mr. Bonanno. You'll be working with me. Those who analyze our accounts don't care where your money comes from. They'll trust my judgment." He wasn't entirely sure if this was true. It had never been a problem with the white-collar clients Goldberg generally worked with.

"Really?" Joe Bonanno was intrigued. Sonny felt he was closing in on the deal.

"Yes, sir."

"Is there any way for me to receive funds, after earning them, without allowing Uncle Sam to…whet his beak?" Bonanno was asking Sonny a question that he most certainly shouldn't answer. But he knew the answer.

Thoughts of his mother and their cramped, damp little

tenement came to mind. "There are several ways to do that, sir. Yes. There are ways to spread your money in a way that no one would ever be interested in tracing."

"Fascinating. I think we will work well together, Vincente Consentino, quite nicely."

Bonanno stood up, and Sonny did the same. His heart dropped, knowing now that he wouldn't get a sale, at least today. Bonanno checked his watch. "I better get going. Duty beckons. Give me a few days to gather up some of my earnings, and I'll come to your office." Sonny thought about Mr. Wallingford's derogatory comments but pushed them away.

"That sounds excellent, sir. I'll be preparing the paperwork."

"And would you mind if I bring along an associate? He would be very interested in the service you provide." Sonny nodded, but Joe continued. "He would compensate you well."

Sonny thanked Fay for the coffee as Joe led him to the door.

"It was a pleasure." Sonny tipped his fedora and made his way back to his route.

Financial District, Manhattan—June 14, 1929

Sonny didn't always like it when Antonello visited him at his Goldberg office. The coworkers that sat at desks around him made it clear that they enjoyed it even less. It didn't exactly bolster the image he was trying to create.

Antonello didn't seem to mind the distasteful glances

he received, and he tried to make small talk with anyone who would give him a chance. Sonny thought he just liked being in a place where he seemed important, well-to-do. He had been working, less discretely then he should, with a bootlegger in East Harlem. He still lived paycheck to paycheck, and sometimes had to borrow for his rent, but that didn't stop him from buying new suits and a pinky ring worth more than Antonello's Model T.

"Make any sales today?" Antonello asked, smacking his chewing gum.

"No, not today. Have some closing appointments lined up for tomorrow, though." Antonello leaned up against Sonny's desk. Sonny hurried to sweep his things into his briefcase, deciding it was better to leave a bit early than to continue to disrupt his coworkers.

"Oh, you ready to go? I can wait. I was thinking we can take a trolley car to Harlem. Some pals of mine found a juice joint that serves the good stuff. I figured we could try it out."

"No, I'm ready to go. Those places are clip joints, though, Antonello. I can't afford those prices." He lowered his voice. He assumed some of his coworkers partook, but they would have probably objected to one of their own attending one of the disreputable speakeasies of East Harlem.

"Mr. Consentino?" The secretary leaned into the shared office room where the salesmen made their calls, which they dubbed the "war room." "You have a visitor at the front desk." Antonello looked the secretary up and down.

"What a peach." Antonello winked. Sonny shot him a discouraging look. "Go ahead. Pretend I'm not here." Sonny stood, and Antonello took his chair.

Out in the lobby, Sonny saw Joe Bonanno.

"Mr. Bonanno, it's good to see you." Sonny kissed his cheek. He was excited to see the man; he'd been afraid he wasn't going to make a sale after he hadn't heard from him in a few weeks.

"You too, you too, Vincente," he said. "I'd like to introduce you to someone. This is Mr. Maranzano." Joe stepped aside and gestured to a man in a fine suit. He was tall and full-bodied, with a thick head of black hair styled to perfection.

"It's nice to meet you, Vincente." The man accepted a handshake as Sonny pondered why the name sounded so familiar. Holding on to Mr. Maranzano's arm was an elderly man, who looked confused and only partially aware of his surroundings. "This is my uncle. He is in need of some of your services. Joseph says you are the man to see."

"Absolutely, absolutely." Sonny looked at the secretary, who nodded to the open conference room. He led Mr. Maranzano and his uncle to the room, and offered them a cola. Mr. Bonanno remained by the door.

"What can I do for you, gentlemen?" Sonny asked, his senses heightening when Mr. Maranzano looked at him.

"What are we doing here?" the elderly man asked, distressed.

"It's alright, little uncle," Maranzano soothed his uncle, speaking in an educated Sicilian dialect. "Joseph tells me that you value discretion, as I do. Is that true?"

"Yes, sir. I do. My father taught me to handle my business hand to mouth." Maranzano smiled. Sonny was compelled to do the same.

"My uncle has a great deal of money," Maranzano said. "A very large sum. He needs somewhere to place it so that his family can receive it when he passes away. He doesn't want anyone taking a cut. Right, Uncle?"

After a moment, the old man nodded.

"There are several ways to do that, Mr. Maranzano." Sonny found himself naturally speaking in Sicilian. It felt more pleasant than forced, as it was when talking with some of the men in Little Italy.

"What do you suggest?"

"Well"—Sonny thought for a moment—"a life insurance policy provides a lump sum of money to the beneficiaries, upon the death of the insured, tax free. And the IRS will see it as an inheritance and nothing more. Regardless of how the policy was paid for."

Maranzano nodded. "And you could get a life-insurance policy on a man his age?" Sonny considered the question for a moment. It was a fair question. Their ideal client was a young man with health and wealth. Then he remembered his mother.

"Was your uncle born in the States?"

"No, he wasn't. He was born in the motherland—Palermo, as a matter of fact." Maranzano was listening intently. The ticking of the clock on the wall seemed to slow.

"Well, I'm assuming he doesn't have a birth certificate, then. Perhaps we don't remember how old he is, exactly."

Maranzano laughed in a low, compelling voice. "That is probably true. Sometimes Uncle still thinks that the Bourbon kings are in control of Sicily, don't you, Uncle?"

"Bastards," the old man snarled.

"Our other options, and one that I would suggest would be to put any remaining funds across the pond."

"Across the pond? In Sicily?"

Sonny shook his head. "No. Great Britain. It's more difficult to track, and after that Mr. Churchill fellow changed up the gold standard, you are buying with pennies on the dollar."

Maranzano leaned back and considered, rubbing his

clean-shaven chin. "I've heard that the economy is turbu-lent overseas. I've overheard the real money is made in this lovely, savage country we now call home."

"That is true, Mr. Maranzano." Sonny reached forward to his coffee mug to steady his hands. "But the best advice I can give you is to be fearful when others are greedy…and to be greedy when others are fearful."

Maranzano chuckled. "Sage advice. I like that. You must be a reader of the ancients. Marcus Aurelius? Seneca, perhaps?"

"I've probably come across them in my studies." He hadn't, but the man seemed so pleased with the connection he had made that Sonny couldn't deny it.

"I will trust your advice, then. Is the amount a problem?"

"Problem? No, no problem. Whatever you would like to invest, I can work with. The life insurance will depend on what he is approved for, but if we handle it correctly, I'm sure he can get what's necessary to cover his needs."

Maranzano stood and gently helped his uncle to his feet.

"I will be back tomorrow, then, after my uncle prepares his funds. How does three million sound?" Sonny was too stunned to reply. "Four million?"

"Four million of coverage?"

"Four million of initial premium. And he can pay whatever afterward to ensure the policy remains in force. Whatever else my uncle has can be invested overseas. As you suggest."

"Whatever your uncle has, Mr. Maranzano, I can help him with."

"Excellent." Mr. Maranzano reached into his pocket and brandished a business card. "If you need me in the meantime, you can reach me here." Maranzano departed, leading his uncle by hand.

Sonny, still too shocked to move, looked at the business card.

"SALVATORE MARANZANO: REAL ESTATE."

The name still sounded familiar, but Sonny couldn't place it. He couldn't focus his mind to consider it. The only thing coursing through his mind was: Who in real estate had four million dollars for a life-insurance policy?

It would doubtlessly be the largest policy ever written by the firm. And the most conspicuous too.

East Harlem, Manhattan—July 29, 1929

Sonny was unused to spending this much time with one of his clients. Generally, the adviser-client relationship didn't extend past his monthly premium collections, but Mr. Maranzano was not an ordinary client. Considering that well over half of Sonny's salary was provided by the business he had done with Mr. Maranzano, Sonny tended to him as much as was requested.

When Mr. Maranzano asked Sonny to go to a talkie, Sonny went to a talkie.

"That was an excellent tale," Maranzano said as they walked out of Warner's Theater in East Harlem.

"I enjoyed it, Mr. Maranzano. I very much appreciate the invitation," Sonny said. *The Virginian* wasn't his favorite nickelodeon of the year, but Gary Cooper was enough to keep any flick interesting.

"There is something about these Westerns, Vincente.

They remind me a bit of Sicily. The fight for survival, the indomitable will, man versus wild, man versus man." Maranzano stared off with wild eyes.

"Mr. Maranzano, I agree with you." Sonny caught a glimpse of one of Maranzano's bodyguards following behind them, reminding him that they were never really alone.

"You understand me, Vincente. You understand what it means to be a Sicilian," Mr. Maranzano said, and Sonny tried to resist blushing. "There is something about the cowboy riding into the sunset, going out on his own terms. I believe it is why the Romans preferred a noble suicide to dishonor. A man wants only to go out on his own terms." Maranzano continued to wonder aloud, and Sonny found himself entranced.

"Yes, Mr. Maranzano. It is the best ending any man can hope for."

"I pray that we both may find such an end." Maranzano's Lincoln pulled to a stop in front of them, its driver ignoring the blaring horns of the traffic around it. Chauffeurs hurried out and opened the door. Maranzano had stopped walking forward and looked to Sonny. "But why would a man want to die on his own terms, if he refuses to live by them?" Sonny tried to think of something to say in response but couldn't develop any thoughts clever enough.

"Do you like where you work, Vincente?"

"Yes, sir…I do." Sonny tried to anticipate what Mr. Maranzano was getting at, but couldn't discern anything.

"And do you live by your own terms? Make your own rules? Or are you held captive by others?"

"I…I hadn't really thought of it, Mr. Maranzano."

Mr. Maranzano shook his head, frustrated. "Sicilians have lived through enough captivity. Decades, centuries, of living under corrupt governments that exploit our labors.

And now, here, in this great land of opportunity, we subjugate ourselves willingly." Maranzano held his hands out to the vast, packed city streets of Harlem before them.

"What do you think a Sicilian should do, then?" Sonny asked.

"If I were you"—Maranzano paused and formulated his thoughts—"I would work for me. My associates would find great value in what you do. There would be money to be made, and less overhead from the privileged men who exploit you."

"How—"

"A man like me is always looking for financial opportunities. I could finance a company, one like your current employer's, but you would be in charge. You would make the rules, conduct your business with your own people." Sonny was stunned. He shuffled uncomfortably and couldn't decide what to do with his hands. "Vincente, let me ask you a question. Do your employers like your Italian clients?"

Sonny remembered the judging glances of his coworkers, and the disapproving glares of Mr. Wallingford. He was bringing in too much business to be reprimanded for it, but it was clear that they didn't like him—or his clientele.

"They do not, sir."

"Exactly. The more Italians you bring in, the richer you become, the more they will hate you. You may work for and with those people, Vincente, but do not ever forget that you are not one of them."

"Yes, Mr. Maranzano." Sonny avoided eye contact. Maranzano's great height made that less difficult.

"You should consider it. I understand you, Vincente, and you understand me. I can see that you are a man who desires autonomy in life, and I can give it to you." Sonny

had never considered himself to be individualistic by
nature, but Maranzano's proclamation had decreed it, so
Sonny assumed it was true.

"And what would you get out of this kindness, Mr.
Maranzano?" Sonny asked just before Maranzano could
enter his car.

"As I've said, a man can never be involved in too many
business ventures, as long as it is with his own people. My
name would be associated with the business, of course, and
some of the money I receive from less-savory occupations
could be reported from there, which keeps the detectives'
watchful eyes off of my private affairs. I would also plan to
use the building for my own work. Namely, the basement.
It would not interfere with anything you do."

Maranzano now wore a gentle, familiar smile. He
smoothed the brim of his homburg and placed it carefully
on his head.

"I hope that you'll consider it, Vincente." He winked
and stepped into the car.

"Wait," Sonny said, and the chauffeur held the door
open. "Mr. Maranzano, how could I get out of my
contract?"

"Don't worry about that, Vincente. I'll take care of it.
As soon as you send the word, I'll make arrangements."
Maranzano nodded to his chauffeur. The man returned to
the driver's seat, and the spotless white Lincoln pulled
away. Sonny stood and watched until it faded into the mob
of traffic, his mind already made up.

MARIA

Every time "Sonny Boy" by Al Jolson came on the radio, Maria noticed a glint in her brother's eye. His lips seemed to tremble, and he'd look to the ground.

> *Climb upon my knee, Sonny Boy,*
> *Though you're only three, Sonny Boy,*
> *You've no way of knowing,*
> *There's no way of showing,*
> *What you mean to me, Sonny Boy.*
> *When there are gray skies,*
> *I don't mind the gray skies,*
> *You make them blue, Sonny Boy.*
> *Friends may forsake me,*
> *Let them all forsake me,*
> *I still have you, Sonny Boy.*

Maria decided it was best if she turned down the volume. When she did so, Sonny looked up.

"I like that song," he said, so Maria turned it back up.

She had remembered him as a mercurial young boy. He had been rather unconcerned with the goings-on of childhood dramas, disinterested in pursuing new friendships or the latest happenings in the world of sports. He was so withdrawn at social occasions that some of her girlfriends asked if he was lame or stupid.

But Maria knew better.

He only wanted to please his family, specifically their father. Sonny had worked relentlessly, toiling alongside Alonzo at the barbershop and at home, indulging in every word of thanks and appreciation. The entire family was of one mind after the news of Alonzo's death spread. Everyone worried about Rosa, and their hearts broke for young Maria and for the two older boys who'd missed out on a chance to know their own father. But everyone asked first about Sonny. They were right to assume he had the hardest time with it.

Every time Maria looked at him, she felt her chest tighten. There was sadness in his eyes, even when he returned home with money and good news that they had one less bill to worry about.

"Mamma, eat your food," Maria said, noticing that her mother was topping off her flask rather than finishing the pasta and veggies on her plate.

"Bah," Rosa said, shaking her head, "your father would never talk to me in such a way." She had reverted to talking only in Sicilian, as if to spite the world that had taken her husband away from her.

"We're just looking out for you, Ma," Sonny said. Rosa didn't reply but picked up her fork.

"When is that nice boy coming back over?" Rosa said after taking a few bites. She meant Buster. Even in her current state, she had taken a shine to him. It was no wonder. He was so polite and so charming, he probably could have won over the Kaiser himself if the army had given him a chance.

"He'll be here in a bit to pick me up. We're going to go to Central Park to watch the stars," Maria replied in Sicilian to please her mother.

"You like him for that fancy car." Rosa shook her head, but Maria picked up on a hint of humor in her weary voice. "Tell him to come say hello when he drops you off."

"Before you leave, Maria, I have some news for the both of you," Sonny said, and scooted closer to the table. "I am planning to move into an apartment in Williamsburg. I went and saw the place today." Maria's mouth dropped, but their mother only shook her head. "I'd bring you both with me, but I know Ma won't leave." He looked to Rosa, hoping she would change her mind.

Maria also hoped she'd change her mind. Their little tenement hadn't gotten any bigger despite Sonny's income. The bathroom was still down the hall, and the closest place to bathe was still a block away.

But the memory of Alonzo was imprinted in that place.

His ghost lingered in every corner of the tenement, still singing Sicilian hymns and telling funny stories he'd picked up from vegetable vendors on Mott Street.

"Go ahead, with your big job. Move away." Rosa turned to Maria. "And you run away with that nice boy and his fancy car. And leave me all alone." She was so frail, she seemed as if it were difficult to even put together her sentences. She had been thin her whole life, even after the birth of four children, but now she was wasting away before their eyes.

"Mamma." Sonny pulled her hands between his own and compelled her to look at him. "I will never leave you alone. Everything I do, and will ever do, is for you and Maria. Don't ever forget that." The glimmer in his eye returned. Sonny wasn't sentimental, and he never had been. He was as tough and stoic as their father. The single tear that gathered along his eyelid was enough to stop Maria's breath.

"I won't," Rosa said, trying to look at him. Her eyes, once sharp and alert, were now dull and unresponsive after years of working in a sweatshop all day, staring through dim light at a single needle.

A horn sounded from outside. Maria stood and ran to the only window in their tenement, and smiled when she caught sight of Buster's Model A.

"That's my ride," she said, and hurried to grab her handbag. She paused and returned to give both her mother and brother a kiss on the cheek.

"Don't worry," Sonny said, noticing his sister's lingering glance. "I'll take care of Ma tonight."

Maria hurried to the hat rack and picked out a cloche with silk roses atop it.

"I don't need anyone to take care of me," Rosa said as Maria slipped on her galoshes.

"Come on, Ma, want me to read to you?" Sonny said as Maria closed the door behind her, hoping that her mother said yes.

VICO

"I don't want to play," the balding man said, and tried to shut the door. Vico stopped it from closing with his boot.

"Mr. Brown is putting on a clean lottery. Everybody in the neighborhood is playing." Vico was already irritated. It was the end of the day, and he had been shaking down every tenant along with his brother and Cargo like some two-bit thug. He didn't like it, but Reina demanded he lay low after the LaDuca murder.

Low-level shakedowns were all he could do to bide his time and stay in front of the people who could tell him something about his father.

"No. I don't want to play," the man said again, and tried to shut the door again, which Vico resisted with ease.

"Just pay up, fella. Maybe you'll win."

"Maybe I'll lose."

"Maybe I'll break your legs if you don't pay me. How 'bout that?"

The man stared back, appalled, like all the others.

After sizing up Vico's chest and biceps, he fetched a nickel from his pocket and threw it in the burlap bag.

"315a. You've been added to the Italian lottery. Mr. Brown will visit you with the payout if you win."

"Go to Naples." The man flicked his hand under his chin. Vico thought about slamming the door into his nose but decided against it. He already had what he needed.

A Model T honked outside the building.

"Hey, Doyle! Come on!" a voice called out. It was the Gap—Vico could tell from the emphasis he always put at the end of Vico's alias.

"I got a few more apartments to hit," Vico said as he exited out to the curb. He jingled the change in his bag to indicate it was still light.

"Never mind that, come here." Petrelli waved him over, a cigarette dangling from the gap in his teeth.

"'Mr. Lucchese won't be pleased if we come back shortchanged'—that's what you told me this morning," Vico said.

"Small potatoes. Mr. Lucchese's priorities have changed." The Gap opened up the back hatch of the Model T, and pulled Vico closer.

Enzo joined them too.

"The zip in 256b pulled a gun on me and told me to go drown in a lake. What do we do about that?" he asked, but quickly forgot what he was talking about. "What's the big idea?"

"Quiet down and get over here."

The Gap pulled a knife from his boot and pried open the lid to the milk crate in the car's trunk.

Within, he scraped back a few layers of straw to reveal several bottles of brown liquor.

"This is Mr. Lucchese's priority now." He turned and smiled, revealing that charming gap.

Enzo's jaw dropped like a child's on Christmas morning.

"What are we supposed to do with that?" Vico closed the lid and peered over his shoulders to ensure none of the locals were watching.

The Gap was perplexed.

"Why, we unload it, Doyle. You really are a few buttons short, aren't you?"

The Gap pried open the crate again, a bit more forcefully than before, and brandished a bottle of liquor.

"And this is the real McCoy too, not like the swill they're cooking up in bathtubs around here. Mr. Lucchese met a Friend of Ours in Canada who's sending it down. They're sending it in through another insider in Atlantic City."

"Whoa," Cargo said, approaching with a bag of coins flipped over his shoulder.

"Yeah, but what about Mr. Gagliano and Mr. Reina? What do they think? They said they wanted to keep their noses clean."

The Gap shrugged and buried the bottle of brown back in the case.

"Don't worry about that. Mr. Lucchese made sure his *i*'s were dotted and *t*'s crossed. As long as he gives them a cut, they'll look the other way."

"Sounds like a win-win to me, Bobby," Enzo said, dollar signs already shinning in his eyes.

"What about Masseria?"

"He and the Castellammarese run rum row. This doesn't interfere with their operations at all. We're gonna steer clear of Manhattan. Everyone can get rich if we play our cards right."

"I don't know, Petrelli. This is on another level. This is how you get caught. Or killed. What about the Prohis?"

"Prohibition agents can be bought off just like the rest of the bulls." The Gap was losing his patience and clearly disappointed that Vico wasn't as excited about the opportunity as he was.

"Sounds expensive. What kind of margin we gonna have after the bulls, the Canadians, the friend in Atlantic City, and everyone up top gets their cut?"

"Mary and Joseph." Cargo rolled his eyes and flicked his wrists.

"What are you, a wise guy now?" the Gap said. "Leave that to the guys with half a brain, Doyle. We're just the muscle. We move the juice and we make a cut. Simple as that."

The Gap wasn't usually this aggressive, at least in Vico's experience. Vico clenched his jaw but didn't mention it. He knew from his time in France that winning a war came down to picking when to fight. If he was going to stand up to a guy on the inside, it wouldn't be over this. He was still hopeful Reina would reveal Alonzo's killer's identity soon, and he didn't plan to jeopardize that.

"Alright. Let's unload it, then," Vico said to a chorus of applause and slaps on the back.

"That's more like it."

"Time to make some real scratch." Enzo rubbed his hands together vigorously.

"What do we do with this?" Vico gestured to the bag of change in his hand.

"Well, if I was you, Doyle, I'd give it to Mr. Lucchese in exchange for a bottle of hooch." The Gap slapped Vico's shoulder, and everyone openmouthed laughed, except Vico. "Get in. I know a juice joint in Yonkers that's going to flip a lid when they see this stuff."

Vico thought about returning to the apartment complex and returning the change to the asshole who'd tried to slam the door on him. But then he followed the others into the Gap's Ford. He'd play along for now. He'd do whatever he had to do. But his patience was starting to waiver. If Reina didn't talk soon, he'd have to figure out another way to get the information he coveted. One way or another, somebody was going to die.

SONNY

Sonny clung to the walls like he once had at Columbia University dance parties. He knew Maranzano and Joseph Bonanno, as well as several other men Maranzano had introduced him to since he had left Goldberg's to form C&M's Investment Firm. Regardless, he felt like an outsider.

The fact that his suit was oversized and had to be fixed with safety pins didn't help build his confidence.

But Maranzano seemed determined to keep him from shying away from the crowd.

He led him by the arm through the auditorium, introducing him to man after man. Each time, Sonny addressed them as a servant does a master, which they seemed to shrug off and respond to by asking him questions about the services he provided. If he could muster the courage, he knew he could walk away from this holiday celebration with double his current clientele.

"This is Vincente Consentino." Maranzano stepped aside, introducing him to another important-looking fellow. "We have recently begun doing business together. He is one of the smartest men in this room, of that I swear."

"Nice to meet you, Vincente." The man shook his hand aggressively, causing Sonny's drink to spill. He was an abrasive man, like many of the others, with big ears and a thick jaw. Sonny privately hoped that the use of "Vincente" would wear off in time, but he still found himself unable to correct Maranzano.

"Vincente, this is Giuseppe Aiello. He is a friend of ours from Chicago, here to spend the holiday with us."

"It's a pleasure to meet you, sir," Sonny said, the handshake lingering.

"Joe. Just call me Joe. I'm not as formal as this guy." Aiello winked at Maranzano.

"One of his many downfalls." Maranzano patted Aiello on the shoulder, and started to lead the forward march to introduce Sonny to every important man in the room.

"Wait, I've heard about you," Aiello said, forcing them both to stop. "Is this the Wall Street guy?" His Chicago accent was apparent in a room of mostly New Yorkers and those straight off the boat from Sicily.

"Guilty as charged." Sonny smiled, and Maranzano did the same.

"You look a little young to be one of those guys. How long you been in the industry?"

"Not long, sir. I left Columbia University last year and got to work right away." Sonny decided to leave out the part where he worked as a day laborer.

"Wow"—Aiello shot a look at Maranzano—"you sure a young buck like him knows what he's talking about?"

"Experience can often cloud our judgment, Giuseppe.

Great minds are not confined to the old, like us." Neither of them was very old, but both laughed as if they were.

"Not a lot of experience, sir. But I've read a lot of books, and that has to count for something." Sonny wanted to join in on the humor while it lasted. "The last job I had was sweeping up after my father gave haircuts at A.C. Barbers." He feared he had gone too far. The smiles evaporated from the men's faces. Aiello looked to Maranzano. Maranzano looked down.

Sonny shifted his eyes back and forth between them, suddenly feeling like quite the fool.

"Excuse me," Maranzano said, clearing his throat, "I need to make a phone call." He stepped off through the crowd, leaving Aiello and Sonny in uncomfortable silence.

"Holler at me if you find any good stocks. The really good ones, I mean." Aiello took a sip of his whiskey and returned to a discussion with other guests.

Sonny hurried through the crowd to the wall. Now, more than ever, he felt it was where he belonged. He had never been regarded as particularly funny, but he wondered what had he said to defuse the men's good spirits so quickly.

At the front of the auditorium, a banister hung with the words "Mary's Assumption" written on it in Italian. It was the reason for their gathering, and it was all Sonny could do not to think about all the times he had celebrated the Catholic festival with his father. He would have much rather been with him and his family.

"Vincente." Maranzano appeared again at his side after Sonny had drained a few more glasses of whiskey. "Can I talk to you privately for a moment?" Sonny's heart began to race, but he nodded for Maranzano to lead the way.

When they had exited into the hallway, with nothing

but a few guards near the front entrance, Maranzano said, "I made a phone call. And I feel very foolish. Did you say that your father owned A.C. Barbers?"

"Yes, Mr. Maranzano. That's correct." Maranzano lowered his head and rubbed his temples with his thumb and forefinger.

"Your father was Alonzo Consentino?"

"Yes." Sonny's hands now trembled in his coat pockets. Maranzano shook his head and closed his eyes.

"I know your father, Vincente."

"You do?"

"Yes. And I believe we've met before. Did he call you 'Sonny'?"

"Yes, he did. Everyone calls me that, still."

Maranzano nodded and finally met his eyes.

"Your father was an associate of mine. I'm not sure how I misplaced it, but, yes, your father was an associate."

"Is that so?" Sonny's Adam's apple danced in his throat as he tried to swallow.

"Yes. And I called him friend. I have so many associates, as you can tell"—Maranzano gestured to the ballroom behind him—"I didn't connect you to him. I am so sorry for your loss, Vincente. I realize he has only recently passed away."

Sonny's breath calmed, and he looked down at Maranzano's shined shoes.

"Yes, sir. That is true. And I appreciate your condolences."

"I wish I had been there at his funeral. I should have been there, but business wouldn't allow it. He was a good man, Vincente." Maranzano looked up, vulnerable for the first time since Sonny had known him.

"He was."

"And…" Maranzano had pulled the leather gloves

from his pocket and now rotated them in his hands. "I know who it was that killed your father."

"You do?" Sonny tried to remain calm.

"I do. His name was Peter Morello."

Sonny froze.

"Yes, his name was Peter Morello. Talk of it spread throughout the men of honor. We were all disgusted."

"Giuseppe Morello?" Sonny's heart leapt in his throat, and adrenaline surged through his veins.

"Yes, that was him."

"That can't be." Sonny looked away and shook his head. "He was arrested years ago. My father and I saw it happen."

"He has been out of prison, Vincente. He was released well over a year ago, but he's laid low to avoid police surveillance."

"I…I…" Sonny couldn't think of what to say, but he couldn't accept it. His mind returned to the fear he once had for the Hook Hand.

"I know this must be a great deal to bear." Maranzano reached forward and placed a hand on Sonny's shoulder. Sonny felt his gaze, and was compelled to meet Maranzano's eyes. "He was released from prison and had an old debt to settle with your father. It seems that it extended back even to Sicily. Old feuds have a way of resurfacing, even after years go by."

"Mr. Maranzano, I saw them together on several occasions. Their relationship, strained though it appeared… I thought they were friends."

"Perhaps they were. But old wounds heal slowly. They fester, even as we bandage them. Morello is a violent man who has offended our people in more ways than one."

"I see…and how do you know this?" Sonny asked, a small part of him still wanting to disbelieve the news.

"Morello himself spread the news. He wanted to make an example of your father. He wanted all our people to see that he was not to be underestimated. That even if time passed, he would exact his revenge eventually." Sonny lowered his head, and Maranzano continued. "When he left prison, his position was weak. He was no longer in control of the organization he'd helped build. He had to send a message that he was still a man who commanded respect. Many knew that he and your father were friends, and by killing him, he let everyone know that there was no one safe from his wrath if he did not get what he wanted."

"I see, Mr. Maranzano," Sonny said, and nodded. In truth, he wanted to beg the man to say no more. His mind was swimming, and he wasn't sure he could handle anything else.

"Vincente," Maranzano said in a low voice, "Morello is not a friend of ours. My associates and I have been looking for an opportunity to punish him for this crime and others for several months now. It has been hard to find him. But I must ask, if the time comes, would you like to hold the gun and the knife yourself? You have the blood right to revenge, if you want it." Sonny kept his feet planted but moved his body back. He couldn't believe what he was hearing. He didn't know what to say.

"I...I cannot do that," he said, his voice barely audible. Before now, he hadn't even believed that his father was involved in the life Maranzano so obviously lived. He couldn't comprehend it all. And now he was being asked to kill? The desire for revenge had been impossible to ignore since the moment he'd seen his father's lifeless body on the linoleum floor of his barbershop. Now that he was offered it, he didn't know what to say. Killing worked better in his mind.

"I understand. Know that your father will be avenged regardless." Maranzano nodded until Sonny did the same.

"Thank you for telling me, Mr. Maranzano."

"Do not thank me." Maranzano pulled Sonny in by the neck and kissed his head. "You are one of ours. Your father would have wanted you to know. But he wouldn't want you to miss celebrating the Assumption of our Lady." He smiled for the first time since they had entered the hallway, and gestured back to the auditorium. "Let's return."

Sonny followed him, exerting extra strength just to keep his legs stable beneath him.

"Bring something good for my friend," Maranzano said to a waiter. As he followed Mr. Maranzano back into the room, his thoughts were numbed by the loud chorus of laughter from the attendees.

The room now felt entirely different.

HEARINGS BEFORE THE
PERMANENT SUBCOMMITTEE ON INVESTIGATIONS
OF THE
COMMITTEE ON GOVERNMENT OPERATIONS
UNITED STATES SENATE
EIGHTY-EIGHTH CONGRESS
THIRD SESSION
PURSUANT TO SENATE RESOLUTION 17
SEPTEMBER 29, 1963

SENATOR MUNDT: Mr. Valachi, you've stated previously that Sonny worked exclusively for Mr. Maranzano during the time that you were acquainted. When do you believe their formal relationship began?

Mr. Valachi: It was certainly by the time I met him in 1930. Or maybe it was '29. He had been with him for a while.

Senator Mundt: Vincente Consentino had been working with Salvatore Maranzano for some time before you met him?

Mr. Valachi: Yes, Senator, that's correct.

. . .

Senator Mundt: You've said that Mr. Consentino was not involved much in Maranzano's bootlegging operation. Is that true?

Mr. Valachi: Yes, Senator, that's correct. He was involved in other ways. He ran a financial racket for him.

Senator Mundt: Can you explain to the court what you mean by "financial racket"?

Mr. Valachi: He worked in finance. Stocks and bonds, or what have you. I'm not so sure, I never really understood all of that.

Senator Mundt: And you believe this was a "racket" in the traditional use of the word?
    (Mr. Valachi laughs.)

Mr. Valachi: Yes, Senator. Most of the guys in my line of work called it that, anyway. He worked for some big-shot company in Manhattan before that, but the owner of the company "retired early" at Mr. Maranzano's request, and Sonny began to work for Mr. Maranzano exclusively.

(Mr. Valachi receives counsel from his attorney.)

Mr. Valachi: That's how I remember the story, to the best of my ability.

Senator Mundt: And the nature of their business together was simply in financial planning?

Mr. Valachi: Sonny worked exclusively with those in Maranzano's family, and helped them hide money.

Senator Mundt: He helped them "hide money"?

Mr. Valachi: Yes, Senator. He helped them put their bootleg money in places where the government couldn't take any of it away. This was before Al Capone got caught on tax evasion, see, but Mr. Maranzano was already thinking about that. We called it a "racket" because Sonny and Maranzano both made a lot of money on it. Several of the men in my line of work began to call Sonny "the Bond Father."

(Mr. Valachi and the court laugh.)

. . .

Senator Mundt: The "Bond Father"?

Mr. Valachi: The Bond Father. A "godfather" was your boss, so "bond father" was because of the line of work he was in, and because he was becoming powerful quickly because of the service he provided.

Senator Mundt: Thank you, Chairman, that's all I have for now.

Chairman: Thank you, Senator Mundt.

SONNY

Williamsburg, Brooklyn—October 29, 1929

Sonny sat in the speakeasy with his hands over his face. He was always careful to disguise his identity in unsavory locations like this, but that wasn't his reason today. He was terrified, hoping to blend into the darkest corner of the room, drowning his sorrow in his drink.

The bar radio played "I Faw Down and Go Boom" by Eddie Cantor, depicting the artist's failures in the stock market, and it was a fitting song. Every few moments, the bartender's ticker-tape machine revealed new information about the stock market. The economy was crumbling. The world itself seemed to be falling apart.

How much money had he lost that day? How much money had he lost his clients in just a few hours? It was impossible to tell. He was afraid that those who shook his hand so pleasantly at Maranzano's dinner party might now be wanting to cut his hands off.

Sonny felt like a wanted man. He jolted with fear when

Antonello pulled up the chair beside him. He had forgotten he had invited him out for a drink the day before.

"What's eating you, fella?" Antonello said, a smirk on his face that revealed he already knew.

"I might be a dead man, Antonello." Sonny winced as he tossed a glass of scotch back. "Another glass of brown plaid," he said to the bartender.

"Come on, it'll be hunky dory." He slapped Sonny on the back and called for a drink of his own.

"What on the earth makes you think that, Antonello?" Sonny was frustrated. Antonello, with his foolish optimism, was not the person he would seek first on a day such as this.

"Everyone's got the screamin' meemies. It's just the jitters. The market or whatever will be fine, just wait."

Sonny lowered his forehead to the glass before him, feeling like he might throw up.

"I staked everything on this, Antonello. And my clients aren't the kind of people to be trifled with. They'll want their money back, and when they don't get it, they'll come after me." Such a promising start, Sonny thought, just to have his empire crumble down around him as soon as he'd begun building it.

"What about that big-shot guy, Marinara, or whatever?"

"Maranzano?"

"Yeah, Maranzano. Nobody is gonna mess with you while he's in your pocket."

"He might be the most dangerous one." New reports came in over the ticker tape, and the bartender preached the gloom and doom.

"Nothing getting oiled can't fix." Antonello raised his glass of whiskey and tossed it back.

"I'll have to go see him, Antonello. And I'll need a

clear head." He pushed away the glass in front of him, ignoring his desire to comply.

"What are you gonna say?"

"I'm going to tell him the situation, and hope he doesn't break my legs."

"Want me to come with you?" Antonello sobered at the thought of Sonny being hurt.

"No, I'll be fine. He's a reasonable man. Maybe we can work something out."

"Well, make sure to ask if he needs a handsome young bodyguard like myself."

Sonny shook Antonello's hand, then paid his tab, adding a tip he was no longer sure he could afford.

He stood at the doorway, peering out into the city streets, unsure if he would see them again.

Midtown East, Manhattan—October 29, 1929

Sonny got vertigo simply looking up at the Eagle Corporation Building. He had never visited Mr. Maranzano at his place of work, and hoped that he was not breaking protocol by doing so now.

"What floor?" the elevator boy asked as he entered.

"Eh, ninth, I believe."

"Yes, sir," the bellhop said proudly.

"I'm here to see Mr. Maranzano. Is that the right floor?"

"Yes, sir. He is located in room 925."

The elevator crept upward, but it was still too fast for Sonny's liking. He still hadn't decided what he was going to say. He tried to formulate something, but the words kept fading into the ether.

"Thank you." Sonny handed the elevator boy a nickel and stepped off. He read the signs pointing him to "Maranzano Real Estate Offices," and allowed his feet to propel him on even though his mind begged him to stop.

"Yes, two shipments should be arriving from rum row this evening. The coast guard shouldn't be a problem. I've made arrangements." Maranzano's Sicilian voice poured through the office. Sonny craned his head to see the man propped up against his desk, his back to the entrance. "That is correct. Mr. Caruso will deliver them to Brooklyn by tomorrow. Yes, the same location." He seemed cool and confident, which eased Sonny's nerves, but only a little.

"Who are you?" The voice caught Sonny off guard. An Italian man stepped into his path, looking him over.

"I'm Vincente Consentino," Sonny said, beginning to think that Maranzano didn't receive many visitors at his place of work.

"Am I supposed to know who you are?" the man said, pointing at Sonny with his beaked nose.

"I work with Mr. Maranzano."

"Is he expecting you?"

"He should be," Sonny said derisively, which was lost on the man. He didn't have an appointment, but Maranzano seemed shrewd enough to expect him on a day like this.

"He doesn't like to be interrupted," the man said. They both heard Maranzano offer a farewell and set down the receiver to his phone. "Alright, this way." The man waved him on. Sonny felt like he was being searched by the watchful eyes of the other employees.

"Mr. Maranzano." Sonny entered and lowered his head.

"Ah, Vincente. I was expecting you," Maranzano said, to Sonny's relief.

"I'm sure you've heard?"

"Yes, I have. I'm certain that every pigeon in Manhattan has heard by now."

"It's been an unfortunate day, Mr. Maranzano." Sonny waited for a response, but found none for some time. Declining to look at Maranzano directly, he admired the perfectly ordered bookshelves behind him, and the entire set of *Webster's* dictionaries and world atlases that they contained. A crystal chandelier hung in the center of the room and lit up Sonny's face more than he would have liked.

"That is business, Vincente. Whenever money is involved, we are gambling. Are we not?"

"Y-yes, Mr. Maranzano," Sonny stuttered, disbelieving that Mr. Maranzano was receiving this news as coolly as he projected.

"We still have the life insurance in force, yes?"

"Yes, Mr. Maranzano."

"Good. Then we shall live to fight another day."

"You are very wise, Mr. Maranzano," Sonny said, keeping his head bowed. He was so relieved, he felt more like prostrating himself before Maranzano and kissing his feet.

"You told me once that it was wise to be greedy when others are fearful, and fearful when others are greedy. Well, Vincente, everyone seems terrified right now, so that means we should be ravenous." He smiled and patted Sonny on the shoulder, seeming to notice his fear. "Would you care for some tea?" He pointed to a stainless-steel vase surrounded by china teacups.

"No, sir, I'm fine. Thank you."

"Vincente, I'm not upset with you. This is how the

economy works. I've seen my fair share of financial crises in Sicily." He gestured for Sonny to raise his head.

No one could wear a suit quite like Maranzano. It was double-breasted with defined shoulders, fitted across his chest and arms. It was a deep blue, and muted compared to the extravagant suits of Maranzano's dinner guests a few months prior. A red rose pinned to his lapel was his only accessory.

"I appreciate your understanding, Mr. Maranzano. I've been sick thinking about this." Sonny finally exhaled in relief.

"Of course. We are business partners, Vincente. You do not answer to me. Unfortunately, you may find some of our other clients to be less agreeable."

"I had imagined as much." Sonny bit his lip.

"Don't be too anxious. They are quick to anger, but quick to forgive, as most Sicilians are. They will not harm you. Of that, you have my word."

"Thank you, Mr. Maranzano. I read that Rockefeller began to amass his fortunes after the crash of 1911. I hope that we can imitate his response in regard to the current crisis."

Maranzano smiled and took a sip of his tea. "My thoughts exactly. Unfortunately, many of our associates are not as well versed in these matters. They will find it difficult to understand."

"It is difficult for all of us to understand."

"That may be true, but those with an even disposition can conquer this. Marcus Aurelius writes that the 'obstacle becomes that way,' that the 'impediment to action becomes the action.' We can use this for good. Not just overcome it, but profit from it."

But only tell me how, and I will do it, Sonny thought.

"Yes, Mr. Maranzano."

"You have earned yourself a great deal of respect for your knowledge of economics. I assume that the community of Little Italy has taken a vested interest in your career?" Sonny wouldn't have put it quite like that, but they certainly responded to him differently when he returned to visit Rosa.

"You could say that, sir, yes."

"I suggest we use this reputation to provide you with gainful employment while we wait for normalcy to return and new clients to appear at your doorstep."

"What did you have in mind?"

Maranzano thought for a moment. "Invest in small companies. We still have capital, and you can give back to the community that reared you by investing in small businesses there. In return, they will pay you a small fee for your protection and guidance."

"Protection? I don't feel capable of protecting much of anything."

"That's not a concern. My men will provide the protection. You will have only to collect the money, and be the spokesperson. When one business struggles, you take a bit more from the others and feed it to your struggling brother. It is a system that has worked for the people of Sicily for thousands of years."

Sonny had never considered it, but he was intrigued, if nothing else.

"And what else could I use my experience for?"

"Well, there is a great deal of money to be made in the mere transportation of alcohol, but I don't believe that suits you. Someone of your education can be useful in other ways."

"I want to be clear, Mr. Maranzano," Sonny said, finding the courage to look him in the eye. "I am not interested in making vast sums of money. I want only to provide for my mother."

Maranzano thought for a moment, then smiled.

"And that is why I favor you so, Vincente. You are a student of the ancients, whether you know it or not. This is about honor, about family. Not wealth. Let other men pursue the boundless riches that fade when they are gone. Sicilians, we believe in something more, don't we?" An idealistic glimmer shined in Maranzano's eye that reminded Sonny of his father.

"Yes, Mr. Maranzano."

"But, if I recall, I offered you the opportunity to exact vengeance on your father's killer, and you denied it?"

"I…I want justice. My goal was to bring the man to court, and have him sentenced." Maranzano's smile faded.

"Perhaps. I cannot fault you for trying. But the police in Manhattan have long since ceased to care about the deaths of Italians. 'Let them kill each other,' they say. With your father's past, they would likely call this another in a string of killings, and let the case fall to the wayside."

Sonny remembered Detective Gallagher's words and struggled to swallow. "You may be right."

"And speaking of our common enemy, we have new intelligence on his whereabouts."

"Oh?"

"Yes. He's been spotted. Peter Morello now lives in New Jersey, safe from the law enforcement that so recently placed him behind bars. Although, he has been working out of East Harlem. He has many powerful friends, and ranks high in their organization. Without working together, neither you nor I will find much success in finding justice for your father."

"I believe you, Mr. Maranzano." Sonny remembered the Hook Hand, and the thought of him prowling the streets of Jersey the way he once had Little Italy made his skin crawl. "I may reconsider your offer."

"You may?" Maranzano seemed surprised.

"All I want is justice for my father and safety for my mother."

"We will need to act soon. Morello is many things, but foolish he is not. He is crafty, and he remains in the shadows far longer than most of his associates are capable of."

"I need time to think," Sonny said, almost disbelieving his own words. Killing someone? He had never considered it, even when Rachel suggested it was his aim, even when he told the detective he would do so if he had to. If it was to be someone, it would be the man who killed his father. The more he considered the pain the man had caused him, the more the urge to agree grew.

"It is an important decision. Take all the time you need. But if we are forced to act, we will. I simply wanted to offer you this opportunity beforehand."

"Thank you for the opportunity, Mr. Maranzano."

"It has been nice talking, Vincente, but I must get back to work." Maranzano reached into his coat and brandished a roll of hundred-dollar banknotes. He flipped through them for a moment and then tossed the roll down on the table. "I suggest we start investing in companies soon. Let them see that we have the capital necessary to aid them in the future, and we have the muscle to make their lives better, or worse."

Sonny tested the weight of the money, and slid it into his pocket.

"I'll do that."

"Calogero will see you out. Let me know if you need anything, Vincente." Maranzano nodded and picked up the phone for another call.

BUSTER

Williamsburg, Brooklyn—December 18, 1929

Maria had demanded that Buster buy a tree. His family out West had never been very festive, and hadn't had money to spend on trivial things like Christmas decorations anyhow. This was his first tree.

"You have to fluff it out, Buster," she said, standing on her tiptoes to delineate the branches perfectly. He tried to ignore the bristles and tree sap that were now covering his living room rug. Maria's flowing white gown made that a little easier.

"Alright, alright, you just have to show me."

"And then you drape the garlands like this"—she looked over her shoulder to ensure he was watching—"and you have to weave it through the branches, to make it look like fresh snowfall."

"I haven't seen a tree since I left Chicago; I don't remember what they look like," he jested. "Now where do we put these?" He held up the three glass ornaments they had purchased in Manhattan the day before, little snowmen painted on one, and angels on the others.

"Three isn't very many for a tree, so we'll have to do it just right." She took them from him one by one, and studied the tree like an architect would a partially constructed building.

"Want me to play some tunes?" He walked to his radio and began to fiddle with it. He could never seem to operate it correctly.

"What I want you to do is pay attention, Buster," she said, giving him a look. "But, yes, music as well."

"And do you want some eggnog? I've got some nutmeg around here somewhere." He left the radio and began searching through his cabinets.

"Buster, stop worrying, I'm fine!" It was true that he worried. When he was with her, he wanted her to be happy. When she went more than a few minutes without smiling, he nearly fell apart. Even after a year of spending time together, she made him feel alive. No matter how much she insisted, he refused to believe he could do the same for her.

"Come on, you've told me how important decorating the tree was for you and your family. I want to make sure this is special." He continued to rummage around until he found the chosen spice. He hoped that this was their first Christmas of many, and he was careful to construct it as the perfect memory. "Here." He handed her a glass of eggnog and toasted it with his own. She took a sip, and he laughed as she ignored the thick white line it left above her lips.

"Sure you don't want a kiss?" she said when she noticed.

They continued to decorate as he partially feigned ignorance so she had to explain every step. He managed to get the radio working, and they sang their favorite holiday hymns with Eddie Cantor. When he hoisted her up by her hips to place the decorative angel on top, he decided he couldn't wait any longer.

"Come on, open your first gift." He retrieved the wrapped shoebox from his closet and presented it to her as proudly as a dog brings its master a bone.

"Buster, presents can wait! We still have a lot more days of Christmas, and you can join us with Mamma again this year."

"No, no, I want you to go ahead and open this one, Maria. I have a few other things for you, and for your mother too. This one is just begging to be opened today." She pouted in mock rejection, but hurried to sit down on his couch.

She shook the box a few times, utterly perplexed. Buster felt quite clever. He had filled the box with socks for weight, and a fistful of nickels for a sound effect. She would never know what to expect.

She took her time peeling back the tape, and watching his reaction as she did so. Buster bit his tongue and did all he could not to shout out what she might find inside.

When she finally removed the top, only a small velvet box remained inside. Her mouth dropped.

"Go on, open it."

Her tiny fingers lifted the lid of the small box. They trembled when she saw what was inside.

She brought a hand to her mouth, and looked up to find that Buster was already down on one knee.

"I've already asked your mother. I want you to be my wife, Maria."

She gasped for air, and fanned air across her flushed face.

"Oh, Buster."

"Do you like it? The jeweler said it was one of a kind. It's real and everything."

"Shut up, you foolish man, and kiss me!" She threw her arms around his neck as he stood. She jumped and wrapped her legs around his waist and kissed his neck and face again and again. "I love it. I love it."

"And I love you," he said, leaning his forehead against hers.

"We're going to have a family!"

"A family, yeah, little Marias running around everywhere."

She kissed him again, her hands holding on to his face.

He could still hear the gunfire of the Argonne Forest. He could still hear the whistles and orders given, the sound of dying comrades and foes. But now, more loudly, he could hear Maria's voice saying, "Don't be afraid," as she had told him so many nights when he had woken up from a nightmare. He finally had reason to believe those words.

PART 4

TURRIDRU

Turridru buried his mother on February 18. His father had been stoic, almost angry, about his wife's death. Turridru was thus tasked to find the location, and then dig the grave himself. A small hill outside the city limits, overlooking their home, under the ancient oak tree he had used to climb as a boy. That was where he had buried her. Without honors, without a funeral, without a procession of mourners. All alone. Quiet. She'd welcomed death silently.

Turridru's father didn't want to share the moment with the community that had disrespected them.

Turridru wept when he thought about it. Not tears of sadness but of anger. He hated that city. He hated Sicily. They had done this, they had done all of it.

He hated the Armettas and what they had done to his family. He hated the villagers that had let his mother bleed out with a stillborn wrapped in her arms. He hated Alonzo Consentino for abandoning them to this fate.

He even hated himself, or who he had become. When he looked at the reflection in his water pail, he didn't know who looked back. He was consumed. He had dark thoughts. He couldn't even bring himself to pray for his mother because he refused to address a God who had allowed his mother to die while evil men lived.

"Need a ride?" the carriage driver asked.

"To Palermo."

"Palermo? That's some ways. It'll cost you quite a bit."

"I have the money." He climbed into the back of the carriage, and the driver snapped the reins.

He had collected the money from the bodies of two dead men.

The boy he used to be would have been ashamed of such actions. Not anymore. Not after spending days wondering where his next meal might come from, not after he'd worn the same shirt day after day. Not after half the city had ignored him as a pariah for his association with a murderer and his clan. It was survival now, plain and simple. The dead didn't need it, and he did. After all, the dead had deserved it.

A sense of relief came over him when he closed his eyes and remembered the day he'd killed them.

The Armettas were known as fighters. Strong men who were not to be trifled with, and not simply because of their connections. But after Frederico's brains were scattered across the dinner table, his little brother had sobbed like a baby boy. He had actually begged Turridru for his life. After receiving teasing gunshots to the shoulder and thigh, he had simply requested a quick death.

Turridru consented, and put a bullet through his eyebrow. It was better than he deserved, Turridru told himself. But at least their womenfolk wouldn't be able to give them an open casket. They would have to be buried in dishonor, just like Turridru's mother.

For the first time since her death, Turridru was able to breathe. He basked in the aroma of their deaths. After taking what he wanted off of them, he had actually sat down at the table and rested for a moment. He took the time to clean the gunpowder of his revolver with the tablecloth.

His heart was beating so slowly, he could have gone to sleep. But he couldn't stop looking at their bodies.

It was kind of beautiful, in a way. He had never felt better. Never. The power, the sweet power to take life. He'd controlled the world in that moment. He was the Roman emperor, giving a thumbs-down to gladiatorial combatants. He had felt powerless when Alonzo abandoned him. He had felt powerless when his family had to scrape their money together to provide a decent meal. He had felt powerless when his mother screamed from her labor pains. But as he analyzed the blood smeared across picture frames, Frederico's broken body sprawled over the spilled pasta bowls, the blood that collected in the cracks of the wooden floor…then he felt powerful.

"So why are you going to Palermo?" the driver asked, distracting him from his pleasant memories.

"What?"

"Why are you going to Palermo?"

Turridru thought about his answer. To escape law enforcement, which would be howling for his arrest. To escape the rest of the Armetta clan, which would be howling for his blood.

"I'm going to seminary," he said. Every time he said it, he had to laugh. It was rather funny. But there was nowhere in the world safer for him than in the robes of a holy man.

"You going to be a priest?" Turridru ignored the man. He had nothing left to say.

Just like killing. Just like taking money from the dead. Just like burying his mother and saying goodbye to his father. It was survival. Going to seminary was staying alive.

It was letting all of Sicily forget about him. And when the time was right, he would make them regret it.

SONNY

The clerk greeted Sonny when he entered Shapiro's Used Clothes, but the man turned sour when he saw him.

"Look, I told you yesterday, I don't want no part of it." The man waved his hands and rolled up his sleeves. "Go on. Fellas have been trying to shake down my joint for years. Get out of here."

Sonny had been following Maranzano's orders for a few weeks now, but it hadn't gotten any easier. He was shut down immediately on most of his first attempts. It wasn't until Maranzano suggested that Sonny take Antonello along with him did the shopkeepers begin to comply. Sonny felt he was playing dress-up and pretending to be someone else. Just like any good actor on broadway, he was beginning to perfect the lines, rehearsing them in his free time. But he never got comfortable repeating them.

"Mr. Shapiro, I wanted to offer you a legitimate opportunity. This isn't a shakedown."

"Says you, fella. I've never had to pay for legitimate opportunities."

"Unfortunately, Mr. Shapiro, the *only* kind of opportunity is one you pay for." Sonny approached the counter and leaned against it, ignoring the man's hostile eyes and clenched fists. "My friends are wealthy and powerful. In times like these, you might need to rely on someone else."

"I've never relied on nobody else. The other business owners have told me what you're doing, and I want no part of it. You hear me, *stronzo?*" He gave an unkind gesture as Sonny shrugged.

"Mind if I take a look around?"

"I'd rather you leave." A bell jingled as the door behind Sonny opened. Antonello entered, as planned, but Sonny ignored him.

"I think you're making a mistake, Mr. Shapiro. I wish we could be friends."

Antonello pushed over a mannequin and then began ripping shirts from their hangers. At first slowly, and then increasing his tempo.

"*Vaffanculo,*" the man cursed them. He stepped out from behind the counter and walked toward Antonello, who straightened in response, ready for a fight.

"Go on, tough guy," Antonello said. The man sized him up, and determined correctly that he was no match, and stepped back. Antonello returned to his destruction. Shapiro lowered his head.

Sonny brandished a roll of one hundred dollar bills, and stamped the floor to draw the man's attention. He counted through them flippantly and then returned the wad to his pocket.

"Men like this will always exist, and problems are sure to arise. Don't you want friends to help you in hard times?" Sonny increased his volume over Antonello's tumult.

"You son of a whore," Shapiro said, his words hot. Antonello ripped a blouse marked with a twenty-five-cent price tag.

"That's not very nice, Mr. Shapiro. That's not the best way for us to begin our relationship."

"Alright. Alright, just call off your dog."

"That's enough, Antonello," Sonny said. Antonello straightened his jacket and departed.

"How much?"

"Standard fee is twenty-five dollars. To show you how reasonable we can be when you cooperate, let's make it twenty. You can use the five dollars to repair the damages."

Shapiro opened the cash register and handed Sonny what was owed.

"I appreciate your trust in me, Mr. Shapiro. I'll be back next month for your next fee." *Just like collecting premiums,* he told himself.

"I don't want to see you until then."

"I assure you, you won't. Unless you have some trouble, or another investor comes by, like me." Sonny slid him a business card. "If so, you call me, and I'll straighten him out." He stared to leave, but paused. "My employer wants you to stay in business. If you don't, then he doesn't get paid. So if you happen to fall on hard times, I can help you. That's what this is about, Mr. Shapiro. One hand washes the other." He felt the tone of his voice change. He hoped what he said was true. He had believed it at first, but after being met with vehement resistance each time he entered a new business, he began to doubt himself.

Sonny left and lit a cigarette as he headed back to Antonello's car.

"Did he pay?" Antonello asked, following behind.

"Yeah, he paid." Sonny flipped through the bills to

ensure it was the correct amount. He knew the man probably needed the money more than he did. The only thing
that soothed his conscience was knowing that whatever was
left after Maranzano's cut was going directly into the hands
of his mother.

"We own half of Elizabeth Street now. What's left?"

"The other half." Sonny took a long drag, slipping into
Antonello's Model T.

"Shouldn't be difficult, after word gets around."

"Elizabeth street has never belonged to the Sicilians.
Others will come back around."

"Then we'll show 'em we plan on sticking around."
Antonello entered the car after he pump-started it.

Sonny pulled out a single dollar and handed it to him.

"Thanks for the help."

"No worries," Antonello said, and slapped his hand
away. "I'm hoping there will be a lot more than a single
simoleon if I stick around with you."

The car rambled forward, and Sonny counted the
money one more time, flipping through the bills like he
used to flip through cards. He hoped it was worth it. He
hoped he was making the right choice.

Williamsburg, Brooklyn—January 15, 1930

Sonny had never been summoned by Maranzano before.
He had heard others mention that they had received
similar invitations, but he wasn't familiar with the nature
of these meetings. As he waited outside of his new apart-

ment, he felt the same jitters that came before giving a speech in college.

He tried to think of reasons for Maranzano's invitation. Sonny had continued to work in protection, and had always given Maranzano his cut. He hoped he wasn't in trouble.

A black Lincoln pulled to a stop in front of him and flashed its headlights.

"Come on, before you let more snow in," the driver said as Sonny opened the door. Sonny didn't recognize him, and was confused when he didn't find Maranzano in the back seat.

"Where are we going?"

"To Mr. Maranzano's house," the man said, straining to see the road behind his windshield wipers. "Do you realize what kind of honor this is?"

Sonny considered before he answered. "I'm not sure what I'm being called for."

"It doesn't matter what it's for. Maranzano will tell you everything you need to know. But this is his private residence. He does his business meetings in Poughkeepsie, so this is personal. Be on your best behavior."

The driver was young and fashionable, with a strong jaw and a handsome face. But there was something about his demeanor that was challenging.

"Of course," Sonny said, hoping the driver would allow them to sit in silence.

"Name's Calogero. Calogero DiBennedeto." Sonny hadn't been sure the driver was even Italian, his English was so refined.

"Nice to meet you, Calogero." Sonny shifted to offer his hand, which wasn't accepted.

"No one calls me that. They call me Charlie Buffalo. Mr. Maranzano called me like he called you, and I had to leave my city. I live here now, and I serve him." Charlie honked his horn at some pedestrians crossing the street too slowly for his liking.

"I understand." Sonny had learned from watching Maranzano's other associates that, when addressed, it was always better to say little, and always in the affirmative.

"Do you know anything about what you're doing, College Boy? Do you understand this thing of ours?"

Sonny struggled to swallow and shifted in the leather seat.

"Not much." He figured this was the desired answer, but he knew enough about Maranzano's work from things he had picked up around Little Italy, and from overhearing his mother and father talking.

"It's more powerful that the Foresters, the Masons, the Sons of Italy, and all of your college fraternities combined." Sonny sat quietly and let him continue. "It stretches across the world. We're in every country in the world, except Japan. And you're just scraping the surface."

Charlie Buffalo turned to him, a glint of humor in his eyes.

"We will last as long as man itself."

Charlie cut the wheel, and the Lincoln pulled to a stop on Avenue J. "Go on in. This is where the old man lives."

Sonny stepped out into the snow and offered his thanks.

"I'll be waiting."

Sonny hesitated before the door, and shook as he knocked. He told himself it was the cold, but he knew he would be trembling just as much if it were burning like the Sicilian sun.

A woman answered the door and greeted him in Italian. She bowed and opened the door, expecting him.

"It is good to finally meet you, Vincente." He shook her hand delicately, and then she called for her husband.

"Vincente, I'm glad you've arrived. I was hoping you could make it before the snow piled up. I hope you're hungry?" Maranzano smiled and kissed his cheek. Seeing Maranzano, the object of his fear, was actually calming. Sonny found his shoulders relaxing and a smile stretching across his face.

"I am. It's hard for a man to cook for himself," Sonny said as Maranzano's wife took his coat.

"Where are my manners? This is Mrs. Elizabetta Maranzano." Sonny acknowledged her again. He couldn't imagine a more fitting woman for his mentor. She exuded grace, her face etched with quiet wisdom and motherly love. She was as beautiful as her husband was handsome. "And this little fellow is my youngest, Marco." He patted the head of the toddler clutching to his leg.

"Hey there, pal." Sonny knelt and offered a handshake to the nervous young man.

Two other young men appeared, and Maranzano introduced his other sons, one of whom was not much younger than Sonny. They were all dressed in nice clothes, and carried themselves like young aristocrats. They were clones of Maranzano himself, in various stages of adolescence.

"It's nice to meet you all. I appreciate this invitation." Sonny lowered his head, ashamed of his humble appearance in their home. He was hoping he might now be afforded a reason for the call.

"I'll return to the kitchen. I hope you like *pasta alla Norma*," Elizabetta said.

"Yes, ma'am. It's my favorite dish."

"Vincente, let's step into my study for a moment," Maranzano said. Sonny followed him, noticing that even despite the presence of three young men in the house, everything was austere. It was nothing like the messy tenement he and his siblings were raised in.

They entered a study where a large desk was the focal point. Behind it was an impressive library to rival the one in Maranzano's office. The host propped himself up against his desk beside a large marble bust of an ancient Roman.

"Marcus Aurelius," Maranzano said, noticing Sonny's gaze. "He is my hero. I idealize him. His strength, his self-control, his wisdom. It was after him my youngest was named."

"I might have to visit the library and pick up a copy of his writings."

Maranzano strode to the bookshelf and handed Sonny a book.

"His famous meditations. May they be as good to you as they have been to me," Maranzano said with the smile of knight passing the torch to his squire.

"Thank you, sir."

"There is a reason I have called you here, Vincente." Maranzano finally became serious, and he met Sonny's eyes. Sonny's heart began to race again. "I trust you. I value you…" Maranzano said, comfortable with the silence that followed. "I want you to be near to me. I need good men."

"I appreciate you saying that, Mr. Maranzano." Sonny flushed.

"You are a good man. You are strong. In many ways, you remind me of myself." His voice faded, and for a moment, they both listened to Maranzano's grandfather clock in the corner. "There are many things that you do not know. I have not told you because I have not wanted to involve you in my own concerns and fears; you have enough of your own. But now I need you."

Maranzano's brows lowered, and Sonny saw vulnerability in his face for the first time.

"I am here for you, Mr. Maranzano. Whatever you ask," Sonny said, and meant it.

"Now, I only ask that you allow me to speak. That you let me pour my burdens on you."

"Of course."

Maranzano gestured for him to take a seat in a leather lounging chair in the corner of the room. He joined him in the chair adjacent to him.

"You are an integral part of a society that you do not know exists. It was your father's society, one he helped build and develop. He cultivated it and watered it as a farmer does a seed. He did so first in Castellammare del Golfo. But you know how we Sicilians are. Our brotherhood is not the least dissipated by distance. Many of our people work together, in unison, here in America. In New York."

"I am honored to be a part of this, Mr. Maranzano," Sonny said, embarrassed that his voice was shaky.

"But we are much larger than New York. We span the United States. And there are those who hate us for what we have built; they seek to take it from us. There is an important man in New York who seeks to control everything, an incomplete man, a tyrant. He has attempted to persuade one of our own in Detroit to betray us, by killing an important brother in Chicago. You met this man at my dinner, Joseph Aiello. Fortunately, our friend Gaspar Milazzo in Detroit refused this bribe, and alerted us."

"Tell me who this man is, Mr. Maranzano," Sonny said, immediately feeling naive. Maranzano didn't mock him, though.

"I admire your courage. In due time. Do you know why the tyrant did this?"

"Because he wanted what you have built."

"What we have built, Vincente. He wants it all. He won't rest until he has it. He seeks to drive a wedge between us, separate us. And division is always a precursor to subjugation. He plans to move on us. And we need good men, Vincente. Offering protection to our brothers in Little Italy will not give us enough to protect ourselves."

"What do you ask of me, Mr. Maranzano?"

"That you stay close to me. That you learn from me, and fight by my side if the need arises."

"I would be honored, Mr. Maranzano."

They stood and embraced. Maranzano clapped his back.

"I am relieved to hear it. I have received much bad news as of late, but this makes up for all of it. But for now, let's put all that aside and eat the food of the old country."

Little Italy, Manhattan—January 19, 1930

Sonny had never liked cemeteries. Sicilians were naturally superstitious, and Sonny had inherited his mother's overwhelming respect and fear of the dead.

Most Sicilians didn't make it a habit of visiting the graves of their fallen loved ones. They could pray for the Virgin Mary to intercede on his behalf just as well from their living rooms. No need to disturb their rest.

But Sonny felt compelled. He wanted to be as close to his father as he could.

At Old St. Patrick's, he paused before the grave that read: "Alonzo Consentino—beloved father and husband. 1884–1928." It still made his knees buckle. It burned to see the words in stone.

"Hi, Papà," Sonny said, placing a few dandelions in front of the grave. "I stopped by Ferrara and bought you a cannoli. I got you a new pack of cards too. I'm sure you and all the saints have been wearing your first deck out."

He set down the cards and the to-go box beside the flowers. He felt foolish. He was talking to the wind.

His nose began to run, but he told himself it was because of the cold.

"I really miss you, Papà." He sniffled. And lowered his head. As the tears began to spill over his eyelashes, he remembered how his father would comfort him as a child. "I could really use you right now. You always knew what to say. You always knew what I needed to hear, even if I didn't listen." He stared at the headstone, unable to look at the earth beneath it.

"You said you would be here for me, Papà. You said you would protect us. Forever and always, that's what you said." Sonny struggled to catch his breath. "Well, where are you now?"

To his surprise, he felt angry. Alonzo had left them. It wasn't his fault, but he was gone. Or, maybe it was his fault.

"I didn't know you were living that way, Papà. You could have told me. You should have told me. I could have protected you. You lied. You made me think..." Sonny smothered his tears with the scarf wrapped around his neck. He was struck with the memory of his father giving him the money to attend Columbia. He could almost hear his father's voice, calm and soothing, saying that he'd done what he had to for his family. Because he loved them, forever and always.

The anger dissipated to a cold emptiness. Sonny stepped forward and bent down to kiss the headstone. It was freezing against his lips.

"I love you, Papà."

Back at his Williamsburg apartment complex, Sonny ascended the stairs one at a time. He was in no rush. There was nothing to go back to but an empty apartment. He sometimes regretted leaving his mother's tenement, but knew it was best to distance his mother from the things he was getting involved with. As he fumbled through his keys to find the freshly minted key for his third-floor apartment, the door opened beside him.

Startled, he let out an exhale of relief when he found only a young woman standing there.

"Oh, sorry," she said, noticing that she had scared him. "My dad is convinced he heard knocking. You hear anything?" Sonny thought her accent was Irish, and her pale complexion and freckles seemed to prove it. Her voice was delicate; it warmed Sonny at the core.

"No, probably my footsteps. I've never been very light on my feet." Sonny forced a smile. He tried to open the door but couldn't take his eyes off of her. Long fire-red locks of hair fell over her shoulders in waterfall curls. She wore no makeup, but her cheeks were rosy from embarrassment. She looked at him curiously but unassuming.

"You look like you're about frozen. Is it that cold out there?"

"Colder than us Sicilians like it."

"I'm only half. My father is Irish, but I still can't stand the cold."

He analyzed the thin chemise she wore and the coat over her shoulders. "Are you going out or just getting in?" he asked, immediately regretting it. That was none of his business. "Sorry, I was only wondering if you had to face the weather. Sure is nasty out there."

He liked to think of himself as at least relatively charming, but he stumbled over his words like the nervous idiot he was when he'd met Rachel at his first college dance.

"I'm in for the night." She smiled at his chagrin. "I don't go out much. I feel like an old maid sometimes."

To his relief, he finally got the door to his apartment open. He almost stepped in before stopping.

"My name is Sonny." He stepped toward her and held out a hand. "I just moved in a few days ago."

She accepted it, modestly holding the coat at the center of her chest with her other hand.

"I'm Millie." She had a far stronger grip than most gals, and maintained fixed eye contact like Sonny had been taught to do. "And I've lived here for a lot longer than I'd like."

"It's nice to meet you." Sonny was already kicking himself for sounding so sheepish.

"It's nice to meet someone who doesn't insult us for being Irish." She shrugged. "We aren't very welcome around here."

"I've never cared much about any of that," he said, lying. Sicilian culture was tight knit, and he had assented to that. But pretty girls were always a clear exception to the rule. He didn't really care where Millie was from.

"Well, then, maybe you'd like to join my father and me

for dinner?" She tilted her head. She held eye contact. Resolved, tender, captivating.

"Maybe some other time. I appreciate that."

"Just let me know, Sonny. It's nice to meet a friendly face." She smiled at him and then went back into her apartment.

Sonny stepped into his apartment, which suddenly felt just as cold to him as the outside.

VICO

"I'm not gonna bother to count this. But if you gyp me, I'll be back. And I'll come in hot." Petrelli patted the restaurant owner's chest. He said it with enough sarcasm to get away with it as a joke, but Vico knew he meant it. They stood in the smoky kitchen of Mezzogiorno's Eatery while Cargo and a few others snuck in four crates of brown plaid.

Restaurants always preferred scotch, and the Gap and his crew were always more than happy to satisfy their needs, for three times the cost.

"If you gyp me, I won't be purchasing from you anymore. The last delivery was three bottles short."

Enzo and the Gap shot Vico a derisive look, which he plainly ignored. He hadn't wanted to get into bootlegging anyhow; of course, he was going to sample the wares. "Our biggest buyer works for us," they had joked. Sometimes, the others did get irritated with him for sneaking a bottle here and there, but he'd toss them half his cut and they wouldn't mention it again.

"I assure you we double-checked it this time."

"Yeah, we'll see. Take them to the cellar," the chef shouted angrily and flicked his wrists at Cargo.

The eggplant frying in garlic burned in Vico's nose and made him feel sick. He was anxious to leave.

All of this felt like a distraction to him, a distraction from his true intentions. "I didn't get involved to make money, Enzo," he had said when his brother continued to sing about what they were bringing in. "Well, I did," his twin had replied. "Bide your time, and we'll both get what we want."

Vico had been biding his time, though. For too long. LaDuca was probably worm food by now, and he still didn't know anything new about his father's killer. He thought he had been pretty patient. But the next time the Gap or Cargo cracked wise, he might just snap.

"Hey, who's Doyle?" a waiter cried, leaning into the kitchen through saloon doors.

"Who's asking?" Vico asked, his guard rising.

"Someone's on the horn for you. It's in the front." The boy exited, expecting him to follow.

"Who would be calling me here?" Vico leaned in and whispered to the Gap.

"Someone worried about who's listening at the Rainbow Gardens." Vico hesitated, so Petrelli continued. "Go on."

"Yeah, who's this?" he asked, tucking the phone to his ear and turning his back to the packed restaurant.

"Someone you should address more respectfully."

Vico's stomach dropped.

"Mr. Reina."

"You guessed it."

"What can I do for you?" He was expecting to hear that someone else needed to get buried. If that was the case, he would comply. Maybe one more body would lead him to the information he wanted.

"I just wanted to let you know something," Reina said before pausing.

"Yeah?" Vico worried the call had dropped.

"I wanted to make sure you were listening. The books are about to open, Doyle. You're going to be brought in. Enzo and Cargo too, if we have the room. I'm going to bat for all three of you."

"Thank you, sir." Vico's hands began to perspire, and he squeezed the receiver firmly to ensure he didn't drop it.

"Then you'll get the information you want. What you do with that is your business. But I don't want any headaches, Doyle. Understand me?" Reina's voice was firm, severe, from the other end of the line.

"I understand."

"You thought I had forgotten. By Gaetano Reina is a man of his word. If you do anything foolish, you'll be the one to pay. But I said I'd tell you, and I will. You just have to get made first. Understand?" Something about Reina's voice told Vico he was doubtful.

"I do."

"Buy a new suit. And lay off the hooch. You'll be summoned when we're ready."

The line clicked without a formal goodbye.

Vico hung up the receiver and straightened his coat. He felt acutely aware of the revolver tucked into his waist-line. And for the first time in a long time, he felt a smile materialize on his face.

GAETANO "TOMMY" REINA

Southwest Bronx, New York—February 26, 1930

Gaetano Reina fumbled through his keys as the girl kissed his neck.

"Come on, want to stay for one more, daddy?" she asked. He sighed and leaned away from her.

"No, I need to get home." He didn't really like sleeping with these bimbos from the Rainbow Gardens, but with six children at home, he couldn't get a moment alone with his wife if he wanted to. And he had to have something.

He had a high-stress job, after all.

He was hoping that after LaDuca got whacked, he could relax a bit, but that was just wishful thinking. It had been two years since the fat bastard was buried, and there was always someone else trying to muscle in on the empire he'd built. Or, someone in his own organization threatening to send it crumbling to the ground.

He handed the girl a wad of money, and she relented. It was what she wanted, after all.

"Keep your mouth shut about this, okay, kid?" He patted her cheek and turned to leave.

He exited out on to Sheridan Avenue, the city still pulsing with energy. Traffic zoomed past him, and the smell of spoiled garbage choked his lungs. It was the city he loved, but sometimes he wondered why.

He finally managed to find the right key and crossed the street to where his Pierce-Arrow was parked. In the streetlights behind him, he saw shadowy legs approaching quickly.

He broke into a dead sprint, not worried about looking like a fool. Gaetano Reina didn't take chances. He grabbed the door handle and jimmied the lock, but gave up as the footsteps approached.

A shotgun burst behind him, the glass of his car shattering before him. He jolted from a few stray pellets but didn't stop to lick his wounds. Reina reached into the car and unlocked it.

He swung the door open as the second shot erupted.

He slumped to the ground, his body hot but numb, blood spilling over the threads of his new suit.

He crawled behind the door and tried to force his guts back inside.

The gunman stepped over him, a fedora covering his face.

Reina looked up and snarled. He wanted to tell the man to go to hell, but he was drowning on his own blood.

"Mr. Masseria sends his regards." The assailant placed the sawed-off shotgun against Reina's forehead.

Reina leaned against it.

"Do it," he managed to say with all the wind left in his body. The gunman shrugged, and then complied.

ENZO

Vico and Enzo burst into the Rainbow Gardens like a shotgun blast, silencing the entire room except for the records playing.

"Is it true? Did they get the old man?" Enzo said as they approached Gagliano. His clothing was uncharacteristically disheveled, and his eyes were puffy and pink.

"Yeah, they got him," Gagliano said, the realization settling in for both of them. "Reina is gone."

Vico's fists were clenched, and his face was twisting in rage. Enzo tapped his arm to calm him.

"What's our next move?" Enzo asked.

"Tell me who did it. Tell me who did this, and I'll kill 'em all," Vico said.

Gagliano grabbed him by the arm and led him to the back of the bar. "You better keep your mouth shut, Doyle. You're gonna get us all killed." He held a finger to his lips, and his eyes darted rapidly around the room. "We don't know who we can trust right now."

"Was it Masseria? Did Joe the Boss call the hit?" Enzo asked.

Gagliano nodded and helped himself to a top-shelf bottle of bootlegged liquor. "We can assume he was behind it in some way or another."

"Then tell me where Joe the Boss is. I'll put him down," Vico said, absent emotion.

"We already told you once, kid, it doesn't work like that." Gagliano winced as he took a pull from the bottle. He offered it to Vico and Enzo, but they both refused. He waved them on, and they followed him into the storage room.

It was dark, with only a single stray beam of light pouring in from a windowpane. There was a man strung up from the ceiling like a prized deer just shot.

"Still working on him," a man gasped, clearly exasperated from the sheer effort of torturing a man. He looked like an accountant with large spectacles and a mustard-colored button-up. But his victim's blood was splattered across his shirt and face, and caked over his hands.

Enzo knew who he was. He was Tommy "Three Finger" Brown, although no one called him that to his face. His real name was Mr. Lucchese, and was one of Reina's most loyal associates.

"We've been trying to get answers out of the little prick for hours," Gagliano said, pointing to the victim.

Lucchese plopped down on the single metal chair beside the victim and dabbed the sweat from his head with a handkerchief. "He's out cold. I'll get back to work when he comes to."

"Who is he?" Enzo asked.

"The driver. Some of our guys saw him trying to get away after the hit. He knows who did it."

"What have you been doing? Just working him over?" Vico asked, sizing up the victim's wounds.

"Yeah. With a steel pipe." Lucchese chuckled.

Vico stepped toward him and flicked the man's eyelids. When the man flinched, he turned around and smiled.

"He's faking it."

"You learn any medieval shit over there in France you could put to good use now?" Gagliano asked, swaying from the effects of the booze.

"Actually, yeah." Vico pulled a dagger from his boot and kneeled beside the man. Suddenly, the captive began to squirm.

"Wha-wha-what are you doing?" he slurred, his lips busted and his mouth swollen.

"I just want to persuade you to help us out." Vico slid the tip of his dagger under the man's big toenail. He turned to his associates and pointed to the insertion and attempted to explain it. "Just like we did to the Jerries. You start slow, just under the big toe, and then…" It wasn't true. Vico had never tortured anyone. But everyone was willing to believe just about anything from soldiers, and most importantly, his victim was willing to believe it.

He slowly carved the sharpened dagger downward. The captive moaned and screamed. Lucchese hurried to replace the gag in the driver's mouth. "You just cut down. We're gonna flay the first three layers of the skin on the soles of his feet. Every step this bastard takes for the rest of his life, he's gonna remember this moment," Vico continued. The victim's moans echoed off the walls, tears ripping from his eyes.

After Vico's dagger had traced the edge of the victim's footprint, the man began to shake his head vehemently.

"Ready to talk?" Gagliano asked. He continued to nod. "Take off the gag."

"Okay…okay…the two guys that done it were Pasqualino Manzelli—they call him Patsy. And Joseph Ronaldo."

Enzo and Vico both looked to Gagliano to see if he knew the men. He nodded his head.

"What else do you know?" Vico asked calmly, like he was comforting a child.

"Nothing."

Vico continued to cut at the man's foot.

"Please, stop! I was just the driver!"

"Who ordered it?"

The man, crying, stopped to consider it. "Come on, he'll kill me!"

Vico grabbed the man's legs forcefully and cut deep.

"Masseria! Masseria ordered it!"

Vico pulled out the dagger and cleaned it on the man's shirt.

"Good." Gagliano bit his thumb nail. "At least we know."

Lucchese cut the rope, and the captive slumped to the ground, barley able to roll his face off the ground.

"We going to war?" Enzo exhaled.

"In time. We ain't ready yet." Gagliano led Vico and Enzo from the room as Lucchese mounted the man and began to strangle him.

"We have to do something," Vico said.

"We will. But we have to wait for the right time." Gagliano, nervous now that he knew who had killed his friend, drained the remainder of his liquor.

"Reina was going to tell me what happened to Alonzo Consentino. We had a deal. Can you tell me?" Vico said, getting to the heart of the matter.

"No can do." Gagliano burped.

"Why not?" Vico's voice was low and threatening. It even intimidated Enzo.

"Because I would get killed." Gagliano looked underneath the bar counter for another bottle.

"Who would kill you? The person who killed Alonzo? You won't have to worry about that," Enzo said. He immediately regretted it, fearing Gagliano would be suspicious. He wasn't, though, as he was too drunk to care.

"No. I'm not sure who would do it. Your pal Alonzo must have been a big deal, Doyle. Hell of a barber, maybe." He chuckled. "They had to take it before the general assembly to get clearance to kill him. That means if I say a word about it to guys who aren't connected, I'll end up in garbage bag floating in the Hudson."

"Connected?" Vico asked.

"Yeah, brought into the family officially."

"I killed LaDuca. I made my bones, and I was supposed to be brought in," Vico said. Enzo nodded, feeling the same way.

"And you were going to be brought in. Both of you. Cargo too. But after the old man got whacked, we can't do anything about it. I received word this morning." He finally turned and paid attention to their queries. "Joe the Boss has appointed a boss for our family. Some old greaseball named Joseph Pinzolo. He isn't even one of ours. They said the books are closed. No new members." Gagliano shrugged, disappointment and resentment present in every word.

"We all know you're the boss. We'll follow you," Enzo said.

"Yeah, well…most of the boys don't feel that way. They don't want to start any trouble with Masseria." Suddenly, he slammed the bar counter with his fist and pointed at them. "But listen to me: this is my family. I am the boss here. I'm gonna kill that old bastard Pinzolo, and then I'm going for Joe the Boss. You hear me?"

"We hear ya," Enzo said for them both.

"If you want in, if you want your information, you kill Pinzolo. When he's dead, I'll see what I can do."

PATSY MANZELLI

Northwest Bronx, New York—March 12, 1930

"Dinner was good, dear," Patsy Manzelli said, dabbing his lips with a napkin.

"Thank you," his wife said. The dinner had passed in near silence. Even his two daughters could sense that something was wrong.

"Girls, have you finished your schoolwork?"

"Yes, Papà," one said.

"I'll finish it in the morning, Papà," his eldest, Rosita, said, keeping her eyes away from him.

"Ah-ah, I don't think so. Go on. Finish it tonight."

Both of the girls stood from the table.

"Don't you have something to say, girls?" he asked. They returned to the table and kissed their mother.

"Thank you, Mamma," they said in unison, and walked off, anxious to get away from the discomfort of the dinner table.

"Can I help with the dishes?" he asked. His wife looked at him, perplexed. The offer was uncharacteristic of him.

"Who are you? And what have you done with my husband?" She was serious, but he laughed anyway.

"Just an offer."

"No, I can take care of it."

He rose and kissed her head. He lingered. "*Mio tesoro*," she said, placing both of her hands around his face, asking him to stay.

He kissed her again and walked away, to his study, where he felt most of his life was spent.

He sat at his desk and poured himself a small glass of scotch. The bottle had been gifted to him by Joe Masseria himself, after his crew successfully moved $100,000 worth of liquor from Canada.

He reached across his desk and put a record on.

He sat back in his chair and breathed deeply, as peacefully as he could imagine, as Act Three of Puccini's *Turadot* graced his ears. He had first heard Puccini's music on a trip to Milan in 1926, and it had been a foundational element of his life ever sense. He told his wife it wasn't just music—it was a way of life. Sometimes he cried while he listened, and he didn't bother to hide it.

He wasn't sad about the way things had turned out. He had made his choices. He had done the best he could. He would be leaving his family with one hundred times what they had arrived in America with, more than any of his compatriots would leave their families with.

But he had made some mistakes along the way. First and foremost was hiring that deadbeat to be his driver. He should have known that he would sing like a canary if he was caught. And that was exactly what had happened. The driver had talked, and spilled everything. He had ratted on himself, Ronaldo, and even Masseria.

Patsy took a sip of his favorite scotch, savoring the bitter smoothness.

He had brought the driver in, he had vouched for him. Now that he had talked, Patsy's days were numbered. Masseria would probably order the hit himself, if he hadn't already.

But Masseria's hit men would probably be too late.

Gagliano's men would most likely be there first. They already found Ronaldo and left him riddled with bullets.

White headlights spilled in from the window facing the road.

Patsy turned back to his record and increased the volume, turning it up as loud as he could. But he could still hear the car doors shut and the approaching voices.

Whoever they were, he was determined to make sure they'd be disappointed. He wouldn't give them the satisfaction.

He reached into the drawer of his desk, pulled out a revolver, and ensured a bullet was chambered.

They'd done their research, surely. They knew where he sat in the evenings after dinner. They were probably approaching the window already.

Finishing the scotch, Patsy smiled at the framed family picture on the wall above the mantlepiece.

He waited until Puccini reached the climax of his song.

"I will win, I will win," he sang along.

Then he put the revolver inside his mouth, and pulled the trigger.

SASA PARRINO

It was approximately 2:49 when Sasa Parrino and Gaspar Milazzo left the Michigan Central Station. Sasa knew this because he looked at his pocket watch every few moments, only raising his eyes to check his surroundings.

Milazzo couldn't have appeared any more careless. He had been dubbed the "peacemaker" for his ability to stop conflicts between the different families in Detroit, but for months, tension had been rising like a tide. Sasa, who had only left Brooklyn for Detroit six months before, had brought the anxious concern of a New Yorker with him.

"Let's grab a bite to eat, I'm starvin'," Milazzo said, pointing to a white brick building across the street, "Fish Market" painted on a sign in big blue letters.

"Is it any good?" Sasa asked, knowing he wouldn't be able to stomach much, no matter what it tasted like.

"The best in Detroit. I had Paulie make a reservation for us. Back room should be empty."

Milazzo was the first to step out into the road, throwing up a middle finger as the halted traffic blared their horns.

"How we doin' today, Sammy?" Milazzo said as the owner waddled to greet them.

"Blessed and healthy, Gaspar. Good to see ya." He kissed Milazzo on the cheek and gave Sasa a nod. "Follow me." He led them to the back room where a single table was set with a snow-white tablecloth and dishes that looked as expensive as the entire worn-out building. "It's all yours. I got some tilapia cooking up, caught this morning."

Milazzo reached into his suit pocket and brandished a roll of dollar bills. He slapped it into Sammy's hand without counting it.

"Take a seat, kid. I'll pick up the tab," Milazzo said. Sammy's assistant uncorked a bottle of wine and poured them both a glass. Sasa checked his watch again: 2:57.

Someone put on a record, and a beautiful Italian sonata filled the room.

"You ever miss New York?" Milazzo sat back in his chair and took off his cream-colored fedora.

"Yeah," Sasa said. He had been waiting on word to return since he had arrived in Detroit. Although born in Castellammare del Golfo, Sasa found anything outside of Brooklyn foreign.

"I know I do. Somethin' about Gotham. Detroit just doesn't have it." Milazzo fiddled with his diamond cuff links.

Sasa took a gulp of his wine, hoping it might calm his nerves. It was 3:01. One hour and fifty-nine minutes until the two of them had their scheduled meeting with Big Chet LaMare and his West Side gang.

"Something is about to break in New York, though. You know that, right?" Milazzo asked.

"I've heard the rumors. What have you heard?" Sasa

said, fearing that Milazzo knew something he didn't. Sasa's brother, Joe, was an important man among the Castellammarese in Brooklyn. If a war popped off, Joe would certainly wind up involved.

"Our people back home...they don't back down. And that Manhattan boss, Masseria, he's getting too big for his britches. He won't like it when we don't get down on bended knee."

"Cola can settle things down," Sasa said, referring to the boss of the Castellammarese Borgata, Nicolo Shiro, who he had known well in New York.

Milazzo shook his head. "Old Shiro has lost his marbles. Gone soft. He doesn't run shit anymore. My old pal Vito Bonventre is the real mover. He and Salvatore Maranzano are the ones calling the shots, and they aren't gonna let Masseria get the best of 'em. So we go to war, and there's gonna be a lot of blood." Milazzo shrugged, resigned to their fate.

The fat chef entered with his assistant and placed two plates on the table, a mound of *pesce spada* on each.

"Thanks, Sammy," Milazzo said. He dug in, moaning with each bite. "Better than sex."

Sasa picked at his fish and vegetables abstemiously, careful not to offend either the chef or his own stomach.

A bell jingled from the entrance. Someone had entered. Sasa turned to the door like a frightened deer, but Milazzo was unperturbed.

"I told Sammy no one is allowed in. He'll turn them 'round," he said through a mouthful of swordfish.

"Yeah, but what if—" The door to the back room busted open, and two masked men entered.

A sawed-off shotgun blasted, the noise ringing off the walls. A bloody mist filled the air as Sasa pushed away from the table, collapsing on the floor beside his chair.

Milazzo hit the ground, a gaping hole the size of a cannon ball in his chest. He gagged on the swordfish wedged in his throat until the gunmen stepped over to Milazzo and shot again, and Milazzo's face dissolved into chunks of skull and brain matter.

Sasa reached into his belt and pulled out a pistol. Then another gunshot ignited. He felt his teeth shatter as a bullet passed through either side of his jaw.

Sasa scurried to his feet, pain suddenly burning hot from two more bullets that ripped through his lower back.

He dropped the pistol and tried to cover his face, trembling like an epileptic and gasping for air like a fish out of water. The gunman with the pistol stood over him.

Sasa lost control of his bowels and his bladder as he waited for the shot. He looked up when it didn't arrive. The gunman standing over him smiled and met his eyes.

"See you in hell, Parrino," he said, his finger tightening on the trigger.

BUSTER

Westchester County, New York—June 1, 1930

"Come on, Maria, put that down! It weighs more than you do." Buster laughed as he hurried to take the box from Maria's arms. Ever since they had begun moving into their new apartment in Westchester, Maria had been determined to carry the heaviest boxes. He was equally determined to stop her, but she was stubborn.

"Hush, you silly man. Leave me alone." She was flustered and panting, her hair in an uncharacteristic mess. He had downgraded to an undershirt and suspenders, but was still burning up. It made their first night in their shared home uncomfortable.

"I'm here to take care of that. You do the decorating stuff, I'm not good at that." He pried the box from her hands and carried it into their bedroom.

Setting it down, he turned to admire her. Even in an old summer dress, she was as lovely as she had been on their wedding day. They had tried to make it a quiet affair, inviting her mother and brothers and only a very few close friends of his. Before it was over, though, many of his New York associates had stopped by to visit. Maria was surprised to find such thick envelopes in her bridal purse by the end of the afternoon, perhaps even suspicious, but she didn't raise any questions or complain about it.

The extra cash would cover their first year's rent, and it had allowed him to select a nice place away from the city, away from those very associates. So he didn't complain either.

"You look beautiful," he said. Irritated and disbelieving, she shook her head.

"Don't lie to me, Buster."

"No, really." He chuckled. The more flustered she became, the more he laughed. "You're the most beautiful girl in New York."

"Say that again with Clara Bow in the room. Now stop pining and help me." He swept her up in his arms, and held her until she exhaled and hugged him back.

She accepted a kiss, less eagerly than on their wedding night, but not without a flush of desire.

The phone rang behind him, disrupting them both.

"Damn it." He let her go, knowing the moment was over.

"Who could that be? I haven't even told anyone the number."

"I had to give it to some of my associates," he said, hurrying to pick it up. "Hello?" There was silence for a moment on the other end of the line.

"Buster Domingo?"

"Yeah, it's me."

"Write this down." The voice was deep and monotone,

serious enough to pique his interest. He grabbed a notepad and a sharpened pencil and flipped to a blank page.

"Go ahead."

"One Hundred and Twenty-First Street, Poughkeepsie, New York. Be there by seven sharp." Buster looked at his watch, realizing he would be pushing it even if he left immediately.

"Got it." The line clicked, and he hung up.

"Who was that?" Maria put a hand on her hip.

"A work call, I got to go." He pulled down his suspenders and hurried to put on a shirt.

"Emergency piano lesson?" she teased.

"Real funny. My other work," he said. They had never discussed his various streams of income. With a brother like Enzo, it made sense that she valued discretion. She didn't ask questions, and that suited him just fine. He didn't want to involve her in any way.

He turned from the door and returned to give her a quick kiss.

"I'll take the Buick," he said.

She smiled. "Damn right you will." He had given her the keys to his Model A as a wedding gift. His friends called him odd for it, and laughed at the thought of a dame driving a car like that. But he was happy to drive a junky 1907 Buick if it meant he got to see her driving the Ford with a big grin and the wind blowing through her hair.

"When will you be home?" she asked as his hand reached the doorknob.

"I'm not sure. Might be a while."

She stared at him, and to his surprise, she didn't seem angry.

"Buster, be safe. Okay?"

"Yeah, of course."

"Promise?"

"I promise." He blew her a kiss and turned to leave. He had never lied to her, but he wasn't sure if that was a promise he could keep.

SONNY

Sonny had never seen Maranzano like this. He had stuck by him for six months, following his every move, obeying his every order. Throughout that time, Maranzano had remained cautious, always believing that something was about to happen, something Sonny couldn't anticipate. When they finally received the news, Maranzano's demeanor changed drastically. He seemed relieved that he had been correct in his hypothesis that war was approaching, but like a general receiving marching orders, he realized what fate awaited them all.

They gathered in the same auditorium where they had once celebrated Mary's ascension. Many of the same faces were present, but the geniality was noticeably absent. The lights were dimmed to match the room's disposition.

"Stand close by me," Maranzano said to both Sonny and Joe Bonanno as they made their way through the whispering crowd. When he had called Sonny to let him know what had happened, he told him to bring Antonello. This surprised Sonny as much as anything, but Maranzano said they would need as much muscle as they could get.

They found their way to a designated table and took their seats. The room waited patiently.

"Don Maranzano, I came as soon as I heard," a man said, approaching Maranzano and kissing his cheek. To Sonny's surprise, when the man turned around, it was his brother-in-law. Maria's new husband, Buster.

They met eyes, and both were equally astonished to see the other there.

"Piano lessons not been going well?" Sonny asked, flushing with anger. He didn't want his sister being cared for by someone in this life.

"Stock market hit you that hard?" Buster retorted, finding a seat beside Maranzano. Sonny looked to Don Maranzano, searching for an explanation. Maranzano only waved to pacify him.

"Gentlemen, please find your seats," a man said, stepping to the center of the auditorium. He had to repeat himself several times before he was heard. His voice was frail and cracking.

Sonny had never met him, but the gentleman had to be the leader of their family, Cola Shiro. He was old, robust, and had a curling mustache that made him look like a nineteenth-century Bourbon king.

"Two of our own have been killed," he continued as the room finally hushed. "We have sent some of our people to Detroit to analyze the situation. At this point, it appears that our dear friend Gaspar Milazzo was gunned down as a result of a conflict that is confined to the state of Michigan."

Murmuring spread across the room.

"No!" Vito Bonventre said, louder than the rest.

"We have no reason to assume that Milazzo's death was connected in any way to our situation in New York." Shiro attempted to calm the room. "We must assume neutrality until we are given reason to believe otherwise."

Maranzano stood, and the room instantly fell silent. He waited for a moment, all eyes resting on him.

"Joe Parrino," he said, waiting until the man addressed stood from a table across the room, "your brother was killed in this attack as well. What do you think about our situation?"

Parrino was on the verge of tears. He looked down and shrugged his shoulders.

"I don't know. What am I supposed to make of it? It was an accident. He was with Milazzo, and if someone was trying to kill our friend, I know Sasa would have fought back. He didn't give them a choice but to fight him as well."

Angry whispers spread again, and Maranzano waited for total silence.

"I have been very troubled since I received this news. I sent a few men of my own to Detroit as soon as I heard, and the reports are damning. Our friend Gaspar Milazzo received two blasts from a shotgun. Your brother Sasa had six gunshot wounds."

The room erupted into a clamor, but still, Maranzano's voice was discernible above the tumult. "This was meant as an attack on our people! A message sent from Masseria!" The men began to roar. Shiro tried in vain to calm them, but eventually gave up and stood silently.

As soon as Maranzano raised a hand, the room stilled. "It is a blemish on the honor of the Castellammare!" Men around the room jumped to their feet and slammed their fists into the tables, Vito Bonventre leading the charge.

Maranzano assumed his seat.

"What would you have us do, Don Maranzano?" Cola Shiro asked, shuffling uncomfortably.

"Why do you ask me? I am only a soldier."

The debate continued for hours. Different men of honor around the room stood to offer their analysis of the situation. Many said that war with Masseria was hopeless. In terms of manpower and resources, Masseria dwarfed the scattered Castellammarese. He was Goliath to their David.

Others combated this, agreeing with Maranzano that they could not accept these insults any longer. Their own people were being eliminated, and something had to be done.

Throughout the rest of the discussion, Maranzano remained silent. He had said all that he needed to say. And from the look on his face, Sonny could tell that Maranzano was confident he had already won.

Williamsburg, Brooklyn—June 4, 1930

Sonny paused at the door and steadied the flowers in his hands. He attempted a breathing exercise he had learned in a Dale Carnegie public-speaking workshop he attended back in college. It didn't really work.

Resigned to his fate, he raised his fist. He knocked three times, carefully not to be too quiet or too loud.

He spent the next few moments contemplating whether he should drop the flowers and run, but Millie was already at the door.

"Well, hello Sonny." She smiled and batted her eyelashes unintentionally.

Sonny had been preparing the dialogue since breakfast, but now that her green eyes were peering into his, he forgot every word.

"Oh, here. I got you these." He extended the flowers, careful to watch how she reacted to them. He had spent hours at the florist, more indecisive about what to purchase than he was about trading stocks. Roses were too forward, he decided, so he'd purchased daisies instead. He was careful to ensure that there were a few orange and red ones included, which reminded him of her hair.

"They're lovely, Sonny, thank you," she said, raising them to inhale the aroma. He didn't say anything, hoping she'd continue. He wanted to hear her voice. Those few words left him wanting more. "I'll have to put them in a vase. Would you like to come in?"

"Who's that?" A thundering voice came from within the apartment before Sonny could reply.

Millie must have thought he looked spooked.

"That's just my father. He sounds meaner than he is."

"I wanted to see what you were doing this evening… and to ask you to come out with me," Sonny blurted out. He was really hoping she'd say yes before he was forced to enter.

"Who's this, then?" A man in stained overalls approached from behind Millie. Sonny assumed Millie's mother had gotten to know the milkman, because he couldn't believe a peach like Millie came from a hunch-backed brute like that.

"He's our neighbor, Papà."

"Well, we're eating dinner. And it's rude for him to interrupt." Sonny could tell what they were eating from the peas caught in his gray beard.

He kept his squinted eyes locked on Sonny, but didn't address him. Mille exhaled and rolled her eyes.

"I'm sorry, Sonny. Bad timing. Maybe another time?"

Her father grunted.

"Of course. Enjoy your dinner." Sonny tipped his hat and watched the door shut before him.

"Why'd you have to do that, Papà? He's a nice boy." The muffled voices came from the other side of the door. Sonny remained planted for a moment, but then admitted to himself that she wasn't coming back out.

He turned to the left and entered his own apartment. There was nothing better to do on a Wednesday evening, so he'd just clean the pistol Maranzano had given him and sit on the couch. Like always.

MILLIE

"He's a guinea. That's why! Greasy hair and fancy threads. He's up to no good," Millie's father, Patrick, said as he returned to his seat at the head of the long table. She took the seat beside him, all the other place mats empty.

"You think the worst of everyone. He was just being kind."

"What were those for, then, eh?" He pointed to the vase of flowers on the haberdasher.

"A kind gesture from a friendly neighbor."

"He wants you to spread your legs. And you'd do it if I weren't here, you whore."

"Patrick!" She threw her napkin down on the table and looked hard in his direction, but he looked away on command and took another pull from his flask. He knew just how to work her up, and just when to stop. She had her mother's temper in her, and she hadn't been gone long enough for him to forget how menacing that could be.

Both of her brothers had fled south to work the coal mines years before, and they'd said it was because of Patrick's drunken beatings, but the whip of their mother's broom wasn't much lighter.

Patrick burped loudly and munched on his potatoes like a horse chews hay. Millie decided he was doing it just to irritate her, but she lost her appetite regardless.

"You should have let me go out with that boy, Father."

"So you could come back with a wee one in your belly? I'm sure an Italian would be around to help you care for it. Bah!"

"I'm pleased you think so highly of me." The truth was, she hadn't been with a man in any capacity since before her mother died four years before. Millie had all but forgotten what it felt like to be wrapped in a strong embrace. But she had spent all those years taking care of her father when he was drunk. Someone had to.

"Fill me up." He held up his flask and wiggled it.

"Say please," she uncharacteristically demanded, and remained in her seat.

He snorted and stood to pour the whiskey himself.

It took both of their combined incomes to provide for their Williamsburg apartment. Patrick worked on the subways being constructed, and Millie worked as a seamstress. She sometimes wondered if her father could cover the cost himself if he didn't spend so much on overpriced rotgut whiskey.

He stumbled his way around the room, stomping like he weighed more than his withered frame really did.

"Mother Mary." She exhaled, stood, and helped him onto the couch. Then she filled up his cup and took it to him. "I'm going to bed," she said once he was situated. She knew she wouldn't be able to fall asleep for several hours, but her patience was wearing thin. This was the third night this week he had been like this.

When she turned for her room, he gripped her wrist with surprising speed and strength.

"Hey." He forced her to meet his eyes, and for a moment, he seemed almost sober. "I'm not ready for sleep. And I need you to take care of me."

She took a seat beside him on the couch, and watched him drink, in silence.

Her thoughts drifted back to Sonny. She wanted to see him again. She wanted to ask him questions. She wanted to see what color his hair was under that fedora.

There was something mysterious about him that made her knees weak. Mysterious usually meant trouble, and she wasn't some spoiled debutante who needed trouble to rescue her from a sheltered life. But she didn't see trouble in his eyes. She saw kindness. Tenderness. Vulnerability.

When she came to, she realized her father was fast asleep, his head back and mouth open, flask still open and in hand. She had been daydreaming for longer than she'd realized.

She froze and waited for a moment before standing slowly to ensure the wood didn't creak beneath her.

Millie leaned in. She waved a hand over his eyes. She snapped her fingers. Patrick didn't budge.

Still light on her feet, she hurried to her room. She brandished the makeup mirror that had once belonged to her mother and applied a little blush, a touch of rouge to her lips.

She was going to see that boy. And she was going to have her questions answered.

Williamsburg, Brooklyn—June 4, 1930

No one answered when she knocked on Sonny's door, but after disobeying Patrick, nothing was going to stop her.

She opened the door and peeped inside.

"Hello? Sonny?"

The music of Eddie Cantor carried through the apartment. She leaned in until she caught sight of Sonny on the couch, bouncing his head with the music and singing along.

"Sonny?"

He jumped like he's seen a ghost, and hurried to slide something under the *New York Times* beside him.

"Millie?"

She tried to respond but couldn't stop giggling.

"Sorry, I shouldn't laugh." She paused again for another fit. "I've just given you a fright a few times now." She continued to chuckle, but she sobered a bit when she considered why he was so on edge.

After a brief moment of embarrassment, he laughed at himself and rubbed the back of his neck.

"You're lighter on your feet than the people I have around here." She stepped in and closed the door.

"Oh yeah, yeah, come in," he said, ashamed that he hadn't invited her.

"Sorry, I should have just gone back home when you didn't answer. That was quite rude of me."

"No, not at all. Did I really leave the door unlocked?"

"I don't have a key."

"*Madonna mia*, I'm not the smartest fella, huh?"

She flushed as she looked him up and down, noticing the muscles his suits hid so well.

"Already in an undershirt? You must have been working diligently at something."

He hastened to pull his suspenders over his shoulders. "I don't usually have visitors. Just the crosswords." He nodded to the paper and grinned. "Can I get you something?"

Her heart began to flutter, but she straightened her back and lifted her chin.

"I want you to take me out."

"Oh? Ah yeah. Sure. Let me grab my coat." He stumbled over his words, which she found adorable. "Did your father change his mind?" He hurried to the coatrack.

She nodded. "Mm-hmm. Said he was sorry for being rude and that you should show me a very special evening."

Sonny's face lit up. It was the first time she had seen his smile, and the little dimples around it. She wanted to see it more often.

"Now the pressure is on. I'm a bit nervous, if I do say."

"You were already nervous. Want me to wait in the hall?"

"No, almost there." He hurried to button his shirt and tuck it in. He threw a coat over his shoulders and didn't bother with a tie. "I better make sure I lock up this time." He winked as they exited out into the hall.

At the front steps of the apartment, he stepped to the curb and hailed a cab.

"Where should we go?" he asked.

"You decide, you silly man." She almost liked that he didn't know the rules of courting. Or perhaps she didn't know them anymore; it had been a while, after all.

When they entered the taxi, she sat an appropriate distance away from him but felt herself nudging closer throughout the ride, her breathing becoming faster along the way.

The cab pulled to a stop in Times Square. It was a rather cliché place to take a gal, and the ride had taken far longer than she'd hoped, but Patrick wasn't going to wake up anytime soon.

She noticed that Sonny paid the driver a handsome tip, a far cry from her miserly father. He wouldn't have taken a cab to begin with.

"I'd ask if you wanted to eat, but I know you already did." His face shone in the blinking lights of nearby buildings.

"Maybe some dessert?"

"Want to see a nickelodeon?"

"We can't talk if we're in a show." She tried to smile flirtatiously, but he seemed to miss it.

"You're a difficult girl to please," he said, a bit more familiar than he had been previously.

"Would you have it any other way?"

"Maybe we could grab a drink?" His eyes widened, and he blushed as soon as he said this. "A tea or something. A decaf?"

"How about something stiffer?"

Sonny looked stunned.

"I don't drink. Do you drink? I drink. Sometimes. In moderation."

He gulped and she laughed.

She touched his arm for the first time.

"Just buy me a drink, you silly man." She realized it was the second time she had called him that, and she felt silly herself. It wasn't as cute the second time, and she was aware of it.

He didn't seem to mind, though. He placed a hand on hers.

"Well, I don't know why you'd think that I'd know where to find a place to drink."

Her laughter carried across Times Square.

Millie never assumed she was street smart, especially in Manhattan, but she could tell they passed by a few juice joints as they walked. Each time Sonny would slow and peek inside. The music would pour out, and for a moment, she'd believe they would enter. He'd crane his head inside and then say the place was no good.

"You better get me a drink soon, Sonny, or you're going to have to carry me. My dogs are barking," she said, pretending to be exasperated.

"Coming up, princess." He feigned a smile, but she felt he was more distant than before, more guarded with each speakeasy they passed.

"Here we go," he said the next time they found one. Sonny slid the doorman a five-dollar bill, and the man quickly stepped aside to let them enter. Maybe Manhattan rules were different, but who had the kind of money to throw it away so flippantly? She was almost intrigued by it. At the very least, she was curious, but she hadn't had a chance to ask her questions yet.

"You sure this is okay?" he asked over the roar of the jazz players and the stomping feet of all the dancers.

"You act like it's my first time!" It was, of course. Not drinking, but going to an establishment like this one. She wasn't going to let her date know this, though.

"And you want a drink with…alcohol in it?" He lowered his voice as he spoke, as if he were afraid the drunks around him would overhear.

"I'll drink you under the table, Sonny." She realized she was peddling papers. She was too busy taking care of her father to partake very often. The only wine she drank was during communion. But Irish girls, even half Irish, were supposed to be boastful, and she was careful to maintain the image.

"What do you want, then?"

"Whatever you're having." Another check she couldn't cash.

"I'll take two brown," Sonny said to the server girl who approached.

"One each?"

"I'll take six, then." He grinned at her and shook his head. Millie was impressed when he didn't crane his head to check out the waitress in that skimpy dress.

The drinks were there quickly. Millie found herself amazed that this "restaurant" could serve alcoholic beverages so flippantly. She was just as impressed that he bought six drinks at two dollars a pop like it was nothing. Even her father would have found that excessive, but Sonny didn't seem to squirm. Perhaps he just really liked her, or perhaps he had more money than a Williamsburg apartment would suggest.

"*Salute*," Sonny lifted one of the shots, and Millie did the same.

"*Slainte*," she said in her native tongue, and took the entire shot in one gulp.

Millie fought back the bile in her throat and pretended she wasn't affected.

Sonny's face scrunched a bit, but she could tell it wasn't his first time. She grabbed the second shot and waited for him to do the same.

He laughed.

"You don't want to enjoy the music for just a moment?"

"I thought you bought these so we could drink them?" she responded.

He shrugged and picked up the next shot.

The both took it again, and this time, neither of them reacted as much.

Her stomach already felt warm from the alcohol, but perhaps it was just the cigarette smog and body heat that clouded the room.

"Another?"

Sonny laughed again. She watched him attentively, and wanted him to keep laughing. That smile sure was handsome.

"Am I going to have to buy more after this?"

"I'll let you know when we're done with this one." She was aware that she was acting like some other girl; perhaps she was pretending to be the girl she figured Sonny wanted. Regardless, she was enjoying herself.

She took the next shot along with her beau.

"Do I need to get more?" he said.

She leaned in and touched his shoulder playfully.

"Do I look like I'm satisfied?"

He tried to stifle a boyish grin, but she noticed it anyway. He turned to signal the waitress, but Millie was already feeling light-headed, in the best sort of way. She wanted to keep drinking because she wanted to make a mistake tonight, and knew she wouldn't do it sober.

"Have you ever kissed a girl before?" she blurted out. Millie was surprised to find that she didn't regret it.

"Why does everyone ask that?" he answered, playfully offended.

"Have you?"

"Of course, I have."

"Want to kiss another?" She leaned in and pressed her chest against him, looking up at his eyes. They had never seemed so handsome before.

And he didn't hesitate. Before she knew what was happening, she was swept up in his embrace, and his lips were on hers.

A shout came from beside them. "Oh, Sonny Boy, enjoying yourself?" Both of them jumped, startled.

"Jesus, Buffalo, I nearly hit you," Sonny said, pulling away from Millie, not hiding his disappointment. The man approaching wrapped his arms around Sonny's neck and rubbed his knuckles over his head. "Stop." Sonny pushed him away and tried to force a smile. His irritation was visible, whether he wanted it to be or not.

"Come on, pal, I had to say hellos to you. Who's this?" He gestured to Millie. The girl who'd approached with the man stood by with a coy grin on her face. She wore a vulgar dress and a flowered headband that made Millie feel inadequately prepared for the occasion. The flat-brimmed hat and yellow chemise Millie wore wasn't nearly as revealing, or accentuating.

"None of your damn business, Charlie." Sonny's patience was clearly wearing thin. Millie didn't want any trouble, but there was a part of her that did want to see Sonny's true side. If it was violent, she was surprised to find that she might still like it. Perhaps it was just the alcohol.

Charlie touched her hip.

"She's a sweet thing."

"Charlie!" Sonny pushed his associate violently. The man adjusted his expensive suit and starting breathing heavily through flared nostrils.

"What's eating you?" Charlie asked, adjusting the stylish hairdo that had momentarily been swept to the side.

"She's not that kind of girl."

Sonny puffed his chest out, and for a moment, Millie thought he might hit the man. She almost wanted him to. She would have liked to see a man defending her rather than demeaning her like her father did.

"I meant no offense, Sonny. I thought she was just a

comare like this one," Sonny's friend said, gesturing to the girl behind him, who didn't seem perturbed by the comment.

Sonny's demeanor relaxed, and he turned to Millie. She could tell from his gaze that he was embarrassed.

"Sorry. Let me get everyone a drink, okay?" He smiled like he meant it and leaned in to give Millie a kiss on her flushed cheeks before he departed. She nearly melted.

But then she was left with Sonny's strange friend. Who was this man? Why did they know each other? And why did both of them have enough money to buy expensive suits?

"That fella is a stand-up guy, you understand?" Sonny's associate stepped closer. He seemed to want to make up for the disruption.

"Is that right?" Millie played along. She wanted to hear more.

"He can take care of you too. He's a big shot. Got me? He owns half of Little Italy. There isn't a business on Mulberry or Elizabeth that doesn't pay him a vig."

"Oh, what do you mean?"

The man Sonny called "Charlie Buffalo" seemed pretty stunned. His jaw dropped, making him look like a Neanderthal. He knew he'd made a mistake. Millie played along like she was really stunned. But she'd had her suspicions to begin with. It didn't change how she felt about Sonny. She still thought he had more sadness and kindness in his eyes than trouble. She still wanted him.

Regardless, the little fellow departed quickly, dragging his woman of the night with him. Millie smiled triumphantly.

"Hey, where'd they go? I got drinks for everyone." Despite the question, Sonny seemed relieved.

"How'd you know that fellow?" she asked. She already assumed the answer, some sort of criminal activity. But she wanted to see how he'd respond. Either way, he still treated her better than how a law-abiding citizen like her father did.

"Oh, him? I know him from work. I work in a barbershop. He gets his hair cut there."

"He seemed awfully familiar."

"What?" The music was picking up, so Sonny had to lean in.

"I said, he seemed awfully familiar!"

"Oh, long-time customer." He smiled but didn't show his teeth like she wanted, and passed her another shot.

"More for us, I guess."

"You sure we should keep going?"

"Just take your shot, silly man." There she went again. Was that the best she had? She drained the shot, and he did too, so perhaps he didn't notice.

They took a few more, at her bequest. She was well aware by now that the alcohol was getting the better of her, but she didn't care.

She locked eyes with him and didn't break it until he met hers. She wasn't quite bold enough to voice her desires. She'd need a few more shots before that. But she wanted to make her body language as clear as possible.

A commotion broke out across the restaurant, disrupting their intimate gaze.

Three men in fine suits stood around a man with his face smooshed into the felt of the table before him.

"And if you don't pay me by tomorrow evening, I'll find you. And I'll make you eat more than felt, *capisce*?"

Millie noticed Sonny couldn't take his gaze off the incident.

"Come on, we should go." He kept his gaze on the

gentlemen across the room, but took her hands in his and started to lead her toward the door.

"Wait, we still have two drinks!"

"I'll buy us more." He picked up his pace.

"*You* don't owe them money," she said, pouting.

"I should have never brought you to a place like this. I'll never be able to look your father in the eye again."

Millie thought she replied, but by now, it was becoming hard to focus. Everything was a blur.

The only thing about the ride home that she remembered was that, this time, they sat side by side, and he had his fingers interlocked with hers. He couldn't quite look at her, but his thumb continued to rub her hand. She took that to mean something.

Next, she recalled when they arrived at her door.

"Good night, Millie." He tried to kiss her on the cheek like their necking in Manhattan hadn't happened. She twisted until he was forced to meet her lips, and then she wouldn't let go.

After she maintained his grasp long enough to ensure he was interested again, she said, "You're not coming in?"

"I couldn't. Your father…"

"He's passed out. He won't wake up."

"That's not the point… I don't want to dishonor—"

She cut him off. Neither of them really wanted to follow that road. She could tell he wanted to come in, and she wanted him to. And she had the right words to convince him.

"My father just doesn't want to be alone. And if you don't come in here, then I'm going over there." She nodded toward Sonny's apartment. "You're choice, sailor."

He said nothing else, but kissed her again, with more abandon than before, and allowed her to lead him inside.

His coat was off before they were in the kitchen.

SONNY

All thirty-five hundred seats in the Metropolitan Opera House were filled. Still, Sonny and Maranzano had plenty of room in their suite, with a few guards behind them to ensure they weren't disturbed.

"Are you enjoying yourself, Vincente?" Maranzano asked as he clapped along with the rest of the audience as the violinists took their bow and began to prepare for the next song.

"More than I can say, Mr. Maranzano." He had grown up loving when his father sang opera, or when classical music came on the radio. His father didn't have quite the same pipes as the lead vocalist.

"I considered inviting the others, but I don't believe any of them have developed the tastes necessary to enjoy this evening. Perhaps Peppino, but I thought it would be nice for the two of us to spend some time together."

Sonny swelled with pride, and averted his gaze to avoid embarrassment.

"More tea, sir?" a waiter asked from the other side of the guards.

"Vincente?" Maranzano deferred to him first.

"No, I'm okay." Sonny wasn't a fan of tea, but he did try to drink it around Maranzano, as the man considered himself a connoisseur.

"I'll take some, then." The guards parted and allowed the man to fill Maranzano's cup.

The stage crew dimmed the lights, focusing in on the lead vocalist.

"Have you ever heard Puccini?" Maranzano asked.

"I don't believe I have."

"I saw him once, in Naples. I was a young man, too young to appreciate it fully. Perhaps this man can do him justice."

The room seemed to take a collective inhale as the vocalist prepared himself.

"Go ahead." Maranzano nodded at the gold cigarette case in Sonny's hands. He had been dying for one since the first act, but had abstained since Maranzano disliked the smell. "No, go on. I want you to enjoy yourself, Vincente."

Sonny nodded with gratitude and hurried to light one for himself.

The lead vocalist began singing, quietly at first. It seemed a relatively tame song for the climax of the show.

"There was a sacred relationship back in Sicily. A man, *il consigliere*, would take a young boy, not his own, and raise him. A sacred mentorship. The man would teach the boy the ways of the world, and how to conduct himself. Even fathers would defer to *il consigliere* in difficult matters."

The opera singer lifted his voice, a deep tenor that

reverberated off the roof of the Metropolitan Opera House, and probably all down Thirty-Ninth Street.

"Did you ever have a mentor like that, Mr. Maranzano?" Sonny asked. He wasn't sure Maranzano had been able to hear him. Regardless, the man didn't answer.

When the volume of the performance died down a bit, Maranzano set down his tea on a saucer between them and leaned closer.

"I did. I loved him dearly. Everything you see before you is because of that man." Maranzano gestured to himself. "He was my father, my brother, my friend…all in one."

"What happened to your *il consigliere*?"

Maranzano moved back in his seat and took a sip of his tea. His eyes seemed to soften with pain.

"He died when I was still a young man, many years ago." He raised his voice over the music, which seemed uncharacteristic. "But not before he taught me all he knew. I've become just like him, but perhaps better. I—" His voice was finally drowned out by the noise as the horns picked up and convalesced with the lead vocalist's beautiful rendition of Puccini: "My name, no one shall know. No… No…"

Sonny felt the hair rise across his arms, legs, and neck.

"I have come to look on you in this way, Vincente."

Sonny's eyes glistened, and he didn't know why.

"I could never be better than you, Don Maranzano," he said. He had never referred to him in this way before. Perhaps it was Maranzano's words of tradition, or the opera singer's voice. Perhaps it was the violin.

"I don't praise those who don't deserve it. And I don't allow people into my life who are not worthy of it." He gestured to the suite he had reserved for the two of them.

"I only want to be like you."

Maranzano leaned across and placed a hand on his knee. Something about the gesture reminded Sonny of his father, so much so that he was forced to avert his gaze to hide the tears. He half expected Maranzano to pull out a deck of cards and tell him he could say curse words while they played.

Alonzo would have been happy for him to have an *il consigliere* like Maranzano.

The two sat in stunned silence as the vocalist reached the climax of the song: *"Vincerò, vincerò, vincerò"*—"I will win, I will win, I will win!"

The entire audience jumped to their feet and belted out their applause as the musicians all took their bow.

"And we will win, Vincente. This war of ours. It will begin soon, and *we will win*."

Williamsburg, Brooklyn—June 8, 1930

Sonny was dragging his feet with exhaustion by the time Maranzano's driver dropped him off at his Williamsburg apartment. As sapped as he was physically, his mind seemed electrified from the music. He could still hear the Puccini ringing in his ears.

Exhausted or not, he was going to have a difficult time falling asleep.

He started fumbling through his keys until he noticed something on the doormat beneath him.

Reaching down to grab it, he realized it was his suit top. The one he had worn when he'd taken Millie out on the town.

His heart began to race, fearing that her father might have found it and realized something had happened. Reaching into the breast pocket, he found a carefully folded note.

The penmanship was delicate and elegant, the kind of practiced script only a seamstress could cultivate.

Sonny,

I had a marvelous time with you. I look forward to the next time my father passes out—I expect you to take me out again.

With kisses,

You know who

P.S. You had a hole in the stitching, so I patched it up.

Sonny found himself smiling as he pulled the suit to his face to see if he could get a whiff of her perfume. He found only the smell of his cigar smoke, but, still, the smile didn't fade.

He really hadn't been expecting to hear from her after what Charlie Buffalo had pulled. He had told himself the next morning that if it hadn't been for the booze, she would have about-faced and run away the moment she'd seen the prick. And she certainly wouldn't have invited him in.

Perhaps Sonny was as wrong in his estimations this time as he was about the stock market before the crash.

Then his grin evaporated.

He wouldn't be able to take her out again if they went to war with Masseria's people.

He wouldn't be able to go anywhere. And he certainly couldn't take *her* anywhere.

HEARINGS BEFORE THE
PERMANENT SUBCOMMITTEE ON INVESTIGATIONS
OF THE
COMMITTEE ON GOVERNMENT OPERATIONS
UNITED STATES SENATE
EIGHTY-EIGHTH CONGRESS
FOURTH SESSION
PURSUANT TO SENATE RESOLUTION 17
OCTOBER 6, 1963

CHAIRMAN: When, Mr. Valachi, do you believe Salvatore Maranzano took over as boss of the Castellammarese clan in Brooklyn?

Mr. Valachi: I can't say with certainty, Senator.

Chairman: Your best estimate, then.

Mr. Valachi: Sometime in the summer of 1930. I was still working out of the Bronx and Harlem at the time, and we didn't keep up much with their family. But things were starting to get hot, and their father, who we knew as Cola, disappeared that summer.

Chairman: He disappeared?

. . .

Mr. Valachi: That's right, Senator. I heard
he left. The strongest boss at that time,
Masseria, demanded he pay a tribute or he'd
find him. So he paid the money and then
left the States, or at least that's what I
was told.

Chairman: That's when you believe Salvatore
Maranzano came to lead the family?

Mr. Valachi: Correct, Senator. There was a
big meetin' in Buffalo. The nationwide
leader of the Castellammarese was Stefano
Magaddino, everyone knew that. So Maranzano
and a few of his guys went to Buffalo to
settle things. Maranzano was going to be
the leader, and he received funding and
weapons for the war from their guys in
Chicago and Buffalo. We even heard about
that in the Bronx. We knew things were
changing.

Chairman: The "war," a war between Masseria
and Maranzano?

Mr. Valachi: Yes, Senator, but it was
bigger than that. Our family was in on it
too. Our godfather, Tommy Reina, was killed

in February of that year, and we all
thought it was Masseria who done it.

Chairman: You believed Joseph Masseria was
behind the murder of your family's boss?

Mr. Valachi: Correct, Senator. We couldn't
prove it, but afterward, Masseria appointed
one of his guys to lead our family. Most of
the guys went along with it 'cause they
didn't want a war, but there was fifteen of
us or so that didn't like it.

Chairman: There were fifteen members of
your organization who didn't like the new
boss?

Mr. Valachi: Yes, Senator. We couldn't
trust everyone, so we didn't talk about it
much. But this guy, Pinzolo, was no good.
We didn't like him. Reina's top lieutenant,
Tommy Gagliano, thought he deserved to be
boss, and we thought he did too. So we were
ready for war.

Chairman: You and your associates were
preparing to go to war with Masseria?

                    . . .

Mr. Valachi: Correct, Senator. We heard rumors about Maranzano's people gearing up, and we figured it was our best shot to take out the boss of bosses.

Chairman: And where did the Consentino brothers figure into this? Were they part of this war effort as well?

Mr. Valachi: Yes, Senator. Sonny was working directly under Maranzano, and the other two were with us.

Chairman: Enzo and Vico Consentino were working with you in your organization?

Mr. Valachi: Correct, Senator. I didn't know they were brothers until after the war. I knew Vico as "Bobby Doyle." He and Enzo the Thief didn't look alike, and they pretended like they barely knew each other.

Chairman: Why did they do this?

Mr. Valachi: Well, the bosses wouldn't say a word if they thought someone would want revenge. It could cause a headache. Vico thought if he changed his name, they might trust him with more information than they would Enzo the Thief.

Chairman: Was his alias successful?

Mr. Valachi: Senator, I didn't know about who he really was until much later—no one did. So I guess so. But he didn't get the answers he wanted. Rumor was Mr. Reina was supposed to sing about it, but then he got clipped.

Chairman: So both Enzo and Vico Consentino were searching for information about their father's killer? And they were using their involvement in organized crime to do so?

Mr. Valachi: That's correct, Senator. They were just like Sonny. They didn't talk to him much, but all three were trying to find answers. The war was a means to an end. They wanted to find the killer, and were prepared to kill anyone that got in the way.

PART 5

SONNY

"The dinner is amazing, Millie," Sonny said. She may have only been half-Sicilian, but she cooked as well as any of the ladies from the old country.

"Less salt next time," her father said, chewing with his mouth open. Sonny hadn't been around the Irish much, but Millie's father, Patrick, fit the bill.

Patrick worked on the subway construction in Manhattan and didn't get home until late. He made up for lost time by drinking his body weight on the way back to their apartment. He was always angry, and held women in low regard.

"Alright, Dad." Millie smiled at Sonny and rolled her eyes.

Sonny remained the friendly neighbor to Millie when her father was around. He was infatuated with, couldn't look away from her every move, but he certainly wasn't going to let Patrick see that. She invited him over for dinner more often than he could accept, and other times, she placed a pan of freshly baked deserts on his doormat. He felt suspended. Was she really interested in something more, or was the night out just an anomaly?

"Would you like something else to drink, Sonny?" she asked when she noticed his cup was dry.

"You gonna start paying us for the room service?" Patrick asked. "You eat here as much as I do."

Sonny, suddenly uncomfortable, reached into his pocket and began to slide a few dollars across the table. Millie leaned across and slapped his hand.

"He's our guest, Pa," she said firmly. Patrick only grumbled in reply.

"At least let me help with the dishes," Sonny said, placing a napkin over his own to signal that he was finished. He didn't want to remain if he was unwelcome.

The phone rang, and Millie rose to answer it.

Sonny watched as confusion spread across her face.

"It's for you." She held the receiver out to him. Equally perplexed, he hurried across the room to answer it.

"Hello."

"Sonny?"

"Who is this? How'd you get this number?"

"You need to go outside. A car will be there to pick you up. Get in and don't ask any questions." Sonny eventually determined that the voice belonged to Charlie Buffalo. He relaxed, but not much.

"Understood." He wanted to ask if something was wrong, but before he could decide whether or not he should do so, Charlie hung up.

"He even takes his calls here now?" Patrick said. "You need to start paying rent."

Sonny set the receiver down and looked at Mille. "I'm sorry. I have to go."

He nodded at the dirty dishes across the table and the pots on the stove.

"Don't worry. I'll take care of that." She waved him off. "It's fine, really."

He kissed her cheek, as a good neighbor should do, and shook Patrick's hand, neither of them pleased to do so.

He waited on the curb, anxiously watching each car as it passed. The vehicle that held his attention the most was the one that eventually pulled to a stop in front of him. A sleek black Pierce Arrow, fast as lightning and worth more than Sonny's apartment.

"Take a seat, padrone," Bonanno said from the driver's seat. Sonny hurried to do so, turning around to find Maranzano in the back seat.

"I'm sorry for the last-minute notice, Vincente. I've been called to a meeting. I wanted you both there."

"Should we make a call to Antonello?" he said, but Bonanno cut the wheel and pulled back out into the dinner-rush traffic.

"That won't be necessary. We need as few men as possible for this," Maranzano replied definitively.

Sonny wanted to ask what was happening, but remembered Charlie's warning to not ask any questions. Luckily, Maranzano seemed to pick up on this.

"I've been summoned by Joe Masseria."

Sonny's hands began to shake.

"Joe the Boss?"

"He has requested a sit-down," Bonanno said.

"Why would Joe the Boss want to sit down with any of us?" Sonny said, disregarding Charlie's advice.

"There are two reasons," Maranzano said, reserved and still. "He either heard about my trip to Buffalo, where I met with Stefano Magaddino, or he hasn't heard of it. In the first case, this is likely a trap. And he will kill me. In the second, he thinks I can be persuaded to betray Magaddino, or perhaps the rest of the Castellammarese."

Bonanno whipped through traffic, anxious to test what looked like a new car.

"You're going to a meeting you believe might be a setup?"

"We can't play our hand too early. If he doesn't know about my activities, then I cannot refuse him, or he will assume I am prepared for war. This should hold him off until we are ready."

Maranzano had materialized a notebook, and he poured over the contents. Sonny didn't know how to feel about being included in what very well might be an ambush. In a strange way, he felt honored.

"Another thing, Vincente. The Hook Hand will be present," Maranzano said. Sonny's mind returned to the image of the Hook Hand that was engraved in his mind. A cold, emotionless face, white as clay with two deep-set black eyes. "This isn't our opportunity to strike. That will come later. But I wanted you to have the chance to look at the man who killed your father. You deserve to see the man who has caused you so much pain."

"I appreciate you bringing me, Mr. Maranzano," Sonny said, just loud enough to be heard over the rumble of the car.

"Thank him when we make it out alive," Bonanno said. All three laughed, but Sonny's smile quickly faded.

They arrived in Morningside Heights just before sunset. Their meeting location was to be a private home that was owned by a respected but mutual party. Maranzano instructed Bonanno and Sonny on how he expected them to behave when they were inside. They were to sit down at a table with Masseria's bodyguards and pretend they were indifferent to the conversation, not even listening.

Bonanno and Maranzano placed their revolvers in the glove box before they exited the vehicle. Sonny would have done the same if he had a piece on him.

A burly enforcer patted them down at the doorway, and once they were cleared, they were instructed to enter.

The home was darker even than the gray sky outside, with only a few candles to illuminate the room. Two tables were set up, and Sonny and Bonanno were led to the smaller one in the corner, where two other men were already seated.

They both gave Sonny a curt nod, attempting to be amiable. They had a look of understanding in their eyes.

After a few moments of deafening silence, Masseria entered. His footsteps were forceful and seemed to shake the wood floor beneath them. Sonny attempted to follow Maranzano's instructions, but kept the fat boss in his peripheral as he entered.

The Hook Hand entered behind him. It was no wonder he had been able to evade detection for so long. He looked nothing like he had before. He was now clean shaven, and his hair was closely cropped and oiled back. What hadn't changed was his eyes. Alert and piercing, the skin around them unmoving as if he were dead.

"*Paisano*," Masseria extended his arms to embrace Maranzano, giving him a kiss on either cheek. Morello offered the same gesture but was far more reserved.

"It's good to see you again," Maranzano said. Sonny

was surprised that even in a room with two of New York's most powerful men, Maranzano's presence still commanded respect.

"Please, take a seat." Masseria gestured, and all three men did so, showing no notice of the others in the room. "These are difficult times, aren't they?" He now spoke in Sicilian. Even to Sonny's untrained ears, it was a harsh rendering of a beautiful dialect.

"They are. But we're all still alive, and we all still prosper."

A man came to Sonny's table and handed them each a demitasse cup of espresso, the steam billowing out to mix with the acrid cigar smoke. Maranzano never smoked, and Sonny assumed he had to be uncomfortable as he inhaled Masseria's fat cigar, and all the hot air of congeniality he was blowing out.

"Let me be direct with you, paisano," Masseria began, leaning across the table forcefully and pointing at Maranzano with his cigar. "Your friend Gaspar Milazzo is dead. There is nothing that can bring him back. But you have so many other friends. So many. You can keep them all alive and well."

"How can I do this?"

"For one, you can persuade your associate Magaddino to come to New York and speak with me as a man. If he doesn't, he is as good as dead. The same applies to Aiello in Chicago, who has offended me before."

"How do you expect me to persuade Magaddino?" Maranzano asked, taking a sip of his espresso.

"Do not insult my intelligence." Masseria smiled and looked at Morello. "We hear that you are leading the family now. And who better to do so? Milazzo is dead, Cola Shiro has disappeared, and Magaddino's days are numbered. But Salvatore Maranzano is alive and well, and thriving in his various enterprises. If he wishes to continue to do so, we must be friends."

Masseria leaned back in his chair, pleased with his words. He was wearing a suit as expensive as the rest of theirs combined, but it didn't flatter him. He looked like a pig with a bow tie, his shirt wrinkled and sloppy, his fat gut rolling out from under a half-buttoned vest.

"I will let Don Morello speak for me," Masseria said, crossing his arms and puffing happily on his cigar.

"Thank you, Mr. Joe." Morello nodded at Masseria, who smiled like a proud child. "First of all, I want to congratulate you on your success in America." Morello's voice was guttural, gruff. His words carefully selected and precisely spoken.

"Thank you, Don Morello. You've done well for yourself," Maranzano said pleasantly, but Sonny could ascertain from across the room that tensions were rising.

He couldn't resist the temptation to look up. His eyes locked on Morello's stone face, and his stomach turned. He knew that this deformed, lifeless killer was the last thing his father had seen.

"Look…" Morello said, contemplating his words carefully. "Milazzo. His death was from our part. We cannot deny it. But, you see, Gaspar Milazzo and Joe Aiello were plotting to kill Mr. Joe. We hope that Milazzo is the only one who needs to die. But what are we to think? When Mr. Joe invites Stefano Magaddino to visit him in the city, offering to buy him dinner and treat him as a friend, and then he is refused…what can we ascertain? We must believe Stefano does not like Mr. Joe either." Masseria nodded along stupidly as Morello spoke. Maranzano kept eye contact and listened carefully. "If Magaddino will only come pay his respects, and talk with his Sicilian paisano, then perhaps we can let the past go. If not, then out of protection, we must consider Joe Aiello and Magaddino threats." Morello's eyes began to narrow as he spoke. "And anyone else who supports them."

"What would you have me do?" Maranzano asked. His voice was softer now. Sonny assumed he was acting, but he played the part of capitulation well.

"That you would put in a good word for Mr. Joe. That you'll tell your friend in Buffalo how kindly Mr. Joe has treated you, and ask only that he will come to New York. We only want to clarify, that's all."

"I will do what I can." Maranzano gave no indication of how he truly felt. Even Sonny began to wonder if he was considering such a generous offer for peace. "But again, I am only a soldier, under the leadership of Cola Shiro."

"Your leader is gone and isn't coming back," Masseria said behind a cloud of smoke, "so try."

"Yes, do try, Mr. Maranzano. If something can't be done, there will be bloodshed. Much bloodshed. And if that comes to pass, I hope that an intelligent man like yourself will do the right thing and remain neutral." Morello shuttered at the thought of such a future.

"We understand each other," Maranzano said coolly.

Morello smiled, the first time Sonny had ever seen him do so, and he reached out to shake Maranzano's hand. As Maranzano attempted to release it, Morello squeezed harder, pulling him to the table.

"If you are fooling us, your fight will be against me. Do we understand each other? You fought many men in Sicily, but you never fought against a man like Don Piddu."

Maranzano leaned closer to him. "And you have never fought against anyone like Don Maranzano."

Williamsburg, Brooklyn—July 2, 1930

Everything changed for Sonny and the rest of the crew after the meeting with Masseria and Morello. If Salvatore Maranzano hadn't been prepared for war beforehand, he certainly was now. He had moved his wife and children from their home in Brooklyn to a safer location in Montreal, Canada. He went nowhere without Bonanno, Charlie Buffalo, Buster, or Sonny. Usually, he traveled with all four. He paid for his Cadillac to be modified with heavy metal plating and bulletproof windows. He installed a machine gun in the back seat that he placed between his legs whenever they would go for a ride. He purchased another Cadillac, with the same upgrades, to serve as his "lead vehicle" wherever he went.

Some of the boys in the family said Maranzano had the screaming meemies and was going a bit mad, that he was all worried for nothing. But, as time went by, and the deadline for Magaddino's visit passed, rumors began to spread. Masseria was outraged, petulant like a child at a dentist appointment.

Masseria boasted, loud and wide, that he would hunt them all down, one by one.

Maranzano said it was a matter of time before bodies started littering the streets. They had to be prepared.

Bonanno followed his instructions and separated temporarily from Fay. Buster told Maria he would away on work for a few weeks, and gave her a number to reach him only in the event of an emergency. Reluctantly, Sonny had approached his mother and told her he wouldn't be able to visit Little Italy for a while. She seemed to understand—or, at least, she didn't protest. He kissed her head and told her he hoped that everything would calm down soon. He didn't explain to Rosa anything about the conflict, or that he was trying to find out what happened to his father, but she seemed to have an idea. Her vision had dulled, but her mind was still sharp.

Sonny really wasn't ready to leave his apartment, though. He had begun to enjoy his little domicile in Williamsburg, and more than that, he delighted in the company of his neighbor Millie. He didn't want to shut any doors. He felt that, on a bad day, when things weren't going well in Maranzano's war, he would like to return to their apartment and do nothing but look into Millie's eyes and listen to her talk about the sweltering heat or the best vegetable vendors in Williamsburg.

But that wasn't an option. He couldn't involve her. He was known as a Maranzano affiliate now. What if someone tried to come for him, and she was caught in the cross fire? What if he was arrested, and she was there to watch him being put in shackles? He couldn't bear the thought.

As he packed a few things, only the essentials, he decided he would have to say goodbye. Permanently. Maybe in a different life, he could sweep her up and tell her that he had fallen in love with her the moment they had met. But not in this life. She deserved someone better than him. Someone who could protect her without putting her in danger, provide for her without breaking the law to do so.

He slipped the pistol Maranzano had given him for safety into the box, and closed the lid. It was surprising how little he needed, and how little he had.

He left, locking the door on his way out. He started

down the stairwell before he stopped. He walked to Millie's
door and knocked.

Patrick answered and strained his eyes to make
him out.

"What?"

"Is Millie here?"

"She's busy."

Just as well, Sonny thought.

"I just wanted to say goodbye. I have to leave for a
while."

Patrick measured him up, scowling while he did so.

"Where ya going?"

"I have to leave for work. I just wanted to tell her thank
you."

"For what?"

"For all the meals…for talking with me all those—"

"You should be thanking me. It was my money bought
it. No respect. Go on now," Patrick shooed him away like
a fly.

Sonny didn't protest. He probably deserved it. Maybe
in another life, he could have been a man worthy of a girl
like Millie. But not in this one.

Poughkeepsie, Dutchess County, New York—July 16, 1930

The news had spread like a tenement block wildfire. It was
in the headlines of every major newspaper: "Another
Gangland Slaying."

It was Joe Bonanno who had called to tell Sonny. He
was sobbing on the phone. "They got my cousin Vito. He's

dead." He wasn't the only one to be disturbed by the events. Maranzano himself was said to be very broken up about it. Vito Bonventre had been a friend of his in the old country, and they both shared a love for the traditional values of the *onorata societa*. He had tried to warn Bonventre that Masseria's people would come after him first because of his wealth and ability to finance the war. Bonventre wouldn't listen. "I am too old and too respected. No one would lift a finger to me," he had told him. Seventy-two hours later, he was dead.

Sonny didn't know Bonventre well, but he always respected the way the man had carried himself. More than anything, though, Sonny was afraid. If the old man could get clipped, who was safe? Who was next? Maranzano, Bonanno, Buffalo…Sonny himself?

Maranzano sent word. Every member of the Castellammare Borgata should travel to his hideout in Dutchess County. He didn't care if they were old, sick, on a stretcher, or all three. Everyone was ordered to be there.

"Masseria has condemned us all," Maranzano said from the head of a long table. Men were crammed in all around it, the most important seated alongside him and the rest standing behind their respective leaders. "He says he wants to eat us like a sandwich." The room let out a collective nervous laugh, except Maranzano. It was only funny because Masseria was probably fat enough to actually do so. "We met before to discuss this man. We talked, and talked, and talked, but it was followed by no action. Now what are we to do? One of our own is dead. One of our very finest men, in fact. What are we to do now?"

Sonny analyzed the reaction of each man at the table, and concluded that opinions differed greatly.

Maranzano seemed to notice too. "Some of you may be thinking that you can pacify this tyrant. You will find yourself unable to do so. Like his penchant for overeating, his bloodlust is insatiable. He will come after each one of us. You may avoid conflict with him for a time, but once the brave among us have fallen, he will come after the rest. He won't rest until the Castellammarese have been eliminated entirely."

"He knows we are the only ones who will refuse to go down on bended knee," Bonanno said from the seat directly beside Maranzano.

"We are a stubborn people," Maranzano said in Sicilian, and shrugged his shoulders. Men around the room smiled and nodded, pride inflating their chests.

"What should be done, then?" Joe Parrino asked, much like Cola Shiro had before. To Sonny, he seemed less disturbed that Joe the Boss had killed his brother than would be expected.

"We go to war." Maranzano stood and paced around the room with his hands clutched behind his back like a commanding general. "In the ancient days, when men of our tradition were embroiled in a war against our French overlords, they bound together. They lived together, ate together, sacrificed together. Nothing like this has ever happened in America. There has never been an event to call for it. But here we are, gentlemen"—heads around the room began to nod—"we are left with little option. We have not sought war. We have not sought a conflict with this tyrant. But we will return the violence that he has given. We will let the world know what happens when you try to fight a member of the Castellammare: you must fight all of them."

"Yes!" some of them said.

"They will know," others said.

"Then we must elect a commander to lead our forces.

Just as the Romans had their Caesar, we must have a war chief to organize and lead our efforts," Maranzano said.

Sonny was surprised to hear Maranzano say this. He had assumed that after Cola Shiro's disappearance, and especially after Bonventre's death, that Maranzano would be the de facto leader. But Maranzano wasn't that kind of man, he concluded. Too sensitive to people's judgments and concerned for the common good, Maranzano wanted to ensure that they were behind him. That they would follow him. Even after receiving Magaddino's blessing when he'd traveled to Buffalo, he desired the Castellammare to elect him.

A few names were put forth. Maranzano, Joe Parrino, and Angelo Caruso being a few. Unanimously, Maranzano was elected, even by Caruso himself.

"It is settled, then. I will lead this family with honor and strength," Maranzano said humbly. Everyone clapped. "We are also here for another reason. Make room at the table." A few of the seated men stood and opened up a space at the center of the table.

Maranzano turned and smiled at Sonny, whose heart began to race.

"We are bringing in three new men to our ranks. They have been with me since the first day, and have shown that they are willing to sacrifice everything for this family. So, 'boys of the first day,' step forward. You know who you are." Sonny kept his feet planted until Buster tapped him on the arm. Buster, Charlie Buffalo, and Sonny approached the opening at the table.

Joe Bonanno stood and smiled at them like a proud parent.

"Gentlemen, this is Vincente Consentino, Sebastiano Domingo, and Calogero DiBennedeto." He gestured to each one in turn.

Bonanno approached them.

"Show me the finger that you shoot with," he said.

"Gentlemen, this is your godfather. You will follow his every command. You will give your life to protect his, and he would sacrifice his to protect yours." A .38 revolver and a knife were placed on the table in front of them, and Bonanno used the knife to prick their extended trigger fingers.

Maranzano materialized three images of the Virgin Mary and slid them across the table.

Bonanno instructed them each to let their blood drip onto the image placed in front of them.

"Cup your hands," Bonanno said, and then leaned in to Sonny. "And it all started with a life-insurance policy," he said. Sonny found himself laughing along with him, and the geniality in the room was unlike anything he had experienced since his father's death. It reminded him of Alonzo, and the way he had cherished tradition and rituals.

Bonanno lit the bloody pictures on fire and placed one in each of their hands.

Sonny watched, mesmerized as the image burned in his palms. As he rotated his hands back and forth to avoid the flames, he saw the Virgin's face dissolve into ash. He wondered if he would go to hell for what he was doing, but he trusted his father. If Alonzo had done this, then Sonny knew it was an honorable thing he was doing.

"Repeat after me: as this saint burns, may my soul burn in hell if I betray this thing of ours," Maranzano said. The three of them chanted the words back in unison. "This family now means more to you than your own family. Or country. Or God." Sonny's stomach turned, but he didn't look up.

"These weapons"—Bonanno pointed to the .38 and

dagger before them—"symbolize that you will live by the gun and by the knife, and you will die by the gun and by the knife."

"The blood you have spilt symbolizes that we are all now your blood. We are one," Maranzano said, and finally Sonny looked up to him. He noticed the kind of loving glimmer in Maranzano's eyes that reminded him once again of Alonzo.

As the flames extinguished and the ashes of the saint's image began to sift through their fingers, everyone in the room stood and clapped for them. Each member at the table lined up, and kissed all three of them on the cheek.

"Welcome to the *onorata societa*," they all said as they passed by.

The table was then cleared, and food was brought out. Glasses of whiskey were given to each member at the table, and everyone saluted the three of them.

They dined on spaghetti *agilo ed olio* and told stories of their tradition. The men around the room spoke to Sonny like his fraternity brothers would speak to members who'd finally lost their virginities. He didn't have time to consider the oath he had just made, to imagine how it would change his life. He simply listened to what everyone said, and reflected on how his father had once sat in the same seat, and had eaten the same meal.

After they had finished their meals, Maranzano stood by the exit, and addressed each member as they left.

Sonny, Buster, and Charlie Buffalo waited at the end of the line. Maranzano had obviously already considered what each man could bring to the war efforts, and he explained it to them as they left.

When Sonny approached, Maranzano's face lit up.

"Vincente, my boy." He kissed his cheek.

"I had no idea this was going to happen," Sonny said.

"You deserve it. You have earned a place in your father's society. I know you will honor our tradition." He embraced Sonny, firmly, like Alonzo always had.

"I will," Sonny said.

"You will be so valuable to this family. We will need you in the days ahead. *I* will need you," Maranzano said. "I believe your business savvy can be used to coordinate weapon and ammo supply chains from our various supporters."

"I can do that."

"And don't forget to keep an eye on my foreign investments," Maranzano said, and laughed, infecting the whole room with geniality. Sonny kissed his cheek and stepped past him, but stopped to listen to what Maranzano said to Buster.

"Sebastiano, I am honored to have you with me."

"Thank you, Don Maranzano," Buster said, and lowered his head with reverence.

"And I feel much safer, as well." Maranzano smiled and looked to some of the elder members who stood around the room. "There is no better sharpshooter in our ranks. When Masseria is eliminated, I would wager any amount of money that it is Buster who pulls the trigger."

"You do me too much honor."

"I do not misjudge people, Buster. I know that you will fight for us well, and will help us defeat this tyrant." He turned again to others in the room. "Buster is from Chicago. I requested personally that he come here to fight for us. Caesar needed his centurions, like Maranzano needs his Buster." They kissed cheeks and parted.

Sonny walked out with Buster, neither of them saying anything as they approached the Cadillac waiting outside. Sonny wanted to say something. He wanted to tell Buster that he shouldn't be doing this, not with a new wife at home. But he couldn't think of the right words.

"The only thing I care about is protecting your sister, Sonny," Buster said as he opened the door and hopped into the driver's seat.

"Is that right? So much so that you'll vow to place these men over her?" The irony of the statement wasn't lost on Sonny, but regardless, he didn't have a wife.

"Sonny." Buster turned to his brother-in-law, who had slid into the passenger seat. "Nothing will ever come before your sister. I will murder half of New York if it means she is safe, if it means I can buy her a new dress and make sure she has food on the table. I'd do anything for her, Sonny."

Sonny fell silent. Buster was exaggerating, but from what Maranzano had been saying, killing half of New York might actually be required.

BUSTER

East Village, Manhattan—August 15, 1930

"I just wanted to hear your voice," Buster said. He pulled the phone closer, as if it would somehow bring him closer to Maria herself.

"I thought you wouldn't be able to call?" she said. Her voice was more concerned than accusatory. He could tell she missed him just as much as he missed her.

"I shouldn't be. I really shouldn't…" He sat down in the Ritz-Carlton phone booth, and looked over his shoulder to make sure the guys weren't watching him too closely. They'd be sure to rib him if they knew he was talking to his wife.

"Are you safe?" she asked. She still didn't know the nature of what was going on, and she certainly didn't know it involved Sonny, but her suspicions had been aroused, as well as her fear.

"Yeah, I'm safe. You have everything you need? Food, money, anything?"

"I'm fine, Buster," she said, her voice soft and sweet.

"I'm glad to hear it. I'm hoping this business will be finished soon. The moment it is, I'll be back on our doorstep."

"You promise?"

"I promise. I wouldn't spend a minute away from you if I didn't have to." He looked again over his shoulder, feeling silly and effeminate for such talk, but it came from the most honest part of his heart.

"Well, then, hurry up and get it finished." He smiled. She had no idea what that meant, but her support meant everything to him.

"And, Maria?"

"Yeah?"

"While I'm out here, I'm not seeing no other girls or anything."

"Don't you know anything about women? I hadn't thought about it once since you left, and now I won't be able to think of anything else." There was just enough humor in her voice to make him laugh.

"Yeah, I guess I don't."

"You foolish man."

"Maria…" Charlie Buffalo beat on the glass of the phone booth and waved for him to come on. Buster held up a finger to quiet him. "Maria, I love you."

"Come on, Buster!" Charlie shouted and knocked against the glass again.

"So nice of you to say so," Maria said, just as defiantly as always.

"Anything you want to tell me?" he asked, gesturing for Charlie to shut the hell up.

"Well, I just don't know what you mean," she said, toying with him.

"Come on, Maria," he said, his irritation with Charlie coming out in his voice.

"Fine. I love you," she said.

"Sorry, Maria. I got to go. I'll call when I can."

"Goodbye," she said, her voice barely audible. He waited until the line clicked to hang up the phone. There was always something more he wanted to say.

"What in the hell is so important?" Buster said, stepping out of the phone booth, moving like he was on a warpath. He noticed that Charlie's face was grim, serious enough that he checked himself. "What is it?"

"Someone spotted Morello. Old Caesar gave us the nod to make the hit."

Buster stopped in his tracks.

He heard Maria's voice: *Well, then, hurry up and get it finished.*

"Okay. Let's take care of him."

SONNY

Sonny's new safe house was lonelier than his apartment. Bonanno came by occasionally to check on him; Antonello, Buster, and Charlie Buffalo visited every few days; and even Maranzano had slept on the couch one evening after refusing to take Sonny's bed. Most of the time, though, Sonny was alone. He busied himself making calls to the Castellammarese allies in Detroit and Chicago, and writing down cryptic ledgers from the orders they would receive.

A cat had appeared on his doorstep a few weeks prior, and Sonny had tried to shoo it away. The cat was determined to make entry, and Sonny eventually let it in. He dubbed the cat Pete, and he shared his breakfast with him every morning. In time, Pete became a source of comfort for him, but more than anything, Sonny was left with a volley of thoughts. Most of them about his father.

As he looked in the mirror and adjusted his tie and

overcoat, he could see bits of his father in the reflection. He hoped his father would be proud. He imagined what it would be like to see him again, and be greeted with a bear hug and a big kiss. "I'm so proud of you, Sonny Boy," he might say when he learned that Sonny had joined the tradition. Alonzo hadn't felt that way with Enzo and Vico, but they had just been kids, and they hadn't followed his instructions. Sonny had always wanted to be everything that his father was, and his father had always been proud of this. Why wouldn't he want him to follow in his footsteps?

The horn of Antonello's car blared outside. It was time to go.

He hoped that by killing Morello, he might be able to put his father to rest in a way that he had thus far been unable to do.

"See ya, Pete," Sonny said, and scratched the cat's chin, then hurried out the door.

"Old Caesar has you all spread so far throughout the city, I wonder if we're even gonna make it on time," Antonello said, throwing up a middle finger to the cars honking at him as he flew by.

"Try to not get pulled over on the way, Antonello. The last thing we need is the bulls seeing a car full of guineas with guns."

The lunch-hour traffic was buzzing past—half of the cars honking along the way—as Sonny and Antonello pulled up outside the Ritz-Carlton hotel in the East Village.

Buster was smoking a cigarette with Charlie Buffalo on

the curb. Buster turned to enter, but Charlie only gave a nod and returned indoors.

"Charlie ain't coming?" Antonello asked.

"No. The fewer we bring, the more likely we are to make it out alive," Buster said, fastening his seat belt.

Sonny noticed the violin case Buster had brought with him.

"You gonna teach us some lessons on the way over?" he asked, still not pleased that Maranzano had ordered Buster to be present for the hit.

Buster slowly unfastened the locks and opened the case, revealing a well-oiled tommy gun.

"We wouldn't make it in there without concealing it. And you can't fit one of these in your overcoat," Buster said. Antonello's face lit up with excitement when he saw the Thompson submachine gun within.

"*Madonna mia*, the Hook Hand won't know what hit him."

"Yeah, he will. He's as slippery as an eel and as cunning as a fox. We can't underestimate him," Buster said, lighting another cigarette.

"You nervous?" Sonny asked.

Buster thought about it, then shrugged. "Yeah. Shouldn't I be?"

"Yeah," Sonny said, feeling the revolver in his jacket and suddenly feeling underprepared.

They arrived in East Harlem just before one o'clock.

"Ready?" Buster asked Sonny. He felt glued to the seat. He could hardly move. He had never killed before. "Sonny?"

The only corpse Sonny had ever seen up close was his own father's. That image was enough to encourage him to unbuckle himself.

"I'm ready. Let's go." Sonny followed Buster out the car door.

"When it's done, hurry up and get back to the car. There are a lot of people here today, so we can use that as cover, but the bulls will be here fast," Antonello said, tapping his fingers against the steering wheel.

Buster led the way into the office building. Sonny followed close behind, but kept becoming distracted by those they passed by. Every suspicious glance concerned him. *Do they know?* he wondered, but he kept moving forward regardless.

They took the elevator to the fourth floor. The bellhop tried to keep his eyes forward but seemed aware of their ethnicity.

"Private lessons," Buster said, tapping on the violin case.

"I'd love to learn," the bellhop said as they arrived on their floor.

Buster strolled out, and Sonny following his example, but as the elevator shut, they picked up the pace.

Buster pulled out the tommy gun as they arrived at a set of oak doors that read: "United Lathing Company." Morello was said to be inside, conducting business as usual, as if he weren't at war.

Sonny put his hand on the doorknob and looked at Buster to ensure he was ready. He returned a nod, Sonny finally experiencing what he imagined his brother Vico had experienced in combat. As he opened the door, Buster took a leap inside. Before Sonny could even round the corner, Buster was unloading.

The sound was deafening, but Sonny could still make

out the screams of the receptionists in other offices across the hall. They had to hurry.

There were three men inside. It was easy to spot Morello. He was the least disturbed. He was hunkered down behind his desk, and remained still as the wood splintered around him. The other two froze like frightened deer, easy targets for Buster's volley of bullets.

Sonny pulled out the revolver. He had six shots. He wanted to save them for Morello. One of Morello's associates crumbled to the floor. The other ran to the window, clutching a bullet in his arm, and lunged out the glass onto the city streets.

"I hit him, Sonny," Buster shouted, shooting off a few bursts to keep Morello pinned.

"Don't say my name!" Sonny cried, realizing now that his breaths were shallow and labored.

Sonny sprinted across the room, and Buster held off the trigger as Sonny entered his lane of fire. His hands shook violently on the revolver extended out from him. But he remembered the image of his father on the barbershop floor, and moved around the desk to where Morello was lying.

Blood was pooling over Morello's scowling lips, but he held a pistol out in front of him. Morello shot, and the bullet ripped through the muscle and tissue of Sonny's shoulder.

Sonny's hand trembled, his eyes flittered, but he fired before Morello could do so again. To his surprise, when he was recomposed, Sonny saw that Morello had a gaping hole the size of a baseball in his chest.

He hurried to the Hook Hand and kicked the pistol from the man's weakening grip.

Morello, still alive, look up to him with hate in his eyes.

"You killed my father," Sonny said, holding the gun out in front of himself like a shield.

"Sonny, hurry up," Buster said, composed as he grabbed his violin case and locked up his tommy gun.

"I didn't," Morello said, his voice carrying the wheeze of shattered lungs.

"You took my father from me!" Sonny pulled the trigger. Then again. In rapid succession, he fired the gun until it snapped into an empty cartridge.

"He's dead, Sonny, come on," Buster said, locking the doors they had entered through.

Sonny reached into his trouser pocket and brandished a deck of cards. His fondest memories were of playing cards with his father. He remembered how he would laugh endlessly when his father would allow him to cuss. Morello had taken that away from him; he had taken that away from Alonzo's future grandchildren. He pulled out a King of Hearts and placed it in Morello's limp hand—to represent the man that Morello had killed.

"There's a fire escape over here." Buster led the way once more. Sonny took one last look over his shoulder, at the mutilated body of the Hook Hand. He was almost sad it would be the last time he would see him. He would have liked to kill him again.

VICO

Vico started drinking again. And probably even worse than before.

The hunt for Alonzo's killer had halted. After Reina got whacked, they had clear targets. Ronaldo was the first to go, and at least Vico received some satisfaction in pumping bullets into him. Afterward, they tried to find Patsy, but he was discovered dead by his wife before they could get to him.

After that, he waited for orders. But days turned to weeks, week into months, months into half a year. Still, Gagliano wasn't ready to move. Pinzolo traveled around with a pack of bodyguards, probably knowing that, as a puppet for Masseria, there were plenty of guys who didn't like him.

Vico spent most of those months alone. Sometimes Enzo would visit him at his new place in Harlem, but it wasn't exactly hospitable. Things were different between them now, anyways. At first, they'd explained the difference by saying they were trying to keep up appearances, hiding the fact that they were brothers. But after a while, it became clear that the tight bond that had once existed between them was now severed. Vico thought he intimidated Enzo. He looked at him strangely, with eyes full of suspicion, as if he was wondering when he might find himself on the other end of Vico's gun.

Vico told himself that it was all cowardice. Gangsters like Enzo were all talk, just like Reina said. They were tough when they were breaking into a joint, terrifying when they were sticking up some rich fool, they could torture a man in cold blood when he was strung up, but when it came down to getting your hands dirty and doing what needed to be done, they shivered. Even Gagliano, with all of his talk about "*my family*" and "*killing that grease-ball*" had come up short. For all of his bravado, Vico thought he trembled internally at the thought of a war with Masseria.

Vico wanted answers, and he wanted revenge. Short of that, there was nothing else he wanted except a bottle of rotgut whiskey and the occasional company of a girl from the Rainbow Gardens.

"Who is going to avenge Dad, if we don't?" he had asked Enzo when he visited one night. "Sonny?" Vico chuckled at the thought.

"Maybe no one needs to, Vico. Dad was obviously involved. That's what happens in this life," Enzo had replied, but Vico knew he hadn't meant it. Revenge was inevitable. Enzo wanted it too, even if he couldn't admit it or bring himself to do what must be done.

But Vico would. He kept his eyes open and his ears pinned back, and the moment he found out what happened, someone was going to die.

The phone began to ring, amplifying the pain in Vico's head.

He stumbled to his feet and walked to the phone, his legs like wet noodles beneath him.

"Yeah?" he answered, rubbing his eyes.

"Doyle. You there?"

"It's me. What is it?"

"You need to go to Lucchese's office in the Brokaw Building on Broadway."

"Where?"

"California Dry Fruit Importers."

Vico scribbled down the info.

"Alright, sure."

"There's a package for you. Take care of it for me." Vico finally discerned the voice as Gagliano's.

"Done."

"You sober?" Gagliano asked.

"Yeah," Vico lied. The rumors of his drinking had been spreading, and he was anxious to dispel the theory.

"You sound fried. Put down the hooch, grab some coffee, and sober up. You're gonna need your wits." Gagliano hung up.

Despite orders, Vico took one last pull of the whiskey and hurried to his car.

Traffic was heavy, as it tended to be on the night of a Yankees game. The bright lights kept Vico's head hurting, but the cars buzzing past him kept him alert.

He arrived at the building and checked for the third time that his revolver was loaded. Six shots. He slid it into his jacket, and pulled his fedora over his eyes. If this was a setup, he would be prepared.

Vico noticed a man standing by the front door. He was adorned in nice threads and was puffing on a long cigar. A bodyguard, Vico decided.

He walked past the building, trying to get a glimpse of the man without raising his suspicion. The face was unrecognizable.

Could be nothing.

Regardless, Vico took an alley beside the building and jimmied the lock to enter through a back door.

He stopped and listened before moving forward, more concerned than relieved when he heard nothing. The office had been closed for a few hours. Whatever was awaiting him wasn't pleasant.

The light bulb in the hallway flickered. He stuck to the walls and moved only when the light darkened. Vico reached into his coat and kept his revolver in hand. He scaled a single flight of stairs to the floor with the 1000 suit numbers, and followed signs for the California Dry Fruit Importers.

As Vico entered, he made out the image of a lone man across the room. The shadowy figure looked up but didn't seem surprised to see him.

"You the guy?" the man asked, his face slightly illuminated by the cherry of his cigar.

"I'm the guy." Vico strained his eyes. The man before him was an old man, a greaseball, as Gagliano would have described him. He matched the description. It was Pinzolo.

"Where is the H? Lucchese told me you'd have a briefcase full," Pinzolo said, noticing that Vico was empty-handed. If Pinzolo thought this was a drug deal, he was wrong.

"I got it tucked away," Vico said, pulling out his pistol. He shot once, and Pinzolo tumbled back onto the floor, his cheekbone shattered. Vico hurried over to him. Pinzolo looked on in dismay, as if he were simply confused and appalled at what was happening. He reached into his coat pocket, fumbling for a pistol, but Vico crouched over him and stepped on his hand.

"This is for Tommy Reina." Vico put the barrel against Pinzolo's chest. He could feel the man's heart beat through the tip of his revolver. He looked into Pinzolo's eyes as he pulled the trigger, and watched them roll back as the last breath escaped him.

ENZO

Coney Island, Brooklyn—September 16, 1930

"Don't say nothin' to nobody," Gagliano had instructed Vico, Enzo, and Cargo before they entered the restaurant in Coney Island. The entire family had been called for a meeting to discuss who had killed their newly elected leader, Joseph Pinzolo.

They found their seats at a table near the Gap and waited for the meeting to commence. The restaurant had been closed early for the evening, no outsiders allowed.

"As many of you know, Joseph Pinzolo was found dead this morning," Steve Rondelli said, the lone man to be standing at his table. "We need to determine who made this hit, and why." He played his part well, Enzo thought. From what he understood, Rondelli had been behind Gagliano since day one. "Our friend Tommy Lucchese has been arrested because Pinzolo was found dead in an office leased by him, but it couldn't have been Tommy. He was with me all yesterday evening."

At the other end of the room, Enzo caught a glimpse of Gagliano, who was puffing on a cigar without a care in the world.

"Could it have been someone from outside the family?" one man asked, who Enzo identified as Sally Shillitani.

"We all know there were plenty of men in this room who wanted him dead," the Gap said, "so no reason to think it came from somewhere else."

"Someone needs to be held responsible. If we don't do something about it, Joe the Boss is going to think we were all in on it," said a man named Frank Callace, who Cargo referred to as "Chick 99."

"Lucchese could have ordered the hit?" another asked.

"Not likely. Lucchese had no reason to have Pinzolo whacked. He doesn't want to be the boss," Rondelli said, and suddenly all eyes fell on Gagliano. It was unspoken, but Enzo thought the room had already made up its mind.

"I did it." Vico stood up. Enzo looked down and away, feeling like he might throw up as he watched his brother forfeit his life.

Enzo tried to analyze Gagliano's response, but the man only squinted his eyes and watched curiously.

"Yeah, I took him out. I didn't have any orders. No one told me to. But we all know that old bastard needed to die, and I was the only one who was going to do it," Vico said. The room collectively silenced.

"Who are you, young man?" one member finally said, appalled.

"Bobby Doyle. I was a loyal associate of Gaetano Reina. Masseria had him killed, so I killed Masseria's guy. It was justice."

"You cannot decide justice by yourself. We have rules!" another shouted.

Vico only jutted out his chin and extended his chest.

He wasn't going to be intimidated. Enzo thought he may have gone too far this time.

The restaurant doors burst open. The men around the room stirred, and many of them reached for their weapons.

It was Lucchese who paced in.

"Tommy?" Rondelli asked, as if surprised.

"I got out." Many of them stood up to congratulate him on getting away from another sentence. "Big news, though."

"What is it?" Gagliano asked, playing his role.

"I heard some of the bulls talking down at the 23rd Precinct. They're keeping it under wraps for now, but they found Giuseppe Morello dead, his body shot up pretty good."

Everyone in the room stirred.

"Somebody else has it out for Joe the Boss," Gagliano said. Together, he and his associates had acted out their parts perfectly. Even Vico had played a roll, even if Enzo hadn't known it at first. It was now established that there were men in their own ranks who wanted Pinzolo dead, even at the cost of a war with Masseria. And now that they knew Masseria had other enemies, maybe, just maybe, they could actually win the war.

Enzo finished the remainder of his whiskey. Time to go to war.

SONNY

After the Hook Hand's death, Maranzano ordered that the entire family lay low. Masseria was howling for revenge, and the police were hunting for suspects. Sonny was moved along with the rest of Bonanno's crew to a new safe house in the Upper East Side, where none of them had been spotted before. Maranzano stayed there most of the time as well, and he sat by the window with a cautious eye to the street.

They ate bread and onions, and drank little. Maranzano said this was a war, and they had to give up certain luxuries if they wanted to be victorious.

Maranzano never stopped cleaning his weapons, and the rest of them followed his example. Even after they went to sleep, Maranzano would stay in the living room, disassembling his weapons completely and inspecting the chamber for any obstructions.

Sonny had arranged for a truckload of ammunition

from Chicago to arrive in New York, and they kept it in their new safe house. Maranzano thoroughly inspected each bullet and shell, but even after they passed the test, he liked to deconstruct the shells and load them with his own ingredients. He would weigh out the gunpowder meticulously on a small scale, and ensure that each shell was filled with the same number of pellets.

"Mr. Maranzano?" Sonny asked one evening after they had finished their meager dinners and were cleaning their weapons.

"What is it, Vincente?" he asked, scrubbing the barrel of his shotgun with a small brush.

"When I killed Morello...he said that he didn't kill my father."

Maranzano sat the gun down across his lap and leaned back against the window.

"Of course, he did. He feared for his life. Even a brave individual like Morello would lie if it meant a chance at survival."

"Yeah," Sonny said, and looked down. Maranzano resumed his cleaning ritual. "Is there any chance you were wrong, though? Is there any chance it was someone else?"

Maranzano looked at him thoughtfully for a long moment. "It's possible. I only know what I am told. But do you actually think it was someone else? Or do you wish it was someone else, so that you could exact revenge again?"

Sonny thought about it, and shrugged. "I just want to make sure I got the right guy," he said, and then returned his attention to the cleaning of his own pistol, anxious to end the conversation.

Buster began to snore. Charlie Buffalo laughed at the sight and made his away across the room. He licked his finger and gave Buster a wet willy.

Charlie laughed as Buster jolted and slapped his hand

away. Maranzano shook his head, smiling like a father does at his children's playfulness.

"Like a couple of schoolboys, these two," Bonanno said, and pointed at them.

"Yeah, and he's the schoolyard bully." Buster wiped the sleep from his eyes.

As they jested, Maranzano turned his attention to the street.

"Someone is coming," he said, and he hastened to put his shotgun back together.

"Who?" Charlie asked. "No one knows we're here."

"We've been here for over a month, Calogero. Someone was bound to find us eventually." Maranzano stood and shut the curtains, leaving only enough room to allow a vantage point of the road.

Headlights passed through the sheer curtains and came to a halt. They all sat silently and tried to calculate the number of vehicles approaching.

"Sebastiano, do you have your weapon ready?" Maranzano asked.

"Yes, I do." Buster stood and grabbed the weapon, slapping a drum of ammo into place.

"Stay inside, Don Maranzano," Bonanno said, moving to the door. "We can handle this."

"That is not how I conduct my business, Joseph, and that isn't how I lead this family." He loaded his shotgun and took one last glance out the door. "I see four cars. There are perhaps more. They'll have the numbers."

"But we have Don Maranzano," Charlie said, spinning the chamber of his revolver and locking it into place.

"Let us go, and let us return," Maranzano said.

The don was the first one to exit the building. He held his shotgun out in front of him, but his disposition was calm. Bonanno, Buster, Sonny, and Charlie poured out the door behind him, weapons pointed at the intruders.

Car doors opened and shut, and men in three-piece suits appeared from everywhere. It was a wonder that all these men could have squeezed into just four cars.

Sonny pointed his revolver at one of them. He hoped he wouldn't have to pull the trigger. They would be massacred.

One giant man stepped out in front of the rest. He took off his fedora and munched on the wet tip of a fat cigar. He smiled coyly.

They stood in silence, appraising each other for a moment. Behind the giant, Sonny spotted two familiar faces he hadn't seen in quite a while. They noticed him too, and seemed just as surprised.

"You're a hard man to find," the giant said to Maranzano. "My name is Tommy Gagliano." He let out a billow of smoke.

"And I am Salvatore Maranzano," the don said. His voice was friendly, but he kept his shotgun pointed at Gagliano's chest.

"I hear we want the same people dead." Gagliano grinned from ear to ear. Maranzano lowered his gun, followed by men on either side of the porch.

Maranzano stepped down to Gagliano and embraced him, with a kiss on either cheek.

NOTE FROM THE AUTHOR

Did you enjoy :)? Leave a review! For every Amazon.com review, Thirteenth Press, LLC will donate $1 to the The Addison Hutchison Foundation.

Didn't enjoy :(? Email the author at Vincent@thir-teenthpress.com and let him know what he can do better!

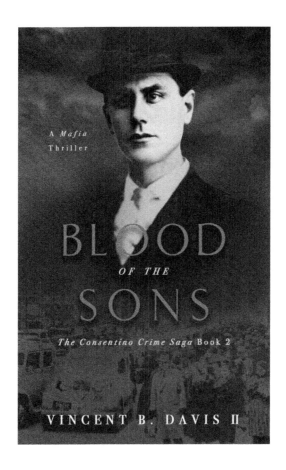

Continue The Consentino Crime Saga in Book 2, ***Blood of the Sons***! Just scan the QR code below!

ACKNOWLEDGMENTS

I'd first like to thank my cover designer, Hannah Linder, who did an incredible job and most certainly brought many of my readers here. I'd also like to thank my editors, Michael Rowley and Michelle Hope, who's fingerprint will forever lay on this story. You all made this story what it is.

This book required an extensive amount of research. At first blush, one might assume that my books on Ancient Rome would require more research than *The Consentino Crime Saga*, and perhaps I even believed that when I began the project. That being said, I wanted to ensure I had the details and historical details correct (as best I could), and therefore I should mention a few of the sources that were invaluable to me during the planning phase of this series.

The Origin of Organized Crime in America by David Critchley was the primary source for all of my research into New York's underground societies, so I'd like to thank both the author and the University of Tennessee library which lent it to me.

The First Family by Michael Dash was consistently on my desk and open during both my research and my writing, and it taught me far more than just about "The Hook Hand", but also about the city during which Morello was active in organized crime.

The Valachi Papers by Peter Maas and *A Man of Honor* by Joseph Bonanno were absolutely invaluable to me, the latter being a first hand account (and written by a main character in this series), and the former being a written account of the man on trial which the series is based around.

Ensuring I had the geography, style, automobiles, and slang authentic was just as important as ensuring the historical events are correct. For this, I used *The Writer's Guide to Everyday Life from Prohibition through World War II* by Marc McCutcheon, *The Historical Atlas of New York City* by Eric Homberger, and *New York: An Illustrated History* by Rich Burns and James Sanders, amongst many others. Without these resources, this story would feel much less authentic.

I'd also like to thank the tour guides of Little Italy, and those that showed me the restaurants (and bakers) where these men congregated and ate.

And as the old saying goes, what mistakes and inaccuracies remain are my own.

Finally, I'd like to thank you, the reader. Cliche as it may be, you are the reason I am able to write. Without your support, I wouldn't be able to continue doing what I love. And for that I truly, humbly, offer my gratitude. Please feel free to email me at vincent@thirteenthpress.com with comments, suggestions, or complaints.

Keep fighting,
    Vincent B. Davis II

ABOUT THE AUTHOR

VINCENT B. DAVIS II is an author, entrepreneur, and soldier. He graduated from East Tennessee State University in 2017, and has served in the United States Army since 2014. His fascination with the development and creation of the Five Families began at an early age, and *Sins of the Father* is the result of many years of research. When Vincent isn't writing or researching for his next book, you can find him playing poker, spending time with his dogs, or watching Carolina Panthers football.

Printed in Great Britain
by Amazon